DIARY OF A
STREET DIVA

D0210191

DIARY OF A STREET DIVA

ASHLEY & JAQUAVIS

www.urbanbooks.net

Urban Books, LLC
1199 Straightpath
West Babylon, NY 11704

copyright © 2005 Ashley & JaQuavis

All rights reserved. No part of this book may be repro-
duced in any form or by any means without prior con-
sent of the Publisher, excepting brief quotes used in
reviews

ISBN-13: 978-1-60162-141-2
ISBN-10: 1-60162-141-8

First Trade Printing May 2006
First Mass Market Printing March 2009
Printed in the United States of America

10   9   8   7   6   5   4

*This is a work of fiction. Any references or similarities
to actual events, real people, living, or dead, or to real
locales are intended to give the novel a sense of reality.
Any similarity in other names, characters, places, and
incidents is entirely coincidental.*

Distributed by Kensington Publishing Corp.
Submit Wholesale Orders to:
Kensington Publishing Corp.
C/O Penguin Group (USA) Inc.
Attention: Order Processing
405 Murray Hill Parkway
East Rutherford, NJ 07073-2316
Phone: 1-800-526-0275
Fax: 1-800-227-9604

Acknowledgments

On behalf of Ashley & JaQuavis
we would like to say thank you to . . .

*Carl Weber for believing in the "KIDS" and putting us on.

*Roy Glenn, we admire your work.

*Teri Woods, for acknowledging our work.

*Shannon Holmes and Kevin Jackson, for showing us the game.

*Arvita Glenn, for your continued support and love. We still got the true story for you!

*Richard Holland, gon' and put out that best-seller.

*Mary and the entire Genesee District Library Staff, thank you for supporting us and promoting our work.

*Chad Swiatecki, thanks for the incredible cover story.

*Veronica at CLUB 93.7, thanks for looking out and showing us love.

* Dwayne Joseph, for helping us get our feet in the door.

*All of the readers, for continuing to support us and buy our book. Without y'all there would be no us. We would like to especially thank the fans from O.O.S.A Book Club and Coast 2 Coast Book Club.

* * * * * * * * * * * * * * * * * * *

First, I wanna thank GOD for continuing to shower me with blessings. I am at a point in my life right now that I never imagined I would be. It's still hard to believe that I have begun my dream career at such a young age.

I want to thank my KING, you are my inspiration and I am so happy to have you in my life. I know that I am meant to be with you because we complement each other. We are partners and I know that our bond is too strong to break . . . I could go on forever with this one, so I'm just gon' end it here. Enough said, you know what it is and how we do. No matter what, please know that you are my world and I love you.

I also want to thank my family . . . my entire family. I love you all so very much. Ma, you have always loved me and supported my dreams to write, thank you for all that you have done—I love you. Daddy, I love you and I know that there is nothing that you would not do for me. I hope I am making you proud. Mar, Syd, Yul, & Yulanai . . . you guys are my heart and I will always be here when you need me. Grandma and Papa, you have been here for me for so long, and I want you both to know that I am proud to be your granddaughter. Grandma Snell, you are my joy, and I admire you for your strength and intelligence. Tammy, I am so close to you and I am fortunate to have you in my life. Raven, I love you so so much. This is beginning to get long, so I'm just gon' list the rest. Aunt Monya, Indie, Jazzy Pha, Court, Amber, Nannie, Uncle Reggie, Aunt Pearlette, Zantofvea, Jatoria, Aunt Lyrica, Aunt Kamela, Ashley C., my godsister Alex, my godson Robin, Joy, Brent, Wayne, Kiara, Jada, lil' Camrin, and last but definitely not least my girl Shay Shay—I love y'all.

I got to thank my BEST friend Char . . . you have been real throughout our friendship and I hope we remain close throughout our lifetime. To one of my closest friends Sharonda, no matter what we go through, I love you very much and will be here forever. We should be able to get through whatever. Rudy, we have been cool for so long, you are a good friend. To my friends La'Troy, Chenita, Shonda, and Jaquetta . . . I didn't forget about y'all. To Lisa Midock, I didn't forget you this time, love ya. To all my Hamady friends, I love and miss y'all. To Margo, (my biggest fan), thanx for keeping my kitchen tight and for supporting me from day one. To my girls, Anita and Quanda, y'all know I had to shout y'all out. To Ms. Blackmon (finally, it's official!), I miss you and I thank you for everything. You are a special and true friend to me. Okay this is the last one then I'ma get out of here. I have to thank Mrs. Couch, Ms. Gulley, Ms. Green, Mrs. Murphy, and all of the rest of HHS. It was there that I learned to strive for excellence and it was those specific teachers that encouraged me to follow my dreams.

Ashley ♥

* * * * * * * * * * * * * * * * * *

First and Foremost, I would like to thank God for blessing me with the talent to paint pictures with words. I would like to thank my environment for giving me the life and knowledge to compose these tales. I also want to thank my better half, my nigga, my love, and my inspiration (you know who you are). We been through hell and back and now the sun is shining down on us. All of those nights we sat at the table contemplating a come up, doing what we had to do is now paying off.

Thank you, Lovie Price, for being my guidance and inspiration: You showed me a lot about life and I just want to say thank you. Thank you Aunt Kamela and Shay for always holding me down. Big ups to the whole 5th Ward (my block), my bro Shelton "Trap" Jones, Johnny "Diddy" Davis, My goddaughter Jada Jones, Nick "Black" Hines, Sam "Spoon" Weatherspoon, John Love, My brother Darrell "Dotta" Campbell (I told you the city was going to be mine), Larry "Two Gunz" Marshall, Glente Wilson, Renny Ren, the whole Bullpen Squad, J. Gerv (Get home), Margo, Eddie's Barbershop, Tammy (my biggest critic and fan), Tammy (my godmother), Aunt Tonya, Pooh-J, Nae Nae, Quanisha, Raven Lindsey, Mildred Robinson (You believed in me when no one did), Shawna Simms, Amir, Izzy, Mr. and Mrs. Johnny

Coleman (Grandma and Papa), Ted and Betty Webster, Aunt Denise, Larry Weatherspoon, Aunt Moink, Johnnie Coleman Jr., Francetta Dixon, Adrienne Niles, Cali, Coby, Double J, G. Almond, Pauletta, Aunt Debra, T.Sims, and Fat Rat. **R.I.P. AC.**

Shout out to my Jersey plug . . . I would never mention ya name.

YaQuavis

Tell us what you thought about our book.

Contact Info

AshleyJaQuavis@hotmail.com

DIARY OF A
STREET DIVA

Chapter One

Cease looked at the picture of his wife that hung on the back wall of his living room. He smiled, thinking of the times that they spent together. He admired his wife's dark mocha complexion and her slightly slanted eyes. He stood in the middle of the room looking at the all-white, Italian-style furniture that Remy had begged him to buy almost a year earlier. She had given him her sweetest face, and he couldn't resist. Cease laughed aloud to himself, knowing his wife was the only person to have ever captured his heart. He didn't have love for too many people. He didn't trust anybody, but Remy was different. He could never tell her no.

He gazed at the portrait with longing. He would give anything to hear her voice and feel her touch one last time. The four years they had spent together didn't satisfy him; it wasn't enough. He was bothered by the way she left him. He had replayed that night over and over in his head, wondering if there was something different he could have done. He was enraged by the fact that he could have prevented it, could have stopped it from ending the way it did. *If I could go back, I would change it. It wasn't supposed to happen like this. She wasn't supposed to* . . . Cease couldn't even think about it without breaking down. The memory was still too fresh in his mind, too painful to recall. *She was everything,* he thought, twisting his wedding band. There were so many things he wanted to say to her, and so many things that he wanted her to say to him.

With his street-savvy demeanor, he lacked in his social graces, but she made up for his shortcoming with her elegance and class. Now that she was gone, his life felt empty. Cease stood up and walked around his home. He stood in front of Remy's room. He had not stepped one foot in it since she left. He thought it would be too painful. As he stood in front of the door, his breaths became shallow, and he was overcome with emotion. He had loved Remy, and just like everybody else in his life, she had disappeared right before his eyes.

Cease grew up in the heart of the ghetto, in the fifth ward of Flint, Michigan. He had learned at an early age that people couldn't be trusted. Before Cease was born, his mother had been addicted to heroin, and to pay for her habit, she walked up and down N. Saginaw Street, tricking, accepting any amount of money for a fix. She was used to living a fast lifestyle and always had traffic in and out of their house. When one of his mother's boyfriends jumped on him at the age of nine, his mother sided with her boyfriend. Cease quickly grew a "fuck you" attitude towards his mother and every other woman who entered his life from that point on. He was surprised when Remy charmed her way into his heart. His thuggish ways seemed to soften around her, and eventually he fell in love with her. She was the only woman he'd ever loved.

He gripped the doorknob as he thought about entering the room, turned the handle, and slowly stepped in. The smell of Remy's favorite perfume filled his nostrils as he inhaled deeply. It was a smell that he missed; it was so familiar that if he closed his eyes he would have sworn that she was standing in front of him, smiling like she always did. Cease walked through the room almost tip-toeing, not wanting to disturb the way Remy had left her things. He sat down on her bed and felt a sense of abandonment. "I miss you," he said, leaning over and resting his head on his fists, trying to fight off the emotions rushing through his body.

He remembered Remy falling in love with the room almost as soon as she saw it when he had first purchased the house. When he asked her why she wanted a bedroom separate from the one they shared she explained, "It will be my personal space. A room I can have when you are getting on my nerves; I need a nice and quiet place, so I can start writing my book."

The memories came rushing back to him as he soaked in the presence of his wife. She had been a "ride or die" chick, and no matter what Cease did, she was always down for him. She did whatever and whenever, as long as she knew she was doing it for him. She never turned her back on him.

He lay down, reminiscing about the many times they'd made love on that very same bed. He reached his hands underneath the pillow and felt something hard. He immediately sat up, knowing exactly what he'd stumbled upon. He pulled out the black book that Remy was writing her memoirs in. He knew it contained her most intimate secrets. All the questions that had been left unanswered when she went away began to race through his mind. He knew the answers would be found on those pages. He opened the diary somewhere in the middle and began to read.

Dear Diary,
I made a lot of money today. It was the first time I did a "side job," and I have to admit, it wasn't all that bad. The men that I entertained tonight were very good tippers. I was scared at first, though, I didn't know that I was gonna have to fuck them. I just thought it would be a little drinking, a little smoking, I would give them a lap dance, and then it would be over. It was much more than that, though, way more than I expected. Once I was in the door there was no turning back, so I did what I had to do. It felt weird exchanging money for sex, especially with so many men. It's not like I had a choice. I need this money.

Cease closed his eyes and lowered his head to his chest. His stomach felt like it was doing somersaults. He did not want to read about his woman having sex with other men. It made him think twice about reading it. The little passage enraged him. He was ready to kill the niggas who'd taken advantage of Remy and he didn't even know who they were. Cease knew that if he continued to read her story it might change the image he had of his wife, but something inside him needed to know the whole story.

Cease knew Remy had a hard life growing up

and that was the exact reason why he never questioned her about anything that happened before him. The only thing he knew for sure was she used to strip before she got out of the hood. He chose to stay in the dark about everything else.

As he sat there with her diary in his hands and the memory of her swarming in his mind, he couldn't help being curious. "I need to know," he said to himself. His voice echoed through the empty room as he clenched the diary tightly in his hands. He wanted to know everything about his wife, and he knew that the only way to find out was by reading her book. "I want to know everything, from beginning to end."

He opened the book and turned to page one. But before he could read one word his Nextel chirped.

"Yo, Cease!" Cease heard his best friend Jodi yell on the two-way.

Chirp!

"Yeah."

Chirp.

"I'm outside waiting for you. It's ten after nine. You gon' be late for court if you don't hurry."

Chirp.

"I'm on my way out."

Chirp.

Cease closed the book and grabbed his blazer off the bed. He stood in front of the mirror and slowly put on his jacket while examining his appearance. He buttoned his shirt up, gradually covering up his tattooed body. Cease reached for his gun that was on top of the dresser, but stopped when he remembered where he was about to go. It had become a habit to grab his gun when he got dressed, a sort of a routine—put on a shirt, put on pants, and strap up.

He ran his hand over his neat, wavy hair and put on the 14ct pinky ring that his mentor once gave him. He kissed it for good luck and headed out of the bedroom. Cease stopped at the door and looked back at the little black book that sat on the bed and walked over to it. He put it in his inside pocket and left out, headed to the courthouse.

* *

Cease sat next to his lawyer in the courtroom with guilt in his heart and hatred in his eyes. He sat and listened to his former girlfriend paint a picture of him as a violent, jealous person. With every false statement that came out of Shay's mouth, Cease grew angrier. He hadn't seen her since their breakup, but he knew exactly why she was on the stand lying and defaming his character. *That bitch mad that I left her dumb ass alone. She envied Remy since the first day she met her, and now that bitch is trying to send me upstate.*

In truth, Cease never really gave a fuck about Shay. To him, she was just another piece of ass. Cease looked back at Jodi, his best friend since childhood, and gave him a look that said a thousand words. Jodi already knew what he was thinking, and he was ready to end her life when the trial was over. Jodi had it set in his mind that she was dead, no matter the verdict.

Cease calmly nodded his head, Jodi nodded back, and it was done—Shay's life was on a countdown. Cease focused his attention back to the character witness.

"He would make me stay in the house for days. He told me if I ever left him—" Shay paused and dropped her head as she gave a performance that should have won her an Oscar.

Cease looked at the jury in disgust because they were actually buying the bullshit. He grew a smug look on his face as he looked at Shay. She avoided eye contact with him, but he stared a hole through her. If looks could kill Shay would be circled in chalk—Cease wanted to put a hollow through her ass right there on the stand.

Cease's murder game was flawless. He had put in work since he was a snot-nosed kid and had a reputation that spoke much louder than any words could ever do. Cease was what you call a straight killer, for real. He got his at any cost and was determined to get rich or die trying. So in the process he had to lay a couple of niggas to sleep in Flint.

Cease couldn't believe what she saying about him. *What the fuck is wrong with her? She is doing all this out of bitterness. She wanted to be in Remy's place. She gon' get hers—that's my word!* Cease realized his face was frowned up and quickly regained his composure and continued to listen to her testimony.

"Drayton Ceaser is an animal," she yelled.

The prosecuting attorney smiled and looked back at Cease. "That will be all," he said and walked to his seat and sat down.

Cease's lawyer stood up, buttoned his blazer, then slowly walked over to the witness stand and stood directly in front of Shay. The lawyer looked Shay directly in her eyes, trying to intimidate her. "Do you have a personal grudge against my client?"

Shay smiled and answered, "No, sir. I'm just up here stating facts."

The attorney looked back at Cease and wiped

his forehead with his handkerchief. "Is it true that you were intimately involved with Drayton Ceaser?"

Shay rolled her eyes and lazily answered, "Yeah."

The lawyer calmly paced the room and took his time, luring the character witness into his trap. If Shay was anything like Cease had described her, it would work like a charm.

"Isn't it also true that he dumped you like a sack of potatoes for his wife Remy?"

Shay shot a look at the lawyer and responded quickly. "Who me? He didn't quit me—I quit his ass."

The defense attorney knew that he had her right where he wanted her and continued to provoke her. "Oh, that's not what Mr. Ceaser stated. He said that you were upset because he left you in the dirt for Remy—you were always jealous of her."

Shay was noticeably getting steamed and couldn't help herself. She had to put the attorney in his damn place. "You got it all twisted. That bitch ain't have shit on me. What I gots to be jealous of? Cease still wants me." Before Shay knew it, she was on her feet and yelling at the attorney.

The attorney smiled. Shay had done the exact thing he wanted her to do—show a personal vendetta against his client. He looked at the judge and said, "That will be all, Your Honor." He walked to the table and sat down. Cease gave him a pound under the table for destroying Shay's credibility.

After a half-hour had passed, the judge adjourned the court for the day. As soon as the judge struck his gavel, Cease immediately loosened his tie and headed out of the courtroom. The allegations that were placed upon him were reminiscent of pure torture. Every time the prosecuting attorney described

Remy's death or called Cease "a cold-blooded murderer of his own wife and child," it hurt him deeply. Jodi waited for Cease outside of the courtroom and they exited the courthouse together. Jodi had never seen his friend like this.

Cease was accused of murdering his wife and unborn baby. Two months earlier Jodi had to post a $250,000 bail to get him out of the county, and since then it seemed like Cease wasn't the same. When Remy died, a piece of him left with her. Jodi drove Cease to his home and as soon as he walked in the door he began reading the story of Remy's life.

Chapter Two

January 1996

Shit had been fucked-up for a long time. It seemed like I was destined to fail from the very beginning. I had been doing the same routine for 11 years, in and out of foster homes, moving from one family to the next. It's crazy how some people are born into this world with everything but still find something to complain about. I never could understand that, but I guess if you've never had anything, you won't understand what it feels like to lose something. I was only sixteen, but it felt like I was forty.

On my own since five, I had seen and done things that no child should've had to experience—stealing, fighting, running, moving—that seemed to be my life story. I didn't like it, but I did what I had to do to get by. I lived in the moment because I never knew if I would be in the same place for more than a couple months.

* * * * * * * * * * * * * * * *

Mr. Jessup was a tall, lean man with deep features. He sat behind the desk of his office with a serious look on his face, staring sternly at me. I was sitting in front of him writing down my thoughts in a diary. I looked up and saw him looking at my profile. The folder sat before him. He shook his head from left to right, and his eyes were wide as if he couldn't believe what he was reading. I could tell he was feeling sorry for me. I knew that to some people my life had been one of chaos. My past had been one of abandonment, betrayal, abuse, and sorrow.

"Ms. Morgan, I know you've had it bad. I know you've had to survive on your own for quite some time, but I'm going to help you put all that behind you," he said.

I heard him speaking, I just didn't care about what he was saying. I closed my diary and made it seem like I was paying attention. While he was trying to read my personality, I was peeping him. He seemed to be a nice guy, but once you got to know them, nice guys usually weren't so nice. I crossed my legs and leaned against one arm of the chair. It was hot in his office, so I took off my jean jacket, revealing the ripped T-shirt I had on. I saw his eyes move to my breasts, and I laughed as he nervously refocused his attention back to my file.

"You are a beautiful young girl, and I know that life has dealt you a shitty hand. I hope that while you are in this girls' rehabilitation home, I can help you straighten out your life. Remy, I am here to help you. We're going to get you on the right path, but you have to want to do right; it's going to take a lot of effort from you.

"We have rules here, and I expect them to be followed. Is that understood?"

I nodded my head. "Will I ever get to leave this place?"

With a look of amusement, he replied, "Yes. You are not in jail, Ms. Morgan. You get one free day per week. Now let me take you to your room."

I got up and followed Mr. Jessup. I saw some of the other girls as I walked through the living room, then through the recreation room, filled with pool tables, ping-pong tables, a TV, and a telephone.

When I arrived at my room, I frowned in disgust. The small all-white room with two twin beds, two dressers, two desks, and two closets looked like a jail cell. The paint on the walls was peeling. I walked in, put down my bags, and looked around at my new home. I reached into my bag and pulled out an old magazine. I flipped through it and pulled out some of the pictures and taped them to the wall. *Anything would be better than looking at the egg-white paint.* I pulled out my diary and began to write.

"When did you get here?" asked a light-skinned girl with badly bleached blonde hair. She was surprised to see someone new in the room.

I could tell by the way she looked at me that she didn't want me there. She wasn't hurting my feelings because I didn't want to be there. I just looked at her like she was crazy and kept writing. She was a bit too friendly, and I hoped that she didn't expect us to get cool. I didn't get along with girls well. It's something about females that I didn't like—they were too damn fake and way too sneaky.

I exhaled deeply, hoping that she would get the hint. I wasn't trying to have a conversation; all I wanted to do was write.

The girl stood there for a minute looking at the pictures that I'd taped to the wall, and after a while she walked over to the bed across from me and plopped down on it. "I'm Shay," she said.

I continued to write, not wanting to pay any attention to my new roommate. She didn't get it—I was not trying to make any new friends. I knew how the girls in group homes could be and I wasn't trying to get caught up in the bullshit. I planned on minding my business and keeping to myself.

I did just that—stayed low-key and didn't talk to anybody. Not even Shay. The other girls had cliques and relied on each other when shit got hectic, but not me. I didn't trust any of them. They all seemed scandalous to me.

I didn't have anyone on the outside waiting for me to get out. No one sent me soap or deodorant. I didn't even have enough panties and bras to make it through one week and was left to fend for myself. I quickly learned the schedules of the other girls, and when they were all doing other things, I snuck into their rooms and stole whatever I needed from them. That was how I got by.

The first week I was in the girls' home Shay tried to be cordial to me, but after she saw that I was not interested in making friends, she stopped trying. I listened closely when she talked, though, and knew all of her business.

Shay had been in the home for almost a year and knew the ins and outs. She had been sent there by her mother, who thought her daughter was getting too wild. After she caught Shay having sex with one of her teachers from school, she saw no other alternative but to send her daughter to a place where they could handle her.

*   *   *

Shay and I sat together in our room completely ignoring each other. I was flipping through a magazine I had stolen from one of the other girls when we heard a lot of commotion in the hall.

"Fuck that! I'm tired of people taking my shit. Where is my watch? My momma just bought me that! Did anybody see who took it?"

Everybody came out of their rooms to watch the scene. The girl was tearing her room up, trying to find the jewelry. I stood outside of the crowd, watching the scene with a smirk on my face.

The girl yelled again, "Who took my shit?"

One of the girls in the home looked at me and crossed her arms. "Remy thieving ass probably got it."

Adrienne, the girl who'd lost her watch, and Sydney, the girl who suggested that I had taken it, both approached me with suspicious looks on their faces.

"Bitch, I didn't steal your shit," I said calmly as the girls stood toe to toe with me. My heart was pounding as a circle formed around us.

"Well, you won't have a problem with us searching through your stuff." Sydney spoke up on her friend's behalf and stormed past me with a group of girls close behind her. Shay sat back watching the scene play off.

I knew if they looked in my dresser drawer they would find Adrienne's watch and a whole bunch of other stuff that had come up missing. I knew Shay had seen me take it too, but she didn't seem to be the type to snitch. So I wasn't worried.

Sydney walked into my room and stormed over to the dresser. She opened it up and started throwing my clothes out onto the floor. The gold watch sitting at the bottom of the dresser caught her eye. She pulled it out and tossed it to Adrienne. "I told you that bitch was grimy." I could hear the aggression in Sydney's voice.

The fact that she had called me out my name made me catch an attitude. I was steaming. "I don't know who you think you calling a bitch, but I didn't take your ol' dollar-store jewelry."

As soon as Sydney started to say something, I decked that bitch in her mouth. It was definitely a fight to see. Growing up on the streets of Flint hardened me, and it showed through my ruthless technique. I didn't care how I won a fight, as long as I did. On top of throwing blows, I was biting, scratching, and pulling out tracks from Sydney's weave job. I was winning until Adrienne jumped in and pulled my hair, trying to get me off her friend. That shit hurt, but I couldn't worry about Adrienne. I had to take those punches. I knew Sydney was the stronger of the two and was determined to beat her ass first.

Sydney managed to maneuver out of my grasp and clawed her nails into my arms.

"Get off my girl." I looked up and saw Shay land a solid punch that made blood spurt from Sydney's mouth.

I let Shay handle Sydney and went to work on Adrienne, stopping only when I felt the muscle of the security guards pulling me off her. The guards grabbed Shay too, but before they could pull her off, she spat in Sydney's face.

The guards broke up the crowd and pulled all four of us into Mr. Jessup's office. He sat behind his desk with a stern, stone-cold look on his face.

"This is unacceptable!" he yelled loudly. "Stealing, fighting. We have to respect each other and their property!" He directed his attention to me.

"I didn't steal that. I got that a couple years ago for Christmas—look on the back."

Adrienne sucked her teeth. "She lying."

Mr. Jessup looked at the back of the watch, shook his head, and then held it up for everybody to see. The inscription read *Remy Princess Morgan*. "Actually she's not. I think you ladies owe Ms. Morgan an apology."

Sydney and Adrienne had "stupid" plastered all over their faces, and when they stubbornly refused to apologize, Mr. Jessup became angry all over again. He began to rant on and on about the rules of the home and the behaviors that are unbecoming of young ladies. I wasn't paying attention to his parental-like scolding; I was too busy wondering why Shay had helped me. It wasn't like we were friends. I wasn't quite sure why she jumped into the fight but was glad that she did.

"You all are on kitchen duty for a month and you can forget about your free days!" Mr. Jessup screamed, interrupting my train of thought.

"But I didn't do shit—that's my watch!"

"Ms. Morgan, your behavior is still inexcusable. Fighting is against the rules, so you will be punished as well."

After almost an hour of lecturing we were allowed to go back to our rooms.

I was silent when I entered the room. I didn't know what to say to Shay; she was the last person I ever expected to help me. "Why did you jump in?"

Shay shrugged her shoulders and sat down on her bed without saying anything more.

I frowned my face and continued, "I mean, we ain't cool or nothing like that. I probably would have watched you get your ass beat if it had happened to you."

"Nah, we ain't cool—I don't like your ass either. I've been wanting to fight Sydney and Adrienne since I got in here; you just gave me an excuse to get it popping."

I laughed at her honesty.

"I just got one question. I saw you when you took the watch—"

Before she could finish her sentence, I waved my hand in dismissal and replied, "I got that shit engraved when I went out last week." We both laughed and that started a mutual respect that eventually transformed into a friendship.

Although we didn't really get along at first, Shay and I began to talk more and more as the months passed by. We were so much alike, it was only natural that we began to click. We formed our own clique in the girls' home and became inseparable. We were all that each other had.

"How did you end up in this place?" Shay asked me one day when we were chilling in our room.

Her question caught me off guard. I never talked about my past and knew it was only a matter of time before she asked. Shay had been itching to know ever since we'd become friends. She would always give me little hints that she was curious. I looked at her, and for a split second I knew she could see the pain reflecting from my eyes.

"I've been in and out of foster homes and girls'

homes since I was little. My momma ran out on me and my daddy when I was a baby. I was only two years old when she packed her shit and left. The funny thing is I still remember her. I remember the day that she walked out on us."

"At least you have your dad."

"My daddy was no better. After my momma left, he saw me as a way to satisfy himself. He started molesting me before I even learned to read . . ." My words broke up as the tears started to fall from the painful memories of my torn and dysfunctional past. "He told me that he loved me and that it had to be our secret. I was in the first grade when some-one finally figured out what was going on. I was in the first fucking grade, bleeding like a grown woman, because my perverted, sick-ass daddy was fucking his little girl." I clenched my diary. Inside it held the story I had just shared with my roommate. I hated my parents more than anything. They were the rea-son why I was so fucked-up.

Shay was speechless for a minute. "I thought I had it bad, but you've been through more than most forty-year-old women have in their entire lives."

The room grew uncomfortably quiet, and then Shay said, "My fault . . . I didn't mean to . . ." She couldn't even finish her sentence. Just imagining what I had gone through would make anybody speechless.

I read the look on her face and wiped the tears from my eyes. "Don't feel sorry for me; I'm dealing with it."

Shay shook her head and replied, "I know—" She paused for a moment, still trying to find the right words to say— "I'm glad that we became cool. You are the first person that I can say I trust."

"Me too."

With that, we left each other to our own thoughts and turned out the lights and went to bed.

I was so tired of being trapped between the four walls of the girls' home. It was April, and I hadn't been out since January. I was growing restless. Because of the fight Mr. Jessup was extra hard on me. He had not allowed me to have any free days for almost two months. I hadn't been anywhere, except to school and back every day. If Shay hadn't been there with me, I would have gone crazy.

Finally, my first free day came, and Shay and I rushed out the building after we checked out. Just happy to be out, I didn't know where we were going. Shay and I stood in front of the home, anticipating the day's events.

"I don't even know where to go?" I stood outside with my hands on my hips.

Shay smiled and said, "I know where I'm about to go—I'm about to go see my friend. You coming?"

I rolled my eyes because I already knew who Shay was referring to. Shay had been messing with this dude named Marcus since she was thirteen, and that's all she ever talked about.

I shook my head and quickly replied, "Hell nah! I ain't trying to be all up in y'all face. You ain't about to make me the third wheel."

Shay walked towards the pay phone at the end of the block. "It won't even be like that, he got friends." Shay picked up the phone and dialed his number. "Hello. Can I speak to Marcus?" she asked into the phone. She paused for a minute. "Hey, this is Shay. Are you still coming to get me?" There was a pause as she listened. "Okay, bring one of your boys, cuz I got my girl with me." Shay hung up the phone and said, "They're on the way."

I laughed. "His friend better not be ugly," I said.

We stood at the pay phone for about twenty minutes waiting for Marcus and his friend to pull up. I saw a beat-up Chevy Caprice pull up on us. I prayed that the one who was driving was for me because the boy who was sitting on the passenger side was ugly as hell. He had some bucked-ass teeth and had the nerve to be hanging out the window, cheesing. He was light-skinned with a fade. (I hated pretty boys.)

We walked over to the car and got in the back seat. "Anthony, this is my girl Remy. Remy, that's Ant."

I gave the driver a quick, "What up," and then smiled to myself.

Ant was fine. He was brown-skinned with corn rows and had a diamond stud in his ear. Ant drove back to his friend's house, where we all went into the basement to chill.

I was uncomfortable at first, but when Ant pulled out some weed and rolled up a fat blunt, I quickly relaxed and started having a good time. We didn't do all that much, but I was just having fun being out of the home.

When Shay and Marcus went into the washroom to handle their business, me and Ant sat back and watched *Comic View*. He put his arm around me, and I sat close to him as we laughed loudly and lit up another blunt.

That night Shay asked me, "So what you think about Ant?"

I shrugged my shoulders, trying to act nonchalant and said, "He cool. He supposed to pick me up next week and he gave me his cell phone number so I could call him."

Ant started picking me up every time I got a free day. I didn't want a boyfriend or nothing like that, I was just looking for a friend. Ant sold weed, so he kept me high and happy when I was with him. I would always come back to the home with money in my pocket, and Shay was impressed at how slick I really was. She knew Ant well enough to know that he would never give a chick money, so she knew that I had to be taking it.

"You either taking it, or you got some bomb-ass pussy." Shay laughed. "Just be careful, girl—Ant do not play about his money," she warned, afraid that eventually my klepto ways would catch up with me.

I had seen Ant every week since we first met after the first couple months, and this week was no different. I signed myself out of the home and walked up the street, where I saw Ant's car sitting at the corner by the phone booth. I quickly walked toward it and got in. I smiled as he drove off. His friends were in the back seat. "What up, Marcus." I recognized Shay's boyfriend.

"What's good with you?" he responded.

I reached across the seat for Ant's hand, but he threw my hand back into my own lap.

I frowned up and said, "What's wrong with you?"

Ant didn't say anything. He just continued to drive with an angry expression on his face. I just figured he was in a bad mood, so I sat back in the seat and chilled. "Where we going?" I asked, expecting to go to Marcus' house, the spot where we always chilled.

"Just ride," Ant replied coldly.

We pulled onto Patterson Street, and Ant suddenly stopped the car. He grabbed the back of my neck roughly.

I cringed and said, "Damn, Ant, quit playing so much. That shit hurts."

Ant tightened his grip and said, "Bitch, you better give me my money. I know you took it—you the only person who been in my car!" His teeth were clenched, and he wrapped his fingers around my neck.

I was scared—I thought he was just being an asshole—so I tried to remain cool while he held me with one arm and pointed his finger in my face with the other.

"What are you talking about? I didn't take your money . . ." I yelled back. I could feel the pressure of his grasp. His hand was wrapped tightly around my neck, and I could barely breathe. My eyes were burning, and they felt like they were going to pop out of my head.

"I know you took my dough. You either gone run my shit or me and my niggas gone run a train on you." The three other guys in the car laughed.

The inside of the car was filled with smoke from the blunts they had lit up, and I was choking. The air that I did manage to squeeze into my throat was rejected by my lungs because of the purple haze that filled the car. I looked Ant in the eyes, and immediately a sense of fear filled the bottom of my stomach. He was serious.

The feeling that consumed me when I knew I

was in trouble invaded my insides, making me feel like throwing up. "I don't have your money, Ant. I swear I didn't take it." I knew that I was in a fucked-up situation because I had already spent the money, rocking his $500 from head to toe. I had gotten my hair and nails done, purchased a new outfit, and bought some shoes with his cash. "Ant, please . . . you are hurting me."

Ant released his grip on me and pushed my head hard against the passenger window.

"Oww! Ant, stop!"

"Give me my muthafuckin' money!" The tone of his voice expressed his rage.

A bitch had never tried to play him like I did, and he seemed to be getting even madder because I was denying it. He knew I had his money and he was going to make me pay him one way or the other.

I scrambled as I tried to reach for the door. I frantically got out the car and started walking fast down the street, figuring they wouldn't try and snatch me off the street in broad daylight.

"Man, bring her stupid ass back," Ant yelled as his boys got out the car and ran after me.

I took off in a sprint, trying to outrun the three dudes.

Ant turned his car around and drove in the direction I was running. He screeched to a stop at the corner, and his boys grabbed me from behind and carried me kicking and screaming. They shoved me into the back seat, and two of them held me down while Ant drove down North Saginaw Street towards Beecher.

I screamed at the top of my lungs. "Stop! Stop!" I tried to kick, twist, and claw my way up, but the two boys holding me down were too strong.

Ten minutes later the car came to a stop, and Ant said, "Get the fuck out." He dragged me by the arm and led me into a garage. His friends followed, laughing at the situation as if they hadn't taken me against my will.

Tears started to fall from my eyes as I tried to think of a way out of this. I knew I couldn't run away from them. "Ant, please . . . just let me go. I'll repay you the money, I swear," I pleaded, wishing I had listened to Shay when she told me not to fuck with Ant's money.

Ant pushed me up against a wall and held my hands up with one hand while he unfastened my pants with the other. "Bitch, you stole from me? You had the nerve to steal from me?"

One of the other guys ran out the garage and came back with a video camera.

"Stop! Somebody, please help me!"

"Bitch, shut the fuck up." Ant smacked me hard across the face.

I tried to muffle my screams, hoping he wouldn't hit me again, but the pain I felt when he jammed his dick hard inside me, ripping my walls, made me cry out, "Stop!"

After Ant was done, he sat back and taped the situation as it unfolded.

I screamed in pain as the boys took turns raping me, each one degrading me in their own way. I tried to keep my thighs closed, but the boys just pried them open, hurting me even more and making me feel like my legs would break.

When they were done, Ant got up and threw my clothes at me. He knelt down beside me and grabbed my face with his hand. "You steal money from me, I treat you like a ho. Bitch, put on your shit and walk home." All four boys walked out of the garage, leaving me alone in the dark.

I was crying hard and trembling as I tried to put my clothes back on. My hands were shaking so badly, I couldn't fasten the buttons on my pants. I heard Ant start his car and his tires screech when he pulled off. "Please, help me," I whispered shakily. I wasn't really talking to anyone in particular, I just wanted help. "Help, somebody. Please, help me!" I tried to get up, but my legs felt like putty. "Help!"

My tears were continuous. I felt the pains run through my body when I tried to move. I tried to stand, tried my hardest to crawl, but my body had given up on me. I tried to breathe deep, but the ninety-degree, mid-August, Flint temperature and the closed garage made it impossible in the claustrophobic space. I could smell the scent of sex, of the blood leaking from my vagina, mixed with sweat and semen, and it made me sick to my stomach.

I cried so hard, my head began to hurt. The pounding on my brain was excruciating. I lay down on the hard cement of the garage and closed my eyes, just wanting to make the pain go away. I felt myself slipping farther and farther into unconsciousness and wanted desperately to wake up. But my body was too weak, and in seconds I fell into a black, cold, restless sleep.

I awoke to darkness. The unfamiliarity of my surroundings immediately put me back in a panic. I looked out the window that sat above the bed and saw the white and black garage. My heartbeat sped up when I saw it. I remembered what Ant and his friends had done to me and prayed that they hadn't come back for me. I got up off the bed that I had been on and found that the strength had returned to my legs. *I had to get out of there.* I didn't even know whose garage it was. It seemed like Ant just chose any place to dump me.

I looked down at myself and saw the dried blood on my legs. The sight made me recall the horror. I was afraid to stay trapped in the room but even more afraid of what, or who, was waiting for me outside the door. I looked around the room and saw a phone sitting on top of one of the dressers and ran over to it. I had to call the home so somebody could pick me up. I picked up the line and heard a man's voice say, "You need to be at the club by nine o'clock. Don't be late." I tried my best to put the phone back on the hook without making any noise, but when I put it down it made a small clank that I was sure both parties heard.

My heart raced with dread as I heard the man say, "I'll call you back."

I looked around the room for something to defend myself with, anything that might help me fight off whoever was getting ready to come into the room. I couldn't find anything and the window was too small for me to climb out of, so I waited as I heard footsteps approach the room. I grabbed a lamp off the dresser and slid my slender body behind the door. The door opened slowly and as soon as the man stepped inside the room I slammed the lamp on the back of his neck and ran out the door. He grabbed the back of his head and felt the blood trickle down his neck. "Shit!" he yelled and ran after me. He grabbed me by the waist and picked me up in spite of my punches and attempts to escape. "Calm down!" His voice was stern. He walked back into the room and placed me back on the bed.

I stopped resisting and sat very still on the bed, hoping he wouldn't touch me.

The man looked down at me and asked, "You all right?"

I didn't reply. I just sat there, my head held low and my eyes on the floor in front of me.

He grabbed my chin and lifted my face so that he could get a better look at it. He noticed a small bruise forming on the right side of my face and saw that I was crying. He could tell I was scared.

I was playing with my fingers, twisting them hard in a nervous reaction.

"I'm not gon' hurt you; I'm the wrong nigga to be scared of." He paused for a minute to see if I would respond. "Who did this to you?"

I still didn't respond. I didn't know him, and after what had happened to me, I wasn't trying to get to know him. I just wanted to get the hell out of there.

"I found you in my garage; I don't know how you got there. Do you have somebody you need to call?"

I nodded my head, and he pointed me towards the phone. I reluctantly got up and walked over to the dresser, trying to keep my eyes on him. I quickly dialed the number and asked for Shay.

"Remy, where you at?" Shay asked in a whisper.

"I don't know—"

"Girl, Jessup is mad. He had the police here looking for you and everything."

My eyes shot wide open. "The police? What did he call the police for?"

Shay lowered her voice even more and said, "I don't know, but if I was you I wouldn't come back here; if you do, he ain't gonna do nothing but have you shipped to another home. You already out, so just stay out."

"Okay. Listen, I'll call you, okay. I love you, girl. Thanks." I hung up the phone and looked at the man standing in the door. "Can I go?" I asked, still not knowing his intentions for me.

"Do you have a place to go?"

I stood there for a minute. I hadn't thought of that yet. I didn't have any family or friends.

He picked up on my hesitation and then walked out the room. I heard the sound of running water. He came back five minutes later with a towel and an oversized T-shirt. "You can get cleaned up here. If you don't have a place to go, you can stay here until you figure something out. I don't know what happened to you, but I want to help."

I didn't reply, but took the towel and T-shirt into the bathroom. I stared at my reflection in the mirror, regretting my situation. Tears came to my eyes, but I shook them away, locked the door, and slowly got into the bathtub.

My body ached, and I could feel every pain as I gently washed myself. I sat in the tub for almost an hour not thinking about anything in particular. I got out of the tub and put on the shirt, which came down to my knees. There was no way I was putting them bloodstained clothes back on. In between my legs ached, and all I really wanted to do was go to sleep. I walked out of the bathroom and out into the living room, where the man was waiting for me.

He took my clothes from me and threw them in the trash. "I'm Dock," he said.

"Remy."

Dock cracked a smile and then said, "Like the drink?"

I cracked a smile too; he wasn't the first person I had gotten that reaction from. "Yeah, like the drink."

Dock walked over to his couch, sat down, and turned on the TV. He seemed to be okay. I walked over to the couch and sat down on the other end.

"Thank you," I said after a couple minutes of silence. "Thanks for the clothes and everything."

Dock picked up a glass of cognac that was sitting in a coaster on the table and poured a shot. "Don't worry about it—you can stay here as long as you need to."

I stayed with Dock for a while and eventually grew comfortable at his place. He had my head—I did whatever he asked me to do and didn't mind, because he treated me okay. I mean, he wasn't the richest or the most attractive, but he was decent to me, and at that time, that was all I could ask.

About a year had gone by when I turned seventeen. Dock was thirteen years older than I, which was part of the reason why I enjoyed his company so much. His brown complexion, high-top fade, and old-school wardrobe were easily overlooked. For a year he kept me in nice clothes and gave me anything I wanted. I was comfortable in the smallest sense of the word—I didn't have to work or go to school. The only thing Dock asked of me was to cook, clean, and have the ass waiting for him when he got home.

Dock owned a strip club, and oftentimes I would find myself jealous of the fact that he spent so much time around half-naked women. I kept it to myself, though. As long as he kept business and personal separate, then I didn't have a problem. But over time things gradually changed. I wasn't as interesting and satisfying to Dock as I was when he first met me, and his true colors slowly began to show.

Chapter Three

August 1997

As I washed the dishes in Dock's small house, I talked to myself aloud, thinking about how unhappy I was living there. He was rude, controlling, and often degraded me just because he knew that he could. I imitated Dock as I scrubbed the dishes. "Clean this, suck this, do that . . ."

Dock had put on a front when I first met him. He used to act like I was all he needed, all that he would ever want. And my dumb ass fell for the game. Now he treated me like the rest of the world did—like nothing.

"When I save up enough bread, I'm out. I can do bad by my damn self," I said as I dried the last dish and headed for the bedroom. I wanted more than anything to get away from Dock but just couldn't. He provided me with a roof over my head and a job. He was all I had, and even though that meant I didn't have much, it was better than being out on my ass. I didn't have any family, any friends, or any place to go—I was stuck between a rock and a hard place.

As soon as I sat on the bed, I heard the keys jingle in the door. I knew that it was Dock, and my heart began to pound. A wave of fear overcame me every time I was in his presence. There was something about him that made me shiver. I heard the door close but didn't recognize the voice that came from the living room. It was a woman's. I quickly heard Dock's voice and walked into the front room just as they were taking off their coats.

It was Dock and a girl who appeared to be around my age. She wore a short hairstyle and dark red lipstick. I stared at her, and she stared right back.

Bitch, I thought, getting defensive.

Dock was hanging up his coat while we were grilling each other.

Who the fuck is this bitch? I put both of my hands on my hips.

Dock noticed that we were looking as if we were about to knuckle up right there in his living room. "Remy, meet Layla; Layla, meet Remy."

I instantly smacked my lips and stormed to the bedroom with my hands folded across my chest.

I heard Dock tell Layla to take a seat on the couch, and he followed me into the bedroom. "What is yo' fuckin' problem?"

"How you gon' bring her into—"

"*My* house. You better remember whose house you living in—I run this! If I don't feed you, you don't eat—remember that shit."

I remained silent, briskly tapping my foot against the ground. I knew he was right and couldn't say a damn thing about it.

Dock calmed down and continued in a calmer

voice. "Now, Layla is going to stay here for a while. Do you have a problem with that?"

I grew angrier with every word he said.

Dock repeated himself in a stronger tone, "Do you have a problem with that?" He stepped closer to me and stood directly above me as I sat on the end of the bed, waiting for me to answer.

"No."

"Good." He smirked at the sight of my submissiveness and then left the room.

I sat on the end of the bed in total disbelief. I couldn't believe him. He was so fucking disrespectful, and there wasn't a damn thing I could do about it. "All I know is she better not say shit to me," I said to an empty room. I eventually calmed down, turned on the TV and watched a movie.

Dock had left us there alone, and I stayed in the room while Layla sat in the living room. We never crossed each other's path.

I looked at the clock and noticed it was almost time for me to go to the club. I walked to the dresser and took out a two-piece, black, nylon outfit and placed it in my duffle bag along with some baby oil and make-up. Just as I finished packing, Layla appeared in the doorway. I ceased all movement and made eye contact with her. I was ready to beat her ass, but she had a different expression on her face than she displayed earlier.

Layla walked in slowly and sat on the bed while I continued to pack. "Listen, I'm not trying to beef with you; I don't even know you. I'm in a fucked-up position right now and I need a place to stay."

I acted as if I didn't even hear her.

Layla tried again. "Look, I know you don't want me to be here, but Dock said he can hook me up with a job. As soon as I get enough dough, I'll be gone." Layla waited for a response but got none. Then she turned around and headed out of the room.

I couldn't be too mad at her; I understood what type of position she was in and realized that we were in the same boat. "Hold on!"

Layla stopped at the door and looked at me.

"I don't have a problem with you; it's Dock—that nigga is foul."

Layla dropped her head, not knowing what to say.

I walked over to her with my hand out. "I'm Remy."

She smiled and shook my hand. "I'm Layla."

* * * * * * * * * * *

Later that night I was in Magic City preparing for my solo performance on stage. I oiled my entire body and looked in the mirror, making sure I looked good. I wore a black, nylon two-piece with net stockings, and some high heels that hurt my feet every time I put them on. I looked over at Layla and saw how nervous she was—that chick was over there sweating bullets. Which made me think about my first time.

* * * * * * * * * * *

I sat in front of the mirror applying makeup to my face. My heart was pounding, and my stomach was in knots. I looked around at the dressing room full of women and couldn't believe what I was about to do. *Damn*, I was only seventeen years old and had somehow managed to find my way into a strip club. I felt my eyes begin to water and quickly fanned away the tears. It had taken me about fifteen minutes to put on my makeup, and I didn't want the tears to ruin it.

I grabbed the baby oil off the stand and rubbed it all over my body. My hands were shaking, and my mouth felt dry. *Come on, a couple of minutes on the stage. That's all it's gonna take. I can do this. I need the money.*

Then I heard a voice say, "You're up in fifteen minutes." Dock stood behind me giving me a brief massage before he returned to the front.

I shook my head lightly and continued to stare in the mirror, hoping that stripping would be as easy as it looked. "I can't believe I'm doing this," I whispered to myself. I looked at the girl sitting next to me and asked, "How is it out there?"

The girl turned her head and looked at me. "This must be your first time?"

I shook my head and lowered my eyes, embarrassed by the fact that I had actually stooped so low. "Yeah, I need the money."

The girl laughed loudly and then replied, "Don't we all?" She looked me up and down and then grabbed my hand.

I followed her over to the clothes rack.

"First you need to change out of that showgirl shit you wearing. Those niggas out there didn't come here for that, all they want to see is you shaking your ass. What did you say your name is?"

"Remy. Remy Morgan."

The girl smiled and replied, "Peaches." Peaches pulled a tiny black thong and fish net top from the rack and threw them to me. "Here, put these on."

I looked skeptically at the outfit, but before I could comment she pushed me towards one of the changing rooms and said, "Trust me, I'm a pro."

I hurried and changed into the outfit. I walked back out and looked into the mirror.

Peaches came up and leaned on my shoulder, waiting for me to say something, I guess. "You look good, don't worry. You're only on stage for three minutes anyway. After that you just circulate through the crowd, trying to make extra money."

I didn't like how Peaches said the words "extra money." *What extra stuff do I have to do?* I knew stripping wasn't actually a good-paying profession, but Dock had drilled it in my head that it was easy as one, two, three, and I finally gave it a shot. I'd heard a lot of stories about how the girls were treated, but I knew Dock wouldn't let things get too out of hand. The ones who did make money from it usually did a whole lot more than stripping. I knew the risks of stripping. I had gone over them in my mind time and time again before I had even applied to Magic City.

"You're up!" Peaches announced.

I felt my heart catch in my throat, and my eyes widened with insecurity.

Peaches saw the look of fear on my face and reached inside her bra and pulled out a small silver container. She pulled off the top and poured a white, powdery substance onto the makeup table. "It makes it easier," Peaches said as she rolled up a dollar bill and hit a line of cocaine.

I was scared. She knew I didn't want to go through with it; I could tell by her expression. I looked around to make sure no one was watching and then lowered my head to the table and sniffed a line of coke. I closed my eyes as the drug started to tingle my nose. It stung for a while, but after a minute I felt my body begin to relax, the nervousness subsiding enough for me to build up some courage to go on the stage.

I walked up the steps and through the curtains that led to the stage. As soon as I stepped out, I heard men yell and saw a couple dollar bills land on the end of the stage. My hands were sweaty, and I didn't really know what to do. The strobe light that bounced around the club made me dizzy, and I felt as if I was about to pass out. *Just dance*, I thought, as I began my routine.

I started to work the pole. I ran my "ass crack" up and down the pole and leaned over sexily, exposing my breasts to the men in the crowd. I took off my shirt and threw it into the crowd. It was hot in the club, and I instantly began to sweat, making my body wet and sticky. I wrapped my legs around the pole and swung around, like some of the other girls did.

I walked to the edge of the stage and turned around, shaking my ass to the beat of Juvenile's hit song, "Back That Thang Up." I could feel the eyes of the men on me. The pressure was intense. As I scanned the room, I noticed the different groups of men scattered around. Some were in cliques, chilling with their boys; others were alone, watching closely and drooling over my every move.

There were all types of men there—white men, black men, old men, and young men. The one thing they had in common is that they all were thinking about what it would be like to have sex with me. I bounced my ass up and down, dropping it to the floor, exposing my vagina to the crowd. Bills filled the stage until I ended my act with a split on the floor.

The crowd erupted, and I saw Peaches laughing and clapping at the side of the stage. I quickly collected my money and walked off. "Oh my goodness, I was nervous as hell!" I said to Peaches.

"I couldn't tell," she said excitedly; "you were good, girl!"

All of a sudden I was plagued with nausea, and a pounding headache began to form behind my temples. I bolted for the dressing room with Peaches following right behind me.

"Relax. That always happens on your first time. You have to let the snow soak in; you'll feel better in a minute."

I rushed to the toilet and threw up the contents of my stomach. "Fuck! I feel sick." I yelled as I draped over the nasty toilet seat.

"It's just the coke," Peaches said as she hit another line.

I was messed up for about thirty minutes before the feeling finally started to fall down. I cleaned myself up, sat at my vanity mirror, and then took a deep breath as I looked into my own eyes. I couldn't recognize the face that stared back at me—it was terrifying. I promised myself at that moment that I would never put another drug into my body again.

* * * * * * * * * * * *

I snapped out of my daydream and continued to lather my body with the oil. I heard my cue and walked out onto the stage. I seductively trotted around, wiping off the poles so I could start my show. The deejay put on a track, and I dropped on all fours and slowly grinded the air. The crowd went crazy when they saw my array of booty tricks. I made one cheek go up at a time, driving the men in the club crazy. A swarm of men gathered around the stage, throwing dollars bills at me. I knew I was going to make a killing that night. I got up and slowly walked over to a man holding a twenty dollar bill and wrapped my right leg around the man's neck and slowly begin to thrust against his face. I placed my index finger in my mouth and teased the other men watching. Every time I got on stage the men went wild. They loved me and they showed it by showering me with dollar bills. I unleashed my grip on the man and headed to the pole. I jumped on the pole and slowly swung down. When I reached the ground I was doing the splits and popping my assets.

I looked over at the group of men and scanned everyone's hand to see who had what I was looking for. *Bingo!* I saw a light-skinned, chubby dude waving a hundred-dollar bill around. I walked over to the man, and just before I reached him, I got on all fours and crawled to him. The man stuck the bill in my top and whispered in my ear, "If you wanna make some real money, shorty, come see me after your set."

I nodded my head and went to the center of the stage and finished up my routine. After a standing ovation I returned to the back. When I was in the back the only thing I could think about is what that guy said to me. I couldn't help but wondering what he had in mind. At that point I was all about that cash, so his words lingered in my head well after he said them.

I returned to the club area in the midst of

drunken men and strippers juicing their asses for everything they had. The club was jumping on this particular night, and I wanted to go home with at least four hundred. Dock usually took most of my money, so I tried to make as much extra money on the side as possible. He knew that I usually made between two and three hundred a night. So anything I made after that I never told his ass about.

I walked around the room, searching for the man that gave me the hundred-dollar bill. I quickly scanned the room and saw the man getting a lap dance from Layla. *Damn! She got to him before I did*. I danced by myself, frequently taking a glance over in their direction. A man grabbed my butt, and I quickly turned around. "Hey, daddy. Wanna dance?"

The man sat back in his chair and opened his legs, signaling for me to give him a dance. I straddled him and began to dance on him erotically. I felt his manhood begin to harden. By the end of the song, I left him broke with a hard dick. When I looked around, the man that Layla was dancing on was heading out of the door. "Fuck!"

I went to the next man wanting me to dance for him.

I was in the back at my locker, taking off my clothes and preparing to go home. I hoped Dock didn't take all day; I was tired and my feet were killing. As I waited, I still couldn't help thinking about the offer that I had been given. I didn't know what he was talking about, but if he had a hundred to just give away, I knew there was more where that came from.

I closed my locker and Layla was right there in my face, standing on the other side of it. It startled me. I dropped what I had in my hands and said, "Girl, don't be sneaking up on me like that."

She smiled, reached into her bra, and pulled out a piece of paper. "That man told me to give you this."

I took the paper and read it. It had a phone number and the name Philly under it. *Philly—so that's his name.* "Thanks, Layla." I put the number in my bag.

Just as I put up the number away, Dock walked in. His lime-green shirt and gator shoes made him look like a pimp from the '80s. His high-top fade was so played out—everyone knew it except him. It was funny because he thought he was the best thing since sliced bread. "Damn, it smells like ass up in here." Dock laughed at his own joke then stopped once he saw he was the only one laughing. "Anyway, I wanted to introduce the newest member of our family to everybody." He walked over to Layla and said, "This is Layla."

No one really acknowledged her. It was a couple of "heys" said but nothing more than that.

Peaches whispered to another stripper. "He must have got tired of Remy. Now his nose is all up her ass. Ain't that a bitch?"

On his way out the room Dock whispered in my ear, "We out of here in fifteen minutes—I got something fun for us tonight."

I smiled and finished getting dressed, excited about what Dock just told me. He hadn't taken me out nor did anything special for me in a long time.

Thirty minutes later, Dock, Layla, and I were all in his long, old-school Cadillac. Dock went straight to the back and put on his robe, Layla lay down in the living room, too tired to even get to the bedroom, and I sat on the couch watching TV.

Dock came in with a bottle of Hennessy. "Remy, why don't you go sit by Layla."

I looked at Dock like he was nuts. "I'm okay right here, daddy."

Dock hit the Hennessy. "I said you need to go and sit by Layla."

I looked at Dock in confusion and walked over to Layla. From the look in his eye I knew he was dead serious.

Layla sat up, wondering what Dock was doing.

He sat in the chair that I just got up from and began giving orders. "Remy, suck Layla's titties."

Layla gave Dock the same look I had just given him a couple of seconds earlier.

I stood up and said, "Yo, Dock, it ain't that type of party—you know I don't get down like that."

Dock stood up, waving the bottle around. "Bitch, you gon' get down like that tonight, or you can get the fuck out." Then he backed off a little. "I just want a little entertainment, that's all."

I tried to plead with Dock. "Baby, let's just go in the back room, me and you—I'll entertain you."

Dock shot up and grabbed my neck. "You heard what I said."

Layla sat there and didn't say anything. I guess she didn't know what to say. This was the only place she had to stay, so she was going to do what she had to do.

I reluctantly got on my knees and pulled one of Layla's breasts out of her blouse. A single tear slid down my face as I began to suck it.

Dock gave us specific sexual orders, and we abided by them. He made us have a ménage à trois with him, but he was the only one enjoying himself. He made me eat Layla out and vice versa. By the time we were finished, Layla and I had tears in our eyes, and Dock had a big smile on his face as he fell out in the middle of the floor, sound asleep.

* * * * * * * * * * * * *

The next morning I woke up early and gave Philly a call. Philly kept the conversation short and sweet. He told me that he had a job for me that earned one thousand dollars a week. He didn't have to say anymore—I wanted to get down. He told me to meet him at the Coney Island downtown. I told Dock I had a doctor's appointment so he wouldn't question where I was going. With his approval, I left on my way to meet Philly.

I caught the city bus downtown. When I finally reached my stop and stepped off the bus, I was contemplating what exactly he had in mind for me. For a thousand dollars a week, I would do just about anything. A G a week—shit, with that I could finally get my own spot and get from underneath Dock's controlling ass. As I got closer to the restaurant, I saw a white SUV sitting square in the middle of the empty parking lot. The sun sparkled off the pearl-white Escalade. Philly's truck was sitting on some grown man's (over 21-inch tires) and his dark tint was the cherry on top.

Philly was getting money and wanted the whole city to know it.

I walked closer to the truck and he rolled down his window letting me see his face. When I recognized his face, I walked over to the passenger side and hopped in the truck.

He looked over at me, and his chubby cheek-bones rose up as he gave me an ear to ear smile. "Remy, right?"

I kept my eyes forward, trying to avoid eye contact with him. "Yeah, right."

My pulse was racing; I was nervous as hell. I didn't know who he was or what the job he had in store for me. All I knew was that there was money to be made and I was about to get on my hustle.

"Remy—what kind of name is that?"

I looked over at Philly and folded my arms. "It's the name my momma gave me."

He smirked and focused his attention back on the road, then turned up his stereo.

I studied his appearance and wasn't impressed at all. Yeah, he was dressed fresh to death and had an iced-out Jesus piece that sparkled every time the sun hit it, but I really wasn't feeling him. Philly's chubby, boyish face and sloppy build didn't appeal to me.

The whole ride to the destination was quiet, except for the Nas CD that blared out of his speakers. He drove into the heart of the fifth ward, an area in Flint where two types of people lived—dope fiends; and the hustlers that were pushing the dope to the fiends. I had to admit, I grew uncomfortable when I saw all of the crackheads on the corners and the old, abandoned buildings that were transformed into crackhouses. I did not show that I was intimidated, though.

Desperate to get out of Dock's house and start over, I finally got up the nerve to ask him, "So what exactly am I going to be doing?"

Philly turned down the radio and replied, "Let's just say, you're about to become a chemist."

I knew exactly what he meant by that and couldn't help cracking a smile. I didn't know the first thing about cooking dope, but I was willing to learn.

We approached a two-story brick house with flowers decorating the porch. It wasn't too flashy. Matter of fact, it was far from nice. Philly hopped out of the truck and motioned his head for me to get out and follow him. We went to the back of the house, and he knocked on the door in a pattern. *Knock, knock, knock . . . knock, knock!*

An older lady that looked to be around fifty or so answered the door, cigarette dangling from the right side of her mouth. "Philly, what the hell you banging on the goddamn door for like the fuckin' police? Shit, I was watching my stories."

He looked at me and smirked at the comment. "Sorry, Betty Netty. I got a new one for you."

She slowly looked me up and down and said, "Hell, you going to stand out there and look dumb with this fool, or you comin' in?"

I smiled, and we entered the house. I immediately noticed that the inside of the house did not match the outside. The inside was plush, with new furniture and a big plasma TV that hung on the wall. *How can a house look like Sanford and Son's on the outside and look like this on the inside?*

Betty Netty was a 60-year-old woman who dressed like youth. You could tell she was a nice-figured fox back in the day and that age caught up with her. Netty walked to her bar and poured two drinks of Rémy Martin.

Philly introduced me to Netty. "Remy, this is the notorious Betty Lynette—she is going to show you the ropes."

Betty Netty walked over to me and handed me a

drink. "Hey, darling, you can call me Netty." Netty looked and examined me and said, "Girl, you sho' is pretty. A lil' bit rough around the edges, but you pretty."

I put my head down and softly replied, "Thanks."

She sat on the barstool and began to chat, "Honey, what you say yo' name was again?"

"Remy."

Betty Netty frowned up. "Remy? Like Rémy Martin?"

I giggled. "Yeah."

Betty clapped her hands together. "That's my favorite drink; we are going to get along fine."

Philly saw that his work there was done, said his goodbyes, and headed for the door.

Netty closed the door behind him and rolled her eyes. "I can't stand his fat ass." We burst out laughing. Netty headed towards the basement, and I followed.

"Now, honey, this job pays well, and it's simple. I will show you what you need to do and how it's supposed to be done. I hope you ain't shy about being naked—Khadafi don't allow no clothes to be worn while on the job."

Khadafi? Who is he? "Nah, I'm comfortable."

Betty waved her hand and put the other one on her hip. "Good!"

In the basement, there were about six topless girls with doctor's masks on their faces, cutting dope on a big table. The table was full of soft and cooked coke. I had never seen so much cocaine before. You could hardly see the wood on the table. There were test tubes and three stoves towards the back of the basement.

Oh my God! So this is what it looks like. It is so

much dope on the table, it looks like a science lab down here.

Betty Netty led the way, giving me a tour of my new workplace. "We have twelve girls that rotate shifts. Every Monday you get paid a thousand dollars. Don't start no shit—it won't be no shit. If y'all bitches wanna fight, do it somewhere else. This is an operation." She paused and puffed her cigarette and looked at me. "You getting all of this?"

I nodded my head, and Betty continued, "This is Khadafi's shit, and I just run it. He doesn't tolerate stealin' either. Lena! Show her what you get for stealing."

A girl walked from the back of the basement and turned her back towards us. Netty lifted Lena's hair and exposed a gruesome sight.

"Shit!" I yelled at the sight of the bubble scar that resembled the letter *T*. I cringed at the sight and turned my head.

"That *T* stands for thief—it would have been worse if she wasn't his friend's niece. Understand?"

I spent the whole day under Betty Netty. She showed me how to cook, chop, and prepare the products for distribution. I caught on very quick; I was a natural. Actually, Betty was surprised how quickly I had caught on.

By nightfall I was topless, chopping up dope alongside the other girls in the basement. Netty made me feel comfortable. She was funny as hell. She talked about everybody and gave me the low-down on all the girls. She was just good people.

I had so much fun with Betty Netty I forgot about my stripping job. I knew Dock would be enraged because I was out all day without calling him. "Oh shit, it's 1:15 in the morning. I have to go."

Betty Netty called Philly, and twenty minutes later, he was in front of the house, honking his horn.

I jumped into the car with him, and he dropped me off in front of the club. As I got out of the truck he said, "You start tomorrow at six. Get there." This would be the last time Philly acted as a cab service and he let it be known.

I yelled, "Okay," and rushed to the front entrance of the strip joint called Magic City.

When I entered the club it was nearly empty. Two strippers were "pussy-popping" on a headstand, trying to make a couple dollars before the last of the crowd left. One of the other strippers approached me with a "you in trouble" expression on her face and almost in a whisper said, "Where you been at? Dock is looking for you and he ain't happy."

I took a deep breath. "Where is he?"

The girl pointed to the back of the club where his office was located. I tried to gather a lie up in my head as I headed towards the back. My heart pounded harder and harder as I approached Dock's office. When I walked in, he was at his desk, counting all one-dollar bills. Without even looking up, he asked, "Where the fuck have you been? You had a lot of requests tonight to go in VIP."

"Baby, I can explain. I—"

Before I could get the lie out of my mouth, Dock jumped up, lunged towards me. He wrapped his hand around my whole neck and squeezed with all of his might, leaving me gasping for air.

"Bitch, you playing with my money. While you was running the streets, I was here missing money because of you." Dock cocked his hand back and backhanded me across the mouth, causing blood to leak from my bottom lip.

I fell to the ground and began to beg him to stop. "Please, Dock."

He paid me no mind and grabbed me by the hair, yanking me from the floor. He had a handful of my hair as he whispered in my ear, "You are going to make this up to me, or I'll put yo' ass right back on the streets where I found you." Dock walked over to the desk and sat on it. He unbuttoned his pants and pulled his penis out.

I knew what time it was. This wasn't the first time he treated me like a ho. I slowly walked over to him, tears streaming down my cheeks.

"That's my girl," he said in anticipation.

I kneeled in front of him and softly gripped his dick.

My hatred for Dock was deeper than the Pacific Ocean, and I regretted the day I met him. I was tired of being treated like a dog. Life wasn't supposed to be like that.

I began to suck the tip, but the thought of going any further made me gag. I looked up at Dock, sweat forming on his forehead and his eyes closed. I gripped his penis with my left hand, lifted it slightly, and punched his balls as hard as I could with my right.

Dock screamed at the top of his lungs in agony. He fell onto the floor, his pants around his ankles, holding his manhood, and rolled around in pure misery.

I stood up and spat on him. "Fuck you, nigga! Suck what? I can't hear you now!" I screamed in frustration. I cried harder as I released everything I wanted to ever say to him. "I hate you, I hate you,

I hate you!" I kicked him square in the nose and rushed out of the door before he could retaliate.

I rushed out of the office with all eyes on me as I scrambled out of Magic City. I walked down Stewart Street at 2:00 in the morning with blood dripping from my face and no specific destination. All I knew is that I'd made a big mistake, but there was no turning back now. I didn't know where to go. I went to the only place I could think of—Betty Netty's house.

An hour and a half later, lip swollen, and my feet aching from my unexpected journey, I was at Netty's doorstep. I knocked on the door and got no response. I broke down and cried on the front porch, not knowing what to do. I gathered myself and began to walk off. Just as I was about to step off the porch, Netty opened the door, wearing a nightgown and headscarf. I looked back at her, and she looked at me.

Netty squinted her eyes, trying to see exactly who was knocking on her door at that time of night. "Remy?" she said, opening her screen door.

I wiped my tears away and was at a loss of words. I was so desperate, I couldn't say a word.

Netty noticed the bruise on my face and opened her door. "Who did this to your pretty face? Come on in, baby." I slowly walked into Netty's arms, and we entered the house.

I told her the whole story about Dock.

Netty dropped a tear, something she said she hadn't done in years. She said that it hurt her to hear what my life had been like and insisted that I stay with her. That night I fell asleep crying in Netty's lap.

* * * * * * * * * * * * * * * * * *

Cease closed the diary. He gripped it tightly in his hands as the different emotions boiled inside him. He never knew that Remy had it that hard, and now that he was discovering her past demons, he was overwhelmed with feelings of anger and grief. His heart ached, and vengeance was the only thing on his mind.

In a way Cease was angry with Remy. He wanted to ask her, "Why didn't you tell me about this?" Cease thought he knew everything about Remy. He knew that she was ashamed of her past, and he could tell from the way she wrote that she was embarrassed.

Remy poured her heart out on a piece of paper, leaving nothing out. She was crying out through a pen.

Cease thought about stopping. It didn't feel right uncovering secrets that Remy tried so hard to keep hidden from him. But he couldn't help it; the curiosity was killing him, and he had to know the whole story. He opened the book and kept reading.

Chapter Four

For the next few months, I had a roof over my head and a job cooking up Khadafi's goods. Netty took me under her wings and began to teach me all of the things my own mother didn't teach me. My mother wasn't around, so I missed out on some of the simple things.

I never had anyone to care about me, so when I met Dock and he showed a little interest, he took advantage of me. When Netty explained this to me, it all started to make a little more sense—I was his plaything; he didn't love me.

Netty treated me as if I were her own daughter, and we grew a strong bond over the months. She told me that I kind of reminded her of herself at an early age. So when she saw Philly dragging me out of the basement, I waited for her to stop him, but she never did, even though I could see the shock and disappointment in her eyes.

* * * * * * * * * * *

"You little bitch. You trying to steal goods and thought I wouldn't find out. Khadafi's not going to be happy when he hears about this." Philly clinched the back of my neck. "I can't believe this. You honestly thought you could get away with it? He's been thinking it was me skimming off the top and all along it was you."

Khadafi's dope hadn't been coming back right and he told Philly to handle the problem or the heat would be on him. Philly knew that Khadafi didn't play when it came to his money. If he even thought Philly was disloyal, he would kill him without question. Since I was the newest girl, I guess he automatically assumed that it had to be me.

I later learned that Philly had placed cameras in the basement to see what was really going on. On every batch I would sneeze or cough. But I wasn't sneezing, I was putting cooked dope in my mouth until I went to the bathroom and hid it for later.

One day I did this about ten times, and it added up. I knew what the repercussions would be if I ever got caught, but I had to take the chance. See, staying with Netty was only a temporary gig, and once that was over, I would be out in the cold again. So I tried to make as much extra money as I could, to save up to buy a place, or at least rent a house in a decent neighborhood. After hiding the dope, I would take it to the block and bang it back dirt-cheap. This routine gained me an extra $250 a week, and it seemed to be worth it at the time. But when Philly snatched me out the basement, I started regretting it.

* * *

He grabbed me firmly by the arm and dragged me out of Betty Netty's house and into his car that was parked on the curb. He was so rough and violent with me, I didn't even have a chance to put on a shirt.

Philly stopped in occasionally to make sure everything was running smoothly, but this visit wasn't the routine check-up. I could tell by the look in his eyes when he entered the basement that something was wrong. He always said things like, "Khadafi likes it this way . . ." or "Khadafi said this . . ."

Khadafi's name reigned in the streets of Flint, and his intelligence kept him above his competition. His ability to network and his numerous business endeavors made him a very successful man.

"Can I at least put on a shirt?" I said as Philly pulled me towards his car.

He ignored me and pushed me into his money-green Mercedes Benz. When Philly slammed the door and started to walk over to his side, I jumped out of the car to make a break for it—I wasn't trying to stick around to see what was about to happen.

Before I could even get two feet out of the car, Philly had a chrome 9mm pointed in my direction. "Uh uh—get back in the car."

I slowly got back in, tears streaming down my cheeks. I knew Khadafi was going to kill me. I'd heard stories about what he did to people who crossed him. I had never seen the man, but I knew he was nothing to play with. "Please don't take me to Khadafi. Please . . ."

Philly ignored me and proceeded to drive to the

outskirts of Flint. He pulled up to a luxurious, fifteen-foot steel gate, rolled down his window, and pushed the button on the intercom. I assumed it was Khadafi's mansion.

A woman's voice came back. "May I help you?"

"It's Philly. Let me through."

Suddenly the gates opened. My heart began to pound harder and harder. I was shaking uncontrollably, thinking about what was about to happen to me. *I never should have fucked with his cash—trying to bite the hand that feed me.* I couldn't believe I got myself in another fucked-up situation—skimming dope off the top for about three months and reselling it to small-time hustlers around the block.

"I wonder what Khadafi is going to do with yo' ass—probably cut off one of your fingers. Or maybe he'll do you like the last bitch that got caught stealing and . . . well . . . she's not around anymore." Philly smiled at the sight of my fear.

"Philly, just let me go. I will disappear and leave town, I swear to God."

He laughed my plea off. "Shut up! You ain't getting off that easy." He hopped out of the car and came over to my side to pull me out. "Come on."

I quickly locked my door so that he couldn't snatch me out of the car. "Please . . . please let me go."

I screamed as he jiggled the door handle, trying to get into his car.

"Unlock the damn door!" He yelled. Philly grew frustrated and pulled a gun from his waistline. He pointed it at me and threatened to put a hole in my head if I didn't open the door.

I reluctantly unlocked the door.

Philly opened the door and snatched me out by

my hair. He pulled me to the mansion's entrance and banged on the door.

An older Hispanic lady, who looked to be at least fifty, answered the door. She stepped to the side so we could enter.

The mansion was immaculate. A crystal chandelier hung above the door entrance and illuminated the room. The wrap around stairs that stood twenty feet away from the door was made of beautiful porcelain, and bodyguards equipped with assault rifles stood in every corner on the main floor, with two atop the staircase. In the middle of the main floor a gigantic *K* was printed in the all-black carpet.

As soon as Philly stepped foot in the door, he began to yell Khadafi's name.

"Let my arm go, you bald-head ass."

Khadafi made his way down the stairs. His 6-foot, 200-and-something-pound frame demanded attention. A well-dressed, forty-two-year-old businessman, the shade of gray in his beard was the only thing that showed his age. He had on a black dress shirt and a loosely tied tie and was unbuttoning the cufflinks on his shirt as he approached us.

I repeatedly tried to pull away from Philly's grasp, but it was useless. His short, bald-headed ass was strong.

"This is the one—this is the bitch that's been stealing the goods all along. The camera caught her ass red-handed."

I looked at Philly, gathered all the spit I could muster in my mouth, and released a glob that landed flush in his eyes.

Philly flinched and wiped the saliva off of his face. He cocked back his hand. "You little—"

Khadafi grabbed his arm. "Phillip, I'll handle

this. Maria just cooked a delicious entrée. Won't you go and have a bite to eat in the kitchen."

Philly calmed down and straightened up his ruffled collar. "All right, call me when you ready to handle this thieving-ass ho—I don't want to miss it."

"Fat muthafucka!" I muttered under my breath as he started to walk towards the kitchen. "I knew yo' fat ass wasn't gon' turn down a meal."

Khadafi focused his attention on me. He just stared at me, gazing into my eyes without saying a word. Handling me for stealing seemed like the last thing on his mind.

I looked into his eyes, terrified of what was about to happen to me. His gaze was deep and intimidating—I knew he was about to dead my ass.

"What's your name?" Khadafi spoke with a strong and deep tone.

I didn't respond. Didn't even look at him. Tears began to fill my eyes as I wondered if that was the day that I was going to die. I thought about taking off for the door, but two black, bald-headed, body-builder-looking men stood in front of it.

(Came to find out later, Khadafi used extreme tactics—usually if someone got caught stealing from him, they would never steal from another soul ever again.)

He ordered one of his bodyguards to go and retrieve one of his shirts for me.

Khadafi had this look on his face that you couldn't associate with anger. A gentleness. A look that told me I shouldn't feel threatened. I had a feeling he couldn't bring himself to harm me.

He gazed into my eyes and placed his right hand on my shoulder.

I flinched at the touch of his fingertips.

"Don't worry"—He gave me a grin—"I just want to talk to you."

I remained silent, not believing a word he said.

Khadafi's bodyguard came down the stairs with a tailor-made shirt and handed the shirt to his boss. Khadafi put the shirt over my shoulders and escorted me to his office.

I was petrified. I stopped crying when I realized my tears wouldn't stop him from doing what he wanted to do.

Khadafi smiled at me and asked, "What do you think I should do with you?"

"Fuck you." I knew he was playing with my head. I had been through so much and the only thing I hadn't seen was death.

To my surprise, Khadafi said, "I want you to go out with me . . . just one night. If you don't enjoy yourself, you can go free."

"So . . . so you mean if I go out with you just once, nothing will happen to me?"

He reached his hand out. "You have my word."

I looked at him in total disbelief. I didn't know if he was toying with me or not. But his eyes were so sincere and honest. I shook his hand and I felt a little better, still not sure.

He looked at me and said, "Nothing's going to happen to you. You can trust me, we will handle this tomorrow." He didn't seem to be the type of man to lie—he was too powerful, and he didn't have to.

"What's your name?"

"Remy."

When the Hispanic woman walked into the room, Khadafi said, "Maria, will you show Remy to one of the guestrooms. Make sure she is comfortable."

Maria nodded her head.

Khadafi stared at me as I walked past him and followed her up the stairs.

My heart was racing when I walked into the room, not knowing what to expect. I sat down on the bed and thought about calling Dock to come get me. The thought quickly passed when I remembered all the bodyguards. And all the shit I went through with him.

All I could do was wait.

Chapter Five

March 1998

I woke up to an unfamiliar setting. At first I didn't know where I was. The shit was far from Dock's house, lavish as hell. I had never slept in a bed so comfortable. (He had his crib laced.) Even the sheets felt expensive. The satin was so soft against my skin, and the king-size bed provided me more than enough room.

After stretching and yawning I noticed a black velvet box on the foot of the bed. I sat up not knowing if I should open it or not. But it had to be for me, cuz it wasn't there when I went to sleep.

I opened the box, "Damn!" I pulled out two huge diamond earrings. They were the most expensive pair I had ever seen. They were blinging and I couldn't imagine myself rocking that many carats.

"Do you need help putting them on?" The deep voice startled me, making me drop the jewelry on the bed.

I looked up and saw Khadafi slowly walking towards me. I ain't know a man in a suit could look so good. I was used to fitted hats and baggy pants, but Khadafi was a whole different breed. He was a smooth-ass nigga; it was something about the way he talked. I didn't know what to say. This fine-ass man was standing in my face and I hadn't even brushed my teeth yet.

Khadafi walked over to the bed and picked up the diamonds. I felt his body heat as he stood behind me. I lifted my hair and felt his touch as he gently inserted the earrings, one in each ear. The warmth of his hands sent goose bumps down my back, and I closed my eyes as his fingertips danced softly on my neck.

"I'll meet you downstairs for breakfast," he said before walking back out.

I was speechless, racing to the mirror to admire my earrings. "Oh my goodness!" I dove onto the bed out of excitement and screamed in the pillow. I thought about all of the jealous stares I would get in the hood.

I rolled over on the bed and noticed Khadafi with a smirk on his face, standing in the doorway. *This nigga had just seen me act like a damn five-year-old.* I was so embarrassed, I could feel the blood rushing to my face.

He turned and walked away, and I just sat there feeling like an idiot.

All the fear that I had felt the night before was gone, I still didn't know Khadafi's intentions, but at least I was still breathing. He could have killed me for stealing but instead I was here, in his company with a new pair of diamond earrings. It didn't make sense, but I didn't really want to figure it out.

I went to the bathroom that was connected to the room. The room looked like a luxurious suite in a five-star hotel. The letter *K* was imprinted on all the towels, and the bathroom was as big as my bedroom at Dock's. I guess all the hype was true—Khadafi was a don; or at least he was living like one. He had to have major chips to afford all of this.

There was a small knock at the door. I quickly walked over and noticed a tiny Hispanic woman holding my clothes and a toothbrush in her hand. She had washed and ironed my jeans and had a plain white blouse for me to put on.

I could definitely get used to this shit.

I grabbed the clothes from the woman and she nodded her head and exited the room. I got dressed as quickly as I could, I didn't want to keep him waiting for too long.

I was nervous as I walked down the spiral staircase and noticed the two bodyguards that I had seen the previous day standing there, like they had never moved.

I admired his house as I found my way to the kitchen.

Khadafi was sitting at the table next to Philly.

I felt Philly's eyes burning a hole through me as I walked in the room. All conversation stopped, and Philly got up and walked out. He slowed down slightly when he passed me, and my body tensed up out of reaction from the harsh encounter just the day before.

Khadafi looked up, and Philly quickly changed his expression and exited the room.

"Good morning, Remy."

"Morning." I walked over and sat in the chair across from him.

A white man with a chef's hat came over to us and asked, "What will you and your guest be having, Mr. Langston?"

"Eggs Benedict." He looked at me, waiting on me to answer.

I was too stunned to reply. It was some shit you saw in the movies. "Is this for real?" I asked him, not believing this nigga had a restaurant in his house.

Khadafi chuckled lightly. "This is for real."

"Bacon and eggs."

The chef nodded his head and went to the other side of the kitchen to prepare our meals.

"So you like the earrings?"

"Yeah, I like 'em—but what I gotta do for these earrings?"

"Nothing. You don't have to do anything except have breakfast with me."

"That's it?"

"That's it."

I relaxed a little.

I wasn't used to somebody giving me something without expecting anything in return. I had been around the block a couple times to know that ain't shit in this world free. I couldn't figure him out, here I was a chick who had just tried to steal from him and I was still breathing. I had seen the scar that he left on the other girl and I couldn't figure it out. I decided to find out what was really going on. "Can I ask you a question?"

Khadafi looked up and nodded his head.

"Why are you being so nice to me? I know I was

wrong for trying to steal from you and I knew for sure that I was gon' be handled."

"Normally, anyone who steals from me would have been; but your beauty struck a chord with me—I've never seen a woman as beautiful as you are."

I smiled. I couldn't believe what was happening. I was sitting at the table eating breakfast with Khadafi and he was telling me how beautiful I was. The situation was unreal—sitting in a house this fabulous was the last place I would have ever expected to be.

"If you don't have any other plans, I would like to spend the day with you.

"I'd like that."

Khadafi smiled at me, and I smiled back.

After breakfast, Khadafi arranged for one of his bodyguards to escort us around the city. Almost instantly we clicked. He had a certain way of getting to people. He made me comfortable and didn't look down on me.

I opened up to him, and before long we were in the limo, having a deep conversation. I told him how I came up and everything I had been through.

Khadafi couldn't believe all of the shit. He immediately wanted to be my savior, the one to turn this gem into a diamond.

I didn't know if he was drawn to me, or my situation, but he had an interest. It was something different about him, and I couldn't put my finger on it exactly. But he looked at me differently than most men did. It was his eyes . . . something about the way he looked at me—he looked into my eyes and not at them.

Khadafi took me on a shopping spree.

We went into numerous stores, and he watched me try on outfit after outfit. He searched for the perfect attire for his newfound friend—me. He sat and watched me strut in different dresses and gave me a thumbs-up or thumbs-down, symbolizing if he liked it or not.

Khadafi only wore the best, so therefore he wanted me to wear the best if I was going to stick around. He had over two hundred suits, from Armani to custom-made designs, by top-notched stylists. Khadafi said that appearance was very important to him, so taking me shopping was mandatory.

He made me feel special. No one had ever treated me this kindly. He was so sincere and intelligent, and I had never met a man of his status.

By the end of the day, I had so many clothes I had to sit some bags up front with Drakey, his bodyguard.

I was overwhelmed by his kindness and kept wondering, *Why me?*

Later that night he asked me to stay the night at his home. I reluctantly accepted the offer, thinking about what Dock would do if he ever found out. I weighed my options and decided to stay.

Maria directed me to the guestroom.

I lay in bed thinking about the man that I had just met. I still couldn't believe what was happening—he didn't want to fuck or nothing. With all the money he spent on me, he could have had his way with me. I stared at the ceiling, trying to make sense out of what was happening and fell asleep with the thought of Khadafi on my mind.

* * *

The next day I was awakened by a knock at the door. "Come in." I sat up and wiped the sleep from my eyes, expecting to see Khadafi.

Instead, Maria came into the room with a platter of fresh fruits and pancakes. I wasn't used to this type of treatment; it felt funny having my every need catered to. "Thank you," I said when she handed me the food.

"You're welcome, Ms. Morgan."

As soon as she left the room, I got busy. I started stuffing my mouth with the food and didn't stop until it was gone. It wasn't often that I ate a meal like that, so I took advantage of it. I was so busy stuffing my mouth, I didn't notice when Maria walked back in.

"Ms. Morgan, would you like any syrup with—" Maria took one look at my plate and already knew that she was too late.

I had finished the plate in five minutes flat; there wasn't anything left to put syrup on.

She quickly smiled and said with her Spanish accent, "Mr. Langston left for the country club this morning. He would like for you to join him when you get dressed. A car is waiting for you outside."

The words that came out of her mouth didn't seem like they were meant for me, but I nodded my head okay.

When she left the room, I felt the nervousness inside me.

I got up and quickly started rummaging through the bags trying to find something to wear. I didn't even know what to put on. It seemed like none of the clothes I had picked out the day before was good enough.

I knew that Khadafi was way out of my league—

and everybody else would too if I walked up in there looking crazy.

After showering, I put on a black Baby Phat dress and some gold heels that laced around my ankles. Staring at myself in the mirror as I put on some makeup, I admired my mocha-colored skin, and soft almond-shaped eyes, hoping I looked good enough. I stepped back from the mirror and took a deep breath before I walked out the door.

Drakey greeted me with a smile to drive me to the club.

When we pulled up, I saw black men in khakis and polo shorts playing golf on the green lawn. I noticed the women walking around with their tennis rackets and immediately knew I put on the wrong thing. "Fuck!" I yelled, scolding myself. I had to realize that I wasn't fucking with any ol' nigga from the hood. I had to keep appearances if I had any chance of staying in Khadafi's company.

After sitting in the car for ten minutes, Drakey rolled down the glass that separated us and said, "It's not as bad as it looks."

Reluctantly, I got out and walked into the glass building. Everybody seemed to whisper when I walked past. I knew that I stuck out like a sore thumb.

Khadafi was sitting at a table in the back of the room, where several people surrounded him. The mayor of Flint was sitting to his right, and there were other men and a bunch of women crowded around. Khadafi smiled when he noticed me, but I was too uncomfortable to return the gesture.

I looked at the women with their pleated skirts

and tank tops and started pulling at my dress that was too tight, too short, and made me look too ghetto.

"Ahh . . . everyone, this is the lovely woman that I've been telling you all about," Khadafi said as I reached the table.

"Remy, this is Mayor Stanley and his wife Mona."

The mayor extended his hand to me and gave me a warm smile, but his wife barely looked at me before giving me a dry, "Hello."

I frowned, but before I could say anything Khadafi continued, "And this is one of my business partners and his wife—Garland and Sophie."

I plastered a smile on my face expecting to get the same treatment from Sophie.

Khadafi motioned for me to sit next to him, and a sense of relief washed over me when I felt his hand reach underneath the table and rest on my thigh.

"Rena is it?" Sophie asked out of the blue.

"Remy," I shot back at her ass. I was born and raised in the fifth ward, she didn't know shit about me, and she wasn't gon' get away with no left-hand shit over here. She heard the hostility in my voice, but I didn't care. The bitch was trying to be funny—she knew my damn name.

"Remy, will you be joining us in the spa?"

"Oh, I'm sure she has other plans," Mona said quickly and gave her friend a look of annoyance.

"That sounds good." Khadafi squeezed my leg softly and gave me a smile. "You ladies can handle that while we're on the golf course." He kissed me on the cheek and rose from the table. "Anything you need, just charge it to my account."

I didn't want him to leave. I wasn't even comfortable around him yet, let alone around the two women who were sitting across the table from me.

He pulled me close to him and whispered, "You'll be fine. Relax and have fun." He walked away, and I was left with two snobbish-ass bitches staring in my face.

"So, Remy . . . what do you do?" Mona sat back and smugly sipped her white wine.

"What do *you* do?" I don't know who she thought she was talking to, but Khadafi wasn't at the table anymore.

"Sweetie, I don't do anything. I was just wondering how, exactly, you know Khadafi." Mona smiled smugly at me.

I was trying to remain cordial, but my fists clenched up. It was something about the way she was looking at me—she was staring at me as if I stunk. Like she thought she was better than me or something. "I know you the mayor's wife and all, but I ain't got to explain shit to you—I'm here with Khadafi—and that's all you need to know."

Mona's jaw dropped to the floor.

Sophie spit out the wine she was sipping on. She cracked an instigating smile and laughed lightly before saying, "Okay . . . that's enough of that. First-class treatment at the spa will make everybody feel better."

Mona got up from the table first and threw down her napkin as she stormed off in the direction of the spa.

Sophie seemed to lighten up instantly. She put her hands around my shoulders and said, "Don't worry about Mona, she'll get over it. She's really not all that bad; she's just pissed off because you told her about herself. Everybody's always kissing her ass, she's not used to people standing up to her."

"Mayor's wife or not, she got me fucked-up."

Sophie laughed. "You just might fit in around here after all—by the way, how did you meet Khadafi?"

"Let's just say, I was his cook."

Sophie laughed loudly. "I remember those days."

I looked at her in astonishment; I didn't think she would know what I meant. "You serious?"

"Girl, please—we all have a past." She glanced towards Mona. "Some of us just forget where we came from."

I was shocked. Sophie and Mona didn't appear to be that much older than me, but I never would have guessed that they were anything like me.

Although I still didn't care for Mona, I still accompanied her and Sophie to the spa. I ordered a terry-cloth robe from the clerk and put my dress and shoes in a locker in the bathroom, before joining the two women out in the lobby.

We made our way to the spa.

Sophie was cool when you actually got to know her. Beneath the surface and beyond the glitz and glamour was a regular, easy-going chick.

Mona was stuck up as hell—she thought she was the shit because she was married to the mayor, so I tried to ignore her and have a good time.

"You look a lot like the last girl Khadafi brought here," Mona said as we all sat in a vibrating chair while wearing face masks and receiving pedicures.

"Which one?" Sophie asked sarcastically.

I shrugged my shoulders. "It really doesn't matter. I'm here right now, so I'm not really worried about it."

"You need to be worried about it," Sophie said; "as many gold-digging women that be after Khadafi. There's always some new girl trying to get their hands on him—or rather, his money. If I was you I would make sure I worry about it."

I didn't get a chance to respond because the conversation ended when the nail technician came over and began scrubbing and massaging our feet. I finished first and made my way back into the bathroom and was in a changing booth when I heard Sophie and Mona walk in.

"Did you see what she had on? This is a country club not a night club."

"Mona, stop. She's all right; she just needs a little grooming."

"Please . . . as much money as Khadafi has . . . he needs a woman of class, not some Baby Phat-wearing hoodrat."

"Look at you, acting all brand-new, like you ain't been there before. Just three years ago, you were her age when Woodrow pulled you out the hood."

"Yeah—out the hood—not the trash."

"Mona, just be cool and give the girl a chance."

Mona smacked her lips. "Why?—She ain't gon' last no longer than the rest of them."

Then I heard their voices drift out of the room as they walked out of the bathroom.

I walked out of the changing booth and looked at my reflection in the mirror. *They were probably right, I didn't match with Khadafi*. He was too powerful, too rich, and too good to be true. Hearing their words in my head I began to feel like a fool. I knew that I was trying to live in a world where I didn't belong. I pulled at my short, form-fitting dress, wishing it was a bit longer and a bit looser. I knew I had the body to rock it, but the country club wasn't the place.

I walked out of the bathroom and was silent as I joined the girls and we went to find Khadafi and their husbands.

Khadafi smiled when he saw me and pulled me close. "Did you have a good time?"

I nodded yes and tried to give him a smile. I could feel everyone's eyes on me and I couldn't help feeling inferior, standing next to such a poised and prestigious man.

"Well, I guess I will see you all next week at the ball," Khadafi said as he shook hands with the men and kissed the women on the cheek.

"And will you be attending the ball next week, Remy?" Mona gave me her arrogant little smile.

I was at a loss for words—Sophie nudged Mona hard with her elbow.

Khadafi spoke up. "Of course she will. That is if she will accept this old man's invitation." He waited and everyone looked at me.

I looked at Mona, who was staring at me tough, and Sophie, who nodded her head yes. "Yes, I'll accept."

"Great. Then we will see the two of you next week." The mayor kissed me on the cheek and patted Khadafi on his back.

Chapter Six

April 1998

A week later, Khadafi arranged for Drakey to drive me to Detroit so that I could prepare for the ball. He told me that there would be a stylist waiting for me and he instructed me to get whatever I wanted.

I noticed Drakey never spoke to me—either he was gay or just flat out scared of Khadafi. I wasn't used to a man not paying me any attention at all, so I wanted to find out why he was so anti-social. I pushed the button to roll down the window that separated us. Music came pumping from the front seat.

Drakey was bobbing his head so hard, he didn't notice that I was looking at him.

"It's Drakey, right?"

He looked at me surprised and turned down the radio. "Yeah, it's Drakey."

"What you listening to?"

"The best rapper of all time—Biggie Smalls."

No, this nigga didn't say that Biggie was the greatest rapper of all time. I had to set him straight. "Get the fuck outta here—Tupac is the greatest of all time."

"How long have you been smoking dope? Biggie's lyrics are legendary."

Drakey and I debated all the way to Detroit about who was the better rapper. Drakey turned out to be pretty cool. His fat ass was funny as hell and he kept me laughing. My stomach muscles felt tight from laughing so much.

When we reached Detroit, we pulled up to a big building with a big sign that read *Emotions*. I'd heard a lot about this salon in the hood. People said that they had a stylist named Delicious and she was the best. She threw the best hair shows and was known throughout the Midwest.

Drakey grabbed his gun from the glove box, and we exited the car and went into the building.

As soon as I walked in the door, a man and two ladies were at the door staring at me like they knew me. The man had French braids and his nails looked better than mine. You could tell he had a little sugar in his tank by his gestures. He was the first to speak. "Are you Remy?"

"Yeah." As soon as I spoke the word, they bombarded me. They sat me down in a chair and went to work. One lady was on my feet, another was showing me magazines of different dresses, and the man was in my hair. I felt overwhelmed. They were talking so fast and were moving so swiftly, I couldn't really catch up.

I frequently looked over at Drakey. He was so busy watching who came in and out that he didn't notice me looking.

After all the chaos settled down, the little man began to talk to me. "Oh, I'm so naughty, I didn't even introduce myself—I'm Delicious."

As soon as the words came out of his mouth, Drakey laughed out loud.

Delicious shot a look at Drakey, and he quickly stopped giggling.

"Anyways, I'm Delicious. Yo' man must care a lot about you—he sent us a big check to make sure you were magnificent for tonight."

"He's not really my man. Just a friend."

"Just a friend? You gots to be more than friends for him to drop five thousand dollars for one night."

As he played in my hair, he kept saying, "What the hell you been doing to your hair, girl?"

I just remained silent and let him go to work. He said that Khadafi requested for me to have an elegant style and he promised to deliver.

I just smiled and listened to him ramble on about how he needed to find a good man.

They refused to let me see my hair and makeup before they were done, so I was excited to see what they had done. Delicious counted down before he spun the chair around towards the mirror. "Three, two, one—"

As soon as I looked at my reflection, I couldn't even recognize myself. It was so beautiful, so elegant, so . . . me.

One of the ladies yelled out, "You are going to drop jaws tonight. You are looking like a diva."

Delicious snapped his fingers and added, "No . . . she looks like a street diva!"

Everyone in the salon started clapping at the job they had done. I looked like a whole different person. My hair was up in a neat bun and my make-up was on point. I couldn't believe I could look that elegant. I said my goodbyes, and Drakey and I headed home so I could prepare for the ball. I only had two hours left before it began, so I had to hurry.

Khadafi walked in the room looking good as hell. That man knew how to hang a suit. The black suit he wore complemented his nice physique well. His head was bald and shiny, and his diamond cufflinks were blinging.

I was sitting at the vanity mirror when he walked behind me and gently began to massage my shoulders. I closed my eyes and imagined what it would be like to make love to him. Just the thought of it made my nipples harden and my inners thighs tingle. His strong hands felt so good on my shoulders.

He kind of had me confused, because he never tried to have sex with me. He was a perfect gentleman. The Khadafi I knew and the Khadafi the streets feared were two different men. He was a very gentle person and I wanted him so bad. The only thing he had to do was say he wanted me and it would have been on.

I felt something cold touch my skin and I jumped as I opened my eyes and noticed the diamond necklace that was sitting around my neck. I looked in the mirror at myself and then up at him.

He kissed me on the forehead.

I was speechless. All I could do was touch the diamonds.

"Exquisite," he said as he looked at our reflection.

"They are." I felt the ten-carat diamond necklace I was wearing.

"I wasn't talking about the diamonds."

I lowered my head in embarrassment. Khadafi made me feel regal, as if I were a queen.

"You look beautiful, Remy. Stand up and let me take a better look at you."

I stood up while holding his hands, and he spun me around. I saw him look at my ass in the mirror and he formed a small grin. I felt so special on that night. He'd bought me a black Versace that hugged my body in the right places. I was feeling myself to the fullest and I knew he was too. I couldn't believe the transformation—I was a completely different person. Never in a million years would I ever have thought I could look like that.

Drakey drove us to the Radisson Inn downtown where the ball was being held. My heart felt as if it was going to leap out of my chest, and my hands were sweaty. I remembered how out of place I felt at the country club and was praying that the ball would not be the same way.

I stepped out of the car petrified and walked side by side with Khadafi. He looked down at me and smiled. I had on a black mink that wrapped around my shoulders. I handed it to the doorman as I entered the hotel.

It was nice inside. Everything was decorated in crème and gold. The room seemed to stop and all chatter ceased as we walked deeper into the room. I could feel the stares of Khadafi's peers, but these stares were different from the ones I had received at the country club. The stares of contempt had become gazes of admiration and awe.

"Everybody's staring at you," I said to Khadafi as we walked through the room.

"No, Remy, they're staring at you. You are breathtaking."

The mayor approached us and greeted me with a glass of champagne. "Remy, you are stunning. Definitely the bell of the ball."

Mona stood next to him, and Sophie and her husband Garland were encircled around us.

"She definitely is a keeper, Khadafi." The mayor could not take his eyes off me.

I laughed as Mona's frown turned into a deep scowl.

"Where did you get that dress? Remy, it's gorgeous!" Sophie exclaimed.

"Oh, it's just a little something I pulled out the *trash*." I kept my eyes glued intently on Mona.

Khadafi put his hand on the small of my back, and we swept past Mona and took a seat at our table. Cameras kept going off in our faces and it felt like my jaw would break, I was smiling so much. You would think that Khadafi had hosted the ball since he was the one getting all the attention. Throughout the whole night people were coming up to Khadafi shaking his hand. I was introduced to so many people, I could barely remember one name.

"Khadafi, long time no see."

"Nice to see you again, Mr. Langston."

"Hey, when can you fit me into your busy schedule?"

That's all I kept hearing all night long.

After an hour or so of business chat, what Khadafi called networking, he turned to me and said, "Would you like to dance?"

I nodded my head yes, and he pulled me out onto the floor. I wrapped my arms around his neck, and he held me close as we danced to the live jazz band that was playing.

"You're a very important man."

"No more important than the next man." He spun me around.

I laughed and held onto him tightly. "I can't help but feel like I don't belong here."

"You belong, Remy. This lifestyle just takes some getting used to. You have to remember that no one can make you feel less than a woman except for you."

"It's crazy. I have never felt so special before. Nobody never took the time to show me that they care."

Khadafi laughed loudly and replied in a joking way, "You probably scared them off with all those double negatives. I guess it's true what they say—you can take the girl out the ghetto, but you can't take the ghetto out the girl."

I hit him playfully, and we shared a laugh as I laid my head on his chest, closed my eyes, and danced to the slow tunes. The song ended way before we stopped dancing and when we realized we were the only ones on the floor, we just stood there looking gently into each other's eyes.

"Would you mind if I took your picture?" We looked up and saw the photographer. We both smiled for the camera and he handed us a card and said, "I'll mail you a copy."

"Join us at the table. Dinner will be served shortly," the mayor said to us, interrupting our romantic moment.

I blushed out of embarrassment, and Khadafi escorted me to the table. I was overwhelmed. There seemed to be some kind of ritual to eating. I watched as all the women unfolded the gold handkerchief that was sitting on top of each plate and placed it in their laps and the men tucked them neatly in their jackets. I followed suit after watching everybody else. I looked down at the silverware that sat beside the plates. Where I came from we only ate with one, so I didn't know which one to use.

The waiter came and placed my meal in front of me. I looked up to see Khadafi smiling at me. He winked his eye and then moved his hand, signaling to me which fork I was supposed to use. I looked around the table to see if anyone had noticed, but they were all too engrossed in their conversations to notice.

I was relieved. The last thing that I needed was to give Mona another reason to look down at me. Khadafi and I followed this same pattern throughout dinner and I made it through my first five-course meal looking like a pro.

The rest of the evening went well.

Sophie and I talked a lot and got to know each other better.

The more time I spent around Khadafi's friends, the more comfortable I became. Khadafi began to circulate around the room.

Meanwhile, Sophie introduced me to everybody she said I needed to make sure I knew. I found myself separated from Khadafi for the remainder of the night, but I was far from lonely. Everybody wanted to meet "the woman who had come with Mr. Langston."

I tried my best to be myself and I seemed to be winning his friends and business associates over.

I was having a conversation with a city councilman when Khadafi came over and said, "Bob, how's it going?"

"Fine. Just chatting with this lovely young woman.

She's very charming and she makes you look good."
He raised his glass to toast my own.

I laughed and held onto Khadafi's arm as he said, "Yes, she does."

The ball was coming to a close, and we were headed for the door. When we reached the limo, Drakey opened the door, and I smiled as we got in.

"Did you have a good time?" Khadafi asked me.

"I did. It was like a fairy tale or something. You have very nice friends."

"I think they fell in love with you tonight."

I looked at him and blushed. I knew we were talking about more than what was being said. "I think I fell in love with them too."

My heart was pounding. I had never felt this way about anyone before. When I was around him, I felt happy. Khadafi made me happy, and it was a feeling that was so unfamiliar to me, it almost scared me.

"Goodnight, Drakey," I said as I exited the car.
Drakey blushed slightly.

Khadafi patted his shoulder and said, "Good night, Drakey." We walked into the house together and up the staircase. Bodyguards were still posted around the house, but it felt like we were the only ones in the room.

I faced him, not knowing what he wanted from me.

We stood close to each other, and he rubbed my face with his hand.

I closed my eyes as he whispered, "You are so beautiful."

I felt his body heat as he stood inches away from me. I would have given anything for him to make love to me right there at the top of the stairs. I was a virgin when it came to that. I had been fucked before, but I had never been loved and I wanted him to be my first. I opened my eyes and saw the look on his face. It was one of uncertainty. Just as I was about to speak he said, "Good night, Remy."

I managed to say a disappointed, "Good night," and retired to the guestroom.

I stared at myself in the black lingerie that I had worn under the Versace and I instantly wanted to feel Khadafi's body against mine. I wanted him and I was almost sure he wanted me.

I walked down the hall where his room was located and knocked lightly on the door.

"Come in," Khadafi said in his assertive, attention-demanding voice.

I walked in slowly.

He stood by the window, his tie loosely hanging around his neck.

I remained silent.

When he turned around, I let the robe drop to the floor. I stood there nervously not knowing how he would react.

He walked over to me and stood close to me.

"Khadafi . . ." I said in between shallow breaths—he was so close to me I could feel his heart racing—". . . I think I'm in love with you."

He didn't respond but he kissed me forcefully, pinning me against the door. He picked me up and carried me over to the king-size bed. We were both silent, but the intensity in the room was high. He kissed me passionately, and I felt his manhood harden as our bodies pressed against each other.

I rolled on top of him and began to unbutton his shirt. I kissed his chest and made my way down until

I reached his pants. I unbuttoned them and took them off and then took him into my mouth. I wanted to please Khadafi in every possible way. I ran my tongue up and down the base of his dick and massaged the head softly with my lips.

He was moaning from the oral sex that I was performing on him and I knew from the tense reaction of his body that it felt good. Just before he was about to reach his climax, I made my way back up to his lips.

Khadafi threw me on my back and ripped the lingerie from my body. He gently went inside me and rocked slowly, in and out, in and out. He was big, and my back arched every time he hit that deep spot. He took his time with me and didn't rush; it was like he was trying to please me.

I felt him speed up. I knew that it wouldn't be long before he burst. I grinded against him and rotated my hips, so he could explore every groove of my pussy.

Khadafi's body jerked, and I began to feel my own orgasm coming. "Oh," I said as he plunged harder and deeper inside my body. My legs began to shake, and just as I got my nut, his face twisted in utter pleasure—he got his too.

"Shit!" He reached for his nightstand. He hit his intercom and said, "Maria, bring me a shot of Hennessy."

I laughed.

He put his arm around me so that I could lie on his chest. "I know I'm old," he said; "I don't ever remember a woman working it like that."

I kissed his chest. "What does this mean?"

"It means that I am in love with you, Remy, and

I would like for you to stay and make a home with me. I knew that you were supposed to be my queen when I first saw you. Will you stay?"

I sat up in the bed and leaned against the huge wooden headboard. "You don't have to say this. I don't want you to just say this because we had sex, I want it to be real."

"Remy . . . I don't have to say anything. If I didn't want you here you wouldn't be here. I would really like it if you'd stick around for a while."

I nodded my head and replied, "I'll stay."

Chapter Seven

March 1999

I couldn't believe how much my life had changed. It seemed like only yesterday I was stripping to make ends meet. Khadafi had been so good to me. He treated me how I needed to be treated. The way I never thought I would be treated. It had only been a year since I met him, but it seemed like I had known him forever. It was kind of crazy because I would have never in a million years thought that I would be with a man like him.

A year ago I didn't have a pot to piss in, but now I had more than I could ask for. He was always giving me something—a diamond tennis bracelet just because . . . or a mink coat when he thought I was chilly. I loved him so much. I knew it was kind of early to be feeling like that, but I couldn't help it. He treated me so good and didn't think twice about showing me how much he cared. I don't know what made him choose me, out of all the women he could have had. I was lucky; I came from nothing.

At first I tried to hide my past from him. I didn't want him to know about what I had been through. Especially what I had been through with Dock. But I knew that eventually he would find out and I would rather it be from me.

I told him everything. At first he was silent. After the initial shock he held me in his arms and told me that we would let the past be the past and we would move forward together. He told me that he never wanted me to keep any secrets from him. He said that my life was his life and that we lived for one another. When he said that to me, I knew that he had me.

I loved that man more than I can describe. I couldn't even begin to describe how I felt. I just felt giddy all the time. Every time I saw his face or heard his voice, I smiled. He just made me feel warm.

He put me in these etiquette classes, telling me I was a diamond in the rough. At first I was offended by it. It was like he was trying to mold me into something that I wasn't, but maybe that's what I needed. Maybe I needed to become a new person, with a new attitude towards life. He always took me out to these fancy dinners with his friends, and I always felt so out of place. We were always flying to New York to see a Broadway musical or an opera. Maybe the new me could learn to appreciate some of that stuff. I needed to be able to socialize in his world. I would be whatever he wanted me to be, as long as he continued to treat me like his queen.

* * * * * * * * * * * * * * * *

Cease closed the diary, unable to read anymore. It was hard for him to read about Remy loving another man. His heart felt weak and he tried to take deep breaths to stop the feeling of pain from invading his body, but he couldn't. The agonizing feeling came over him as he pictured Remy happy with somebody else.

Although Cease knew about Remy's involvement with Khadafi, it was hard for him to actually understand how much he meant to her. Cease was selfish with what was his, and the words written in the diary by Remy enraged him. Especially after everything that had happened, and after all that had went down. The fact that Khadafi and Remy's love was so real made her death so much harder to bear. He couldn't really blame her for loving Khadafi, though, because he was a noble man.

At one point in his life Cease himself had a great amount of love and respect for the same man. The words in the diary made Cease think back to the time when Khadafi was like a father to him. Khadafi taught Cease a lot, and Cease knew Khadafi's life story. Cease went from respecting Khadafi to hating him.

One particular encounter with Khadafi stuck out clearly in his mind.

"A dead man can't pay his debt," Khadafi told Cease; "he is worthless to me now. You got to be smarter than this, young blood! If you want to last in this game, you have to think before you act. I have watched you grow from a boy into a man and I'm proud of that. You are like my son. But on my block you don't make those types of mistakes. You don't create friction when it's not necessary. Conflict is a bad thing. It slows down business. That's what gets young cats like you locked up or killed. My operation is flawless—that's what separates me from the rest—perfection."

Khadafi knew that Cease was a don in the making. He knew that the boy was ruthless and had the heart of a hustler. He just needed to be groomed.

Cease sat inside Khadafi's office listening to what he had to say. He was not intimidated by Khadafi, but he respected him. He knew that Khadafi was a gangster. Khadafi's Armani suits and extravagant lifestyle sometimes confused people, but Cease knew the deal. He knew what Khadafi was capable of and how much power he had.

Khadafi was the reason why people were eating in Flint. He was the reason why there was money to be made and corners to be hustled. Cease took Khadafi's words to heart, making sure to apply them to his own hustle.

Khadafi finished his meeting with Cease and sat down at his desk, shaking his head side to side. Cease reminded Khadafi a lot of himself when he was younger. He knew that Cease was a little proud and hard-headed young hustler who thought that he was untouchable. Khadafi had the same mentality, but he could afford to—he had put in work and had moved his way to the top. Cease was still at the bottom, trying to come up, and needed to be patient. Khadafi told Cease back about his younger years when he got his first taste of the drug game.

Khadafi Martin Langston was born in 1963. It was the era of civil uproar, the time when the African-American community was rising against the injustices of racism and discrimination. On September 15, 1963, four little girls (Cynthia Wesley, Denise Mc-Nair, Addie Mae Collins, and Carole Robertson: RIP) were attending Sunday school when a bomb exploded in the basement of the 16th Street Baptist Church in Birmingham, Alabama. It was August 28, 1963 when Dr. Martin Luther King, Jr. delivered his famous speech, "I Have a Dream."

Khadafi was conceived in this time of conflict and was born right in the middle of the protests. His mother was nine months pregnant in May of 1963. She marched down the streets of Birmingham, holding her bulging stomach and screaming at the top of her lungs for what she believed in. She didn't know if it was the pressure from the fire hoses that Bull Conner had ordered on the protestors or all of the walking that she had been doing, but she went into labor right there in the middle of the chaotic streets. She was rushed to the hospital with her husband, not knowing if her baby would be okay. She was frantic and sick with worry as she pushed the 6-pound baby boy from her body. All she kept thinking was that her baby wouldn't survive. She was praying that the force of the water pressure hadn't injured her child.

When she heard her son cry out loud for the first time, she knew that he would be a strong, intelligent, independent black man. She was determined to see that he was. "If you can survive this, you can survive anything," she whispered into his ear when they put him in her arms.

Khadafi's father, a member of the Black Panther Party, was sent to a federal prison on some bullshit charges shortly after his birth. Although he was absent from his son's life, Khadafi adapted the same leadership skills that his father so proudly displayed. His mother continued to stay active in the movement, but because she was now a single parent, she had less time for it and had to focus on providing for her son.

Lacking a male role model, Khadafi was pushed into the streets at an early age. The local drug dealers quickly filled the void in his life. With his mother working to make ends meet, Khadafi spent a lot of time in the streets. He got a taste of what getting money was like at an early age and quickly found out that he was good at it.

There was one thing that distinguished him from the other hustlers—he was smart. His mother stayed on him about school and drilled a strict discipline of knowledge into his head. By the time he was seventeen, he had graduated from high school with a 4.0—and from "nickels and dimes" to pounds of cocaine.

After graduation he applied to Michigan State University. It was there that his most valuable friendship was made. His freshman year, he was paired up with a young Colombian roommate. At first Khadafi was livid, but as the school year progressed, he became good friends with Poe. They began to understand and respect each other because they were both seeking the same thing—power. They remained roommates the entire time that they were in college, and after they graduated they quickly became business partners.

Poe, a member of a notorious drug family in Colombia, and Khadafi, a young, business-minded hustler quickly sparked an empire. Poe supplied Khadafi with the cocaine that he needed to flood the streets of Flint, and Khadafi paid Poe well for his services. They were the perfect pair.

By the time Khadafi was 30 years old he had obtained a master's degree in psychology, his own record company, and connections with the Colombians. After his funds began to grow, his reputation did too. He was often seen in restaurants with the mayor of the city or with the chief of police. He established these relationships because he knew that they were valuable to him

Khadafi opened a prestigious country club for Blacks, which attracted important people within the city of Flint. Khadafi flooded the streets with pure Colombian cocaine. Even though he was pushing dope, he maintained his position as a prestigious figure in the community. Every year Khadafi took a poverty-stricken family and bought them a furnished home. He also closed his club on Sundays and provided hot meals for his community. At times he felt bad that he was poisoning his own people with cocaine and felt obligated to give back. He told himself that once he had enough to survive, he would give up the drug game, but that day never came. He knew if he had told the Colombians their number one customer wanted out, it wouldn't be taken lightly.

Khadafi had masterminded an underground network of drug dealing, ranging from street hustlers, to judges, to political leaders throughout Michigan. He was too deep in the game to quit and was at a point of no return.

Khadafi had the type of personality that was pleasing to be around. He could charm anyone. Psychologically superior to most of the people he came in contact with, his deep tone of voice and slow speech demanded attention. He didn't let too many people get close to him and kept friends and associates at a distance.

With this mentality he was bound for success.

Philly was his head street-man and he had to put in years of work to get in good with him. Besides Philly, Khadafi never let anyone get too close, until he met Cease.

* * * * * * * * * * * * * * * * *

Cease stopped the memory short. "Khadafi is a bitch," he said to himself. Khadafi had done the unspeakable and no matter how much time passed, he would never forgive him. Trust was something that had to be earned with Cease. There were no second chances with him. If you fucked up once, you were done in his book. He wasn't the type of nigga that made the same mistake twice.

Cease, a product of the streets, thought back to his childhood. His single parent mother was addicted to drugs and seldom took any time out for her son. Her priority was getting high, and she didn't care what she had to do in order to feed her habit.

Cease had two younger siblings, each of whom had different daddies. Their fathers quickly took them away, and Cease was left alone in the unfit household. The streets called for him, and he fell into the wrong crowd at the age of twelve. He quickly learned that school was not for him because while he was sitting in a classroom, niggas were making money outside.

The allure of the dope-game intrigued him, and he craved the fast money. He remembered the first time he'd met Khadafi. He was sixteen at the time. On the block late one night, one of his loyal customers approached him.

"What you need?" Cease asked as he stood on the corner.

"Give me a twinky."

Cease took the hoody from over his head and examined the block. "Hold up," he said. He slowly walked over to the tree that was about five feet from where he was standing and grabbed a Doritos bag. Cease took another look around to make sure the coast was clear and stuck his hand inside the bag. He pulled out a nice-sized "twenty rock" and walked back over to the fiend.

The fiend was waiting for him with his hand out, and Cease dropped the rock into his palm and took the money with his other hand simultaneously. As the fiend walked away, Cease pulled out a wad of money and wrapped the twenty over his stack. "Another day, another dollar."

He leaned against the stop sign waiting for the next sale. After about two hours of just standing at the corner without making a sale, he wanted to go home but decided to stay a little longer to try to make a little more dough. Though Cease was just sixteen, he already had five years of hustling under his belt. Having a fiend for a mother and a no-show father, his circumstances forced him to get on the grind. He had to do what he had to do.

His mother used to have sex with different men to support her drug habit, so she didn't know exactly who her son's father was. She slipped up and told Cease the truth one day while she was high. After that, Cease had no desire to know who his father was.

Cease had been on the corner for about two hours before his partner in crime and best friend, Jodi, showed up.

Jodi approached Cease with his hand extended to show him love. "Yo, what's really good, Drayton?"

Cease cut his eyes at Jodi. "Man, don't call me that shit."

Jodi knew Cease hated to be called by his first name and occasionally used to fool with him. He giggled. "I'm just fucking with you, Cease. What's good?"

Cease smiled, and they slapped hands.

Jodi leaned on the other side of the stop sign and asked, "Has it been poppin' this morning?"

Cease pulled out a wad of money. That gesture spoke louder than any words. Cease put his money in his pocket. "The early bird gets the worm."

Jodi lived in the apartment right under Cease in the projects. They had been best friends since they were five years old. Their mothers used to get high with each other, and they were left to fend for themselves. Naturally they became close.

The two of them stood at the corner alternating crack sales for about an hour when a black sedan pulled onto the block. The windows were tinted, so they couldn't see inside of the car. The same car had been posting on the corner for the last three days around the same time. Cease knew it wasn't cops because the first time he had noticed the car, he had just finished making numerous sales. He knew that if it was the "hook," he would have been nabbed. They immediately grew suspicious and began to walk in the opposite direction.

"Who the fuck is that?" Jodi asked as they swiftly walked towards the other end of the block.

"I don't know, but I got the strap on me if something pop off." Cease patted his waist, reassuring Jodi.

The car slowly crept down the street following them. Cease had enough of the cat and mouse game and turned towards the car and lifted his shirt, exposing his gun. The car still crept towards the boys.

Cease didn't budge, but Jodi pleaded, "Man, let's just bounce. This ain't the time for you to be pulling that Billy the Kid shit."

Cease ignored Jodi and kept his eyes on the approaching car.

Jodi wanted to take off running but wasn't about to leave his best friend, so he walked towards Cease and stood right next to him. The car pulled right alongside them, and the window slowly rolled down. A man's face emerged.

Cease and Jodi just looked at the man in the back seat, not knowing what he was about to do. A man smoking a Cuban cigar looked at the young boys and asked, "Do you know who I am?"

The boys immediately recognized Khadafi's face. He was the most talked about man in the city. He practically owned it. Khadafi spoke again, "Well, you see, this is my block, and y'all getting money on it—I have a little problem with that."

Cease looked Khadafi straight in the eyes and was on his p's and q's. He kept his hand near his gun and was ready to shoot if he needed to. Cease responded to Khadafi. "Look, man, I'm just trying to eat."

Khadafi put out his cigar and rubbed both of his hands together. "This is my area, and you making it hot. Niggas don't stand on the corners no more—this is the '90s. You are making my block hot, and I need for you to leave."

Jodi immediately began to walk away, expecting his friend to be behind him, but he wasn't.

Cease stayed there and stood his ground.

Jodi yelled, "Man, let's just go." Jodi had heard stories about Khadafi and didn't want to witness any first-hand.

Cease looked at Khadafi and said, "You might as well kill me . . . cuz if I leave the block right now I'm going to come right back when you leave—this is how I eat."

Khadafi's bodyguard motioned to get out of the car and handle Cease, but Khadafi threw his hand up to signal him to keep calm. Khadafi looked into the young hustler's eyes and saw that he had heart. He liked that. "Young blood, you got more balls than brains, I'll tell you that. You remind me of myself; you just don't give a fuck."

Khadafi smiled and asked Cease to get in. Cease was skeptical, but he knew that if they wanted to do something to him, then it would have already been done. He told Jodi that he would meet him at home and got in the car.

Khadafi took Cease under his wing and showed him the ins and outs of the drug game, keeping him close so that he could see how a successful hustler ran his business. He treated Cease very well and made sure that Cease was taken care of.

He knew about Cease's home life and eventually helped his mother kick her drug habit. Ironically, Khadafi had gone to school with Cease's mother back in the day. Khadafi even helped her get her own hair salon after she got clean.

Cease admired and respected Khadafi. As the years passed he observed Khadafi and watched him become a millionaire. Khadafi always kept Cease around and frequently sprinkled him with game. Cease watched as Khadafi gave his corner hustlers bonuses and sometimes dropped off shoes and jewels. Khadafi even let some hustlers pay for half of what they bought and give the rest to him later, called consignment.

Khadafi made it a point to never give Cease anything.

Cease never knew why and asked him one day. "Yo, Khadafi. I ain't trying to be difficult or anything, but why I can't get my work on consignment. My block make twenty a day and I have the whole east side on lock."

Khadafi looked at Cease and smiled, cigar hanging out of his mouth. "No one gave me work on credit; I had to grind for mine."

Cease began to speak, but Khadafi cut him off and said, "You will thank me in the long run, Cease. I'm giving you something more valuable than an ounce of dope, I'm giving you independency and game."

Khadafi gave Cease specific blocks to run, and Cease came to be known in the streets as "Khadafi's boy." Only eighteen years old and knee-deep in the game, people often wondered how Cease had moved up the ranks at such an early age.

Khadafi often took Cease along with him to conduct business and taught him how to read people and distinguish the real from the fake. Khadafi used his master's degree in psychology to his advantage. He would always tell him, "A man's eyes do not lie. Real recognizes real, and you can sense when you're not dealing with your own kind."

Cease admired Khadafi's savvy and knowledge. The streets called Khadafi "the man that made it snow," and that's exactly what he did. Cease was the man behind the man and Khadafi knew that he would eventually take his place at the top.

Philly and Cease didn't see eye to eye on many

occasions. Cease sensed jealousy from him and never really liked him. He knew that Philly had a problem with him being so young and working so close to Khadafi. Philly felt that he should be the one holding the east side down. The east side had the biggest clientele, and he wanted that position. It was only their mutual respect for Khadafi that kept them from being at odds.

* * * * * * * * * * *

Cease had come to see Khadafi as a father. He would never see him that way again. He opened Remy's book and forced himself to read on.

<u>Chapter Eight</u>

October 2001

For the first time in a long time I was happy. It was crazy because before I met Khadafi, I don't think I'd ever been happy. I was so in love with him. He was everything that I could ask for in a man. My love for him was unconditional and I was sure that he felt the same way about me. *He has to—he treats me too good not to be in love with me,* I thought to myself as I looked at the man that lay next to me in the bed that we shared. I stared at him for hours as he slept soundly, snoring lightly. I laughed to myself as I remembered back to when it used to get on my nerves.

We had been together for three years, and all of the things that used to irritate me quickly became the things that I loved most about my man. Khadafi was a strong, intelligent, business-minded man. I loved him more than I could say. I was 21 years old and I had finally found a man who had my best interest at heart.

Khadafi was almost exactly twice my age. At forty-two, he was the man that I loved, respected, and hopefully one day would marry. I got out of bed and walked over to my bay window, which I had asked him to build me in the bedroom. I sat down and watched the sunrise as I looked out at our beautiful home. It was a dream house. And I loved the fact that Khadafi had chosen me to share it with.

I looked into the mirror and admired myself as I slipped out of the lingerie I had worn the night before. I brushed my teeth, washed my face, and slipped on some running pants and a sports bra. I made my way into the kitchen and fixed a light breakfast for myself and then went for a run along the suburban neighborhood.

Khadafi had built his house on the outskirts of the city, in a small town called Grand Blanc. He didn't want his business to ever get mixed up with his personal life with me, so he kept them very separate.

I ran for about thirty minutes. Thick in all the right places, my stomach was flat and firm. I liked my shape and made sure I worked out to keep it that way. (I hated when bitches thought they were looking good but was really looking sloppy.)

Well into my run, a black Lincoln Navigator rolled up on me. I stopped running, walked over to the car and got in. "You slipping; you're late today. It took you an extra ten minutes to come and get me." I smiled as I kissed Khadafi on his cheek.

He had a stern look on his face. I knew that he was about to give me his daily speech. "Remy, you know that I do not like you out running by yourself. It is dangerous. I have money, Remy. Everybody wants a piece of the pie, and they will do anything to get it—even if that means getting to my woman . . . getting to you."

I smiled sweetly. "I know. I know. But Drakey can't keep up with me." Drakey was one of Khadafi's soldiers, more specifically the one who escorted me when I went out. I leaned against Khadafi and relaxed as his driver drove us the ten blocks home.

When we arrived Khadafi looked at me and said, "Go and get dressed. We have plans today." Then he kissed my forehead.

I went into the bedroom to dress. I opened up my walk-in closet and rummaged through the many clothes and shoes that he'd bought me over the years. Loaded with stuff from top designers, my closet looked like a small store. I pulled out a white summer dress with a light jean jacket and some white flip-flops and placed them on my bed. I went into the bathroom and took a quick shower, excited to spend the day with him. It was very rare that he didn't have business to tend to. It would be one of the few times that we spent time together alone.

I put on the dress and jean jacket and then quickly accessorized my outfit with white diamonds that he'd given me for my birthday. My hair was layered shoulder length and the light-brown highlights accented my dark-brown skin. I was five feet six inches, with a figure that most women tried their entire lives to get. My eyes were dark-brown, and when the sunlight hit them just right, you could see the passion of amber burning inside them.

After admiring myself in the mirror, I met Khadafi at the car. I saw Drakey standing next to Khadafi as they both waited near the car. Khadafi had made Drakey my personal bodyguard and never let me go anywhere without him.

"Hey, Drakey," I said as I kissed him twice, once on each cheek.

Drakey nodded his head in acknowledgment but he didn't speak. A trained killer, he always stayed very professional, especially when Khadafi was around.

Khadafi opened the door for me, and I kissed him on the lips before entering the car. "Where are we going again?" I asked when I got in.

He smiled at my eagerness.

I knew that I acted like a little girl sometimes, and that was one of the reasons why he fell in love with me so quickly. I was not only his little girl, but also his woman. I was obedient and respectful without losing myself. I listened to what Khadafi had to say and did most everything he asked of me.

I had been through a lot in my lifetime and had trusted Khadafi enough to share my past demons with him. Khadafi felt that I deserved to be spoiled, and that's exactly what he did.

"We are gonna spend the day together. I've been noticing you moping around the house lately." He sat back and enjoyed the ride into the city.

"You've been gone a lot lately. It feels like I haven't spent time with you in months. I just miss you."

Khadafi rolled up the window that separated us from Drakey. "Remy, business is hectic right now. A lot of stuff is going on. I didn't want to tell you this because I knew you would worry, but my record company has been under investigation. The Feds are riding our books hard, and I am under suspicion for money laundering—"

"Khadafi, why didn't you tell me? That is something serious. What if they take you to prison—I can't survive without you; I love you—that would kill me. When were you going to tell me?—when they came into the house and handcuffed you?"

Khadafi reached for my hand. "It's not going to get to that point. Remy, I don't make mistakes. They won't be able to prove the money laundering. It will die down in a couple weeks," he said, trying to comfort me.

I could tell he was lying but remained silent as I thought about the bomb he just dropped on me. *I can't believe he is acting like this is no big deal— the Feds are nothing to play with. If they are investigating the record label, then something is up; they have some kind of proof, or they wouldn't even bother. He can't go to jail—I need him . . . more than he knows.*

I want to believe him when he tells me that it will die down, but I know him. There is something that he's leaving out, hiding from me.

I stared out the window as we entered into the city. Flint was so run-down. The hood of all hoods, Flint was the gutter for real. Born and raised there, I knew the ins and outs of every borough. People died there everyday.

It was the middle of the summer and I knew people were gonna start acting a fool. I looked through the window as we rode down the streets of the small city, where everybody knew everybody, and if something went down everybody knew what happened and who done it.

Drakey drove past the city and out into Linden, one of the local suburbs. When we pulled up to the beautiful beach, I immediately pulled Khadafi out of the car.

"You didn't tell me to bring my swimsuit." I reached up and hugged around his neck.

Khadafi laughed and pointed to a blanket that sat on the sand. It had a picnic basket and a card sitting on top of it. We walked down the steps and onto the hot sand. I beamed from ear to ear. I loved when Khadafi surprised me. Planning a picnic wasn't something he would normally do. I figured he was trying to make things up to me for keeping me in the dark about the Feds.

I sat down on the blanket and opened the card: *I love you.* That simple note sent butterflies through my heart. Khadafi and I ate lunch on the beach and enjoyed each other's company.

Both of us were equally infatuated with the other, and the love we shared was evident—it was written over everything that we did and said. Everything that Khadafi did, he did to provide a better life for me. He wanted me to have everything that I didn't have and thought I deserved.

I wanted him to have me and was determined to make myself the perfect woman for him, molding myself to his liking and catering to him in every sense of the word. I was his support system. Whenever I thought he needed me, I was there for him.

Our picnic lasted for a couple hours, ending abruptly when Khadafi received a phone call from Philly. The ringing of his phone seemed awkward on the serene beach. I don't know what was said on the other end of the phone but it interrupted Khadafi's good mood. "We have to go," he said sternly as he helped me up and escorted me to the car.

Drakey drove us back into Flint and onto the street where Betty Netty lived. She was standing outside with her hands on her hips, pacing back and forth.

"Khadafi, them muthafuckas tried to come up in here," Netty yelled as soon as Khadafi opened his door.

He quickly shut it so I couldn't hear what she was saying, and I rolled down the window just a crack to eavesdrop.

"Khadafi, those pigs tried to come up in here. They interrupted the whole operation and had your girls scared to death. I told them that they wasn't coming up in my house without no warrant. I told them that I would shoot a trespasser without thinking twice," she said, a Virginia Slim dangling from her lips.

Khadafi didn't think the Feds would find out about the small factory in Netty's house. "Close down shop and send everybody home. Keep cool, and make sure you don't let them in your house without a warrant. I'll take care of this."

Betty Netty turned around and walked back up to her house, cursing about the Feds trying to raid her house.

"What was that all about?" I asked as soon as Khadafi got back in the car.

He placed my head in his lap and stroked my hair gently. "Nothing. Just business."

The next couple days were filled with movement in and out of our house. He told me that he had a lot of business to take care of and that I would have to stay in the house until he completed it. The phone rang constantly, and every time he answered it he grew angrier and angrier.

It had to be more than just the Feds.

I had never seen Khadafi so stressed out. Every day he began to yell at me more and more, but I knew that it had nothing to do with me.

I sat on our king-size bed watching TV when the

phone rang. "May I speak with Khadafi?" I heard a voice say when I answered. My suspicions grew because the voice on the phone had an accent. I knew that Khadafi's connect was from Colombia, but he had never called the house.

I walked over to the intercom system and paged Khadafi. *Beep*. "Khadafi, you have a phone call." I wanted to be nosy, but instead I placed the phone back on its cradle and continued to watch TV.

Less than five minutes later he came into the room. "Remy, I have to talk to you."

I turned off the television and sat up in the bed.

"I have to go on a business trip. It's only for a couple days, but I need you to be very careful. If you go anywhere—"

I interrupted him and said, "I know, I know. Take Drakey with me."

Khadafi quickly replied, "No, take Philly with you. Drakey is easily distracted and the two of you have become friends; I need you with someone who will tell you no."

I shook my head. "Okay. When do you leave?"

Khadafi walked over to the closet and pulled out a suitcase. "Now."

* *

The next morning I got up, put on my running clothes, and was ready to walk out the door when Philly stopped me.

"Where you going?" he asked.

I stopped in my tracks. I forgot he was supposed to be watching over me while Khadafi was out of town. "Out for a run."

Philly kicked back his fat ass on the couch and

said, "No, you're not—sit your ass down. Khadafi said if it's not necessary you don't leave the house."

I turned up my face at him; I never really cared for Philly, but I was cordial. (He was Khadafi's best friend.) I slowly closed the front door and walked over to the couch and sat down next to him.

Philly was a leech in my opinion. He was the worker out in the streets that made sure all Khadafi's commands were followed. Philly was light-skinned with a sloppy build and got on my nerves most of the time. Having grown up in the Regency projects, one of Flint's most notorious neighborhoods, Philly was born a hustler. He knew what an ounce of dope was and how much it went for before he knew how to tie his shoes, and Khadafi thought of him as his most trustworthy companion.

I looked at Philly and wondered why Khadafi took Cease with him instead of Philly. *At least Cease was around my age; I wouldn't have been stuck in the house with Philly's old ass.*

"So what have you been up to? I haven't seen you around here in a while." I asked Philly, trying to make conversation.

Philly didn't reply. He just sat back and watched TV. When he didn't respond to me, I grabbed a magazine off the table and went up to my bedroom to relax.

A couple hours later, I took a shower and put on a white terry cloth robe. I walked downstairs, soaking wet and holding my robe together. Philly was still sitting on the couch and looked at me when he heard me come down the steps.

"Do you call going to get something to eat a necessary trip out the house?" I walked over to him and stood directly in front of him, with my hands on my hips.

Philly's eyes roamed my body. He gazed at the water rolling down my breast line.

I quickly closed my robe before he got any ideas.

He got up off the couch and moved a little too close to me; I could feel his body heat. He said, "I'll be in the car when you ready."

I smacked my lips and walked upstairs and put on some clothes.

We went to eat at Applebee's, and Philly kept up his silence as we ate dinner.

"Why don't you close your mouth when you eat?" I asked him, wishing that he would stop making smacking noises at the table.

"That's how I eat."

Philly was rude to me, but I knew that I was safe with him. He wouldn't let anything happen to me, so I sucked up his bullshit. He had been very loyal to Khadafi, so I knew he would be loyal to me as long as I was Khadafi's woman.

After we ate, we went directly back to the house. I kept wishing that he'd left Drakey there with me. At least I would have had laughter while stuck in the house. Drakey should have been on *Comic View*, as funny as he was. Too bad I was the only one that saw his comedic talent.

* *

Ccase stopped reading, remembering the time that Remy had just described. Business had been crazy. There was some kind of mix-up with the Colombians, and Khadafi had asked him to come to Colombia with him to figure things out. Cease reflected on their trip to the drug capital.

Cease could smell the narcotic in the air. He and Khadafi were being escorted to Poe's house, and neither of them knew what to expect. Khadafi had received a phone call the day before. "We need to meet" is all Poe's messenger said, but Khadafi knew something was up.

They arrived at an enormous villa in Bogotá that sat on the edge of the Colombian coastline. They rolled up to a black steel gate, reached their hands out the window and put their fingertips on the sensor. The device ran their fingerprints, and then a computerized voice announced, "Khadafi and his guest are here to see you."

The gates opened to let them in. They got out at the back of the house where Poe was sitting enjoying the company of a few women. Bodyguards were posted all over the house, and they watched closely as Khadafi and Cease approached their boss.

"My good friends . . . Khadafi, how are you?" he said in a thick Colombian accent.

"Poe, how's business?"

Poe, Khadafi, and Cease sat down at the table that sat next to his swimming pool.

"That's what I brought you here to talk about." Poe pulled out three cigars and offered two to Cease and Khadafi.

Khadafi sat back as a beautiful woman in a swimsuit that covered nothing came over to him and lit his cigar. "What about it?" Khadafi puffed on the cigar.

The woman then moved to Cease and lit his cigar. Cease looked at the woman and she smiled at him.

Poe looked at Khadafi. "We have word that you are under investigation by the Feds."

"It was a small inconvenience—it is being taken care of." Khadafi's stern tone indicated that he didn't want to discuss the subject any more.

"Well, you see that is not what we heard. We hear your entire operation is being shaken up by this. We also heard that somebody gave us up as your supplier—that is not how we handle business."

Khadafi was enraged but didn't show it. He didn't know anything about one of his people giving out information. He couldn't even figure out who did it. Only he, Philly, and Cease knew about Poe. *The Feds must have the house wired*, he thought. "I assure you that is not how I handle business; we are operating on the same standards, Poe. My business is operating just fine . . . without any worry to you."

"You see, Khadafi, that is just it—your business is shutting down. If you keep operating you are putting us at risk, and my people and I are not willing to take that risk."

Khadafi continued to puff on his cigar. He took his time smoking the good Cuban cigars. "Poe, my operation will continue. I keep you in business, and if you want to continue to live this lavish lifestyle, you will handle your business in Colombia and let me worry about your connections in the States. If not, you and your people can be replaced. I have another connect; you only have one: Khadafi."

Khadafi knew what his business meant to the

Colombians. He spent millions of dollars with them a year. They were one of the top suppliers in the world, thanks to Khadafi, and if he took his business elsewhere, then they would have new competition. He knew they would go to war with him if he didn't stop his operation. But Khadafi was sure that it was a war that he would win, so he didn't back down.

Poe laughed heartily and sipped the drink that sat in front of him. "That's what I get for fucking with a nigger."

Cease reached for his 9mm, and Poe's guards instantly swarmed over the table.

Khadafi put his hand on Cease's, signaling him to put his weapon away. Khadafi wanted to smack the shit out of Poe but, instead, kept his composure. He looked Poe in the eyes and said, "Well, I guess we know what this means."

Poe raised his glass. "I guess we do."

Khadafi and Cease got up from the table and headed for the airport. Khadafi knew he'd just started a war and had to go prepare his camp for the battle.

* * * * * * * * * * *

Cease shook his head. "That was some crazy shit," he said to himself. He thought he was going to die that day in Colombia and felt he was lucky to leave with his life. He continued to read the diary where he left off.

* * * * * * * * * *

"Khadafi, I am tired of sitting in the house. Can I go shopping today?" I rubbed his shiny, bald head. He'd been back for almost a week and hadn't let me step foot outside the house.

"Remy, this is not the time. I am in the middle of a war—we've been over this a million times."

I sighed and continued to rub his head as he sat at the office desk. "I know, Khadafi, but damn, they got beef with you; that has nothing to do with me."

Khadafi stood up and gently grabbed my shoulders and softly said, "It will be over very soon, but until then I have to keep you safe. I'd go crazy if anything ever happened to you." Khadafi kissed me on the forehead.

With that, I left the room just as Cease entered. I gave Cease an evil look and walked out, leaving the door cracked so that I could still see inside the room. I was tired of not knowing what was going on.

Khadafi looked out the window overlooking the lake in the back. Cease sat down and, knowing that Khadafi was deep in thought, waited for him to turn around.

Khadafi finally turned around and acknowledged Cease's presence. "What's going on, young blood?"

"Nothing much. I got the message that you wanted to see me."

Khadafi nodded. "Cease, you been working for me since you were a young boy. I hope that you have learned a lot, you should have been watching and observing. As you know, the business is in trouble. The Feds are watching my every move, and we are at war with the Colombians. I'm getting too old for this game. I've been watching you, trying to see if you are ready to take over the city, come into your own, young blood. I'm about to get out of the game, settle down with Remy, and enjoy life. If you are ready, I will put you on."

I couldn't believe what I was hearing.

Cease nodded his head up and down. "I'm ready."

Khadafi had confidence in Cease, who he thought was going to be the next big thing once he himself stepped down. Khadafi kept messing with the encrusted diamond ring on his pinky finger. He took it off and handed it to Cease. "Young blood, this was my father's ring—it was his lucky ring. He gave it to me, and now I want to give it to you. This ring gives me strength, and in a business like this you are going to need it. You are about to take all this over. You are my protégé, and I want you to continue this legacy."

Seeing the meeting was getting ready to end, I went up to my room and turned on the TV.

After Cease left the house, Khadafi came up to check on me.

"How long is this going to last, this war that you say you're in? Philly called and said—"

Khadafi covered my mouth with his hands and pulled me into the bathroom. He turned on the shower and ran the water in the sink and then whispered sternly in my ear, "Never talk about my business in this house—the Feds have it wired. I've put a blocking system in my office. It scrambles the signal in there, but the rest of the house is bugged."

I shook my head up and down, and Khadafi uncovered my mouth. I hugged him closely, just wanting everything to be over. "I just want everything and everybody to go away," I said as he held onto me, making me feel safe.

"I am going to figure something out. I'll make it go away, I promise you."

<u>Chapter Nine</u>

December 2001

"**I** have to end this feud with the Colombians. I can't deal with Poe and the Feds at the same time—it's too much for me and for Remy. She's restless and tired of sitting in the house. I know I can't keep her inside forever. I know the games that Poe plays. If he is anything like me, his first target is going to be her. She is my weakness, and he knows it. If anything happens to her, I will kill him. I will kill that man with my bare hands. That's why I need to end this. He's already gotten to some of my street workers, and I have gotten some of his, but us going back and forth is not going to end this war. The Feds been coming around, showing their faces, asking questions. The dealers in Flint are becoming hesitant to buy from me. My record company is under investigation, and I can't make a move until this is over."

I stood outside of Khadafi's office door and peeked inside. I watched silently as he paced his office, walking the same back and forth pattern, while he talked on the phone and rambled on and on about his beef with the Colombians. His situation seemed to have his mind running in circles.

Khadafi always prided himself on being strategic. Outsmarting the enemy and the competition had always been his strong point. But from the way he was stressing, I knew that somewhere along the way he had fucked up, drawing the attention of the Feds and being at war with a very powerful man, one perhaps even more powerful than he was.

As I walked into the kitchen to get something to eat, the doorbell rang. I looked up and saw Khadafi go to the door. He opened it and Cease stood on the outside. "Come in," Khadafi said.

Cease walked into the living room, and I listened in on their conversation.

"Young blood, I wasn't expecting to see you until later today. This must mean you have some information for me."

"I didn't mean to drop in on you, but I thought you should know that the streets is talking."

Khadafi looked back at me then turned to Cease and said, "Let's handle this in my office." Both men walked down the hall and into Khadafi's office.

I was itching to know what they were talking about, so I walked out of the kitchen and crept quietly down the hall and stood outside Khadafi's door. I peered inside just as Khadafi sat down behind his desk and folded his hands on top of it. "What do you mean 'the streets is talking'—who?"

"Man, the Feds are shaking things up in the hood. They asking questions to the wrong people. People who don't know all the facts. A lot of people are speaking your name right now; everybody got something to say about you. The block is hot right now, and nothing's moving. The Feds are bold. They just be sitting in unmarked cars all day, watching everybody, but we know it's them. I'm telling you, Khadafi, everybody's shook."

At that moment, I walked in. "Sorry for interrupting, I just wanted to know if Drakey could take me to the store. I need to pick up some things."

Khadafi didn't respond to me. He was so busy thinking about his situation, he didn't even hear what I had asked him.

"Khadafi!" I said impatiently.

My voice caught his attention, and he waved his hand in a dismissing way. "Yes, Remy, whatever you want."

I smiled to myself and quickly closed the door before he changed his mind. Cease was the distraction that I had been waiting for. Once I heard what they were about to talk about, I knew that it was the perfect chance for me to get out of the house. I ran and put on a pair of oversized dark shades, a black headscarf that wrapped around my head, and got my Prada handbag.

I hurried to find Drakey and found him in the living room talking to some of Khadafi's other soldiers. They all stiffened up when they saw me approach them. "Relax, Khadafi is in a meeting. Hey, Drakey, I need you to take me to the mall."

Drakey was huge. He stood about 6 feet 5 inches and was over 300 pounds. His fat ass had a sweating problem too—no matter how cool a room was, he always had sweat on his forehead. He was cool as hell, though, and we had become good friends.

"Let's go," I said as I walked out of the house and opened the back door of the Lincoln.

Drakey followed me out to the driveway and looked at me in confusion. "Khadafi said that I couldn't take you out."

I closed my door and said, "I already asked him; he said it was fine. Now let's go!"

Drakey was still hesitant. I knew he was seconds away from going to ask Khadafi himself.

I walked close to him, knowing he had a little crush on me. I was determined to use what I had to get what I wanted. The closer I got to him, the more his fat ass began to sweat. I spoke in my most seductive voice. "Drakey, I haven't been out of this house in a long time. I just want to go buy one pair of shoes." I put my hands on his chest. "Please?"

Drakey couldn't resist. He used to sneak peeks at my ass when Khadafi's head was turned. "Just one pair of shoes?" he asked.

"Just one pair and I'm done." I kissed him once on each cheek and then got into the car. I was so relieved.

Even though Khadafi told me I could go, I knew that he was distracted when I asked. Had Drakey gone behind me and asked again, Khadafi would have definitely come to his senses and said no.

Khadafi was smothering me with confinement. It felt like I had been in a prison. I knew that he was going through some stuff right now but I highly doubted that I was in any kind of danger. I was just happy to be out of the house.

Drakey drove into Flint and took me to the Genesee Valley Mall. The mall was packed, and I couldn't wait to swipe the numbers off my credit card. "Come on, Drakey!" I practically dragged him into the mall.

Drakey lazily got out of the car, knowing he was in for a long day of store hopping.

I shopped all day, roaming from store to store and trying on almost everything they had, figuring it would be a while before I convinced my man to let me out again. By the time I was done, the mall was closing. I knew I would hear Khadafi's mouth about being gone too long.

Drakey escorted me to the car. "One pair, huh?"

I couldn't help laughing. "Oh, Drakey, it didn't kill you."

We got into the car and began the drive home. Halfway down the road, we came to an intersection that was blocked off. There was a police officer waving a stop sign. Drakey stopped the car and rolled down his window.

"Sir, this road is closed. You'll have to take the detour."

I looked around and noticed that there were other officers. Even though the police wore uniforms, I still felt like something was wrong. All of them were of Colombian descent. I frowned my face up, recognizing an accent.

It sounded like the same guy on the phone. "Drakey, drive!"

Before Drakey could put his foot on the gas, the Colombian opened the door and shot Drakey twice, once in each leg.

"Oh shit!" Drakey yelled out in pain. He immediately went for his gun that sat in the passenger seat, but the man shot him in his hand, causing blood to splatter all over my face.

The Colombian rushed to the back door, but I was already on my way out the other side of the car. I was worried about Drakey but I couldn't help him. The Colombian opened the door and grabbed hold of my right ankle. I kicked him with all my might with my left foot.

"You fucking bitch!"

I scrambled across the seat. As soon as I opened the door, I was snatched out by two other men who pulled up on the other side of the car.

"No . . . let me go!" I screamed and struggled to free myself from their hold.

I watched in slow motion as two other cars full of men pulled up. They pulled Drakey out and threw him into the back seat of one of their cars. They put a pillowcase around my head and pushed me into the back seat and drove off.

I was terrified. Being in a car with three men who were at war with Khadafi meant they were at war with me. I couldn't see anything, and that's what scared me the most. I didn't know where they were taking me. The last time that I had been forced into a car, I was raped. *What's gonna happen to me now?*

I tried to calm down. Wherever they took me wasn't far, because a couple minutes later the car stopped moving. They dragged me out and forced me into a building. All I knew was that I was headed down some stairs.

"Please, don't do this—I have money; I can pay you," I said, trying to bargain for my life.

The Colombians laughed and pushed me down the rest of the steps. I felt my body bang against each step as I fell to the bottom of the staircase. Pain shot up my leg and made me cry out. A strong sense of desperation swept over me as I heard the men descend the steps. I crawled backwards, trying to create as much distance between me and my kidnappers.

One of them walked over to me and snatched the pillowcase from my head.

"Tie her up," another instructed. I was pushed into a wooden chair and my hands and legs were duct taped to it.

I watched helplessly as they pushed an injured Drakey down the stairs. His legs were bleeding badly, and he could barely stand. Drakey tried his best to get up. The men walked around him, taunting him and kicking him repeatedly.

"Stop it! Please, stop!" I screamed, seeing that Drakey couldn't take anymore.

"You hear that?—she wants us to stop," one of them teased.

"Set him on that table," he said, pointing to a wooden table that sat directly across from me.

"What do you want?" I asked boldly.

"What do we want?—we want you to deliver a message to Khadafi from Poe," one of them said. He pulled out a knife and stabbed it through Drakey's uninjured hand.

I turned my head and heard Drakey's piercing scream echo through the basement.

"Don't touch her! Don't hurt her; she has nothing to do with this," Drakey cried out in agony.

One of the men came behind me and held my head in place so I could watch them torture Drakey.

"Stop it!" I yelled as the men began to cut pieces of Drakey's flesh off the bone.

Drakey looked at me and called for me as the men tore him apart. The tears flowed down my face, like a river, and they kept coming. Drakey was more than a bodyguard to me, he was a friend.

I didn't know what they were going to do to me, and I prayed to God that I wasn't next. I was in agony as I watched them slaughter Drakey. "Please, just stop!" I pleaded.

"Shut her up!" one of them yelled.

The other men placed a piece of tape over my mouth.

There was blood everywhere. I could even smell it. It was dripping from the table where they had placed Drakey and was forming a pool on the floor in front of me. Drakey's body twitched furiously, and he jerked with every piece of flesh they cut from his body. "Please, just kill me," he managed, as blood ran from his mouth.

One of the men walked to the head of the table and stabbed a long hunting knife through his neck. He then ran it horizontally in jagged motions until he had ripped his head from his body.

I vomited from the sight and began to choke because the vomit was stuck between the tape and the back of my throat. I couldn't breathe. As soon as they removed the tape, more vomit came up. They picked me up, still taped to the chair, and carried me back up the stairs and out the door. I screamed to the top of my lungs.

They put the pillowcase back over my head and placed me in the van. I didn't know where they were taking me until they pulled me out the car and sat me on the curb of my own home. One of the Colombians snatched the pillowcase from over my head.

The sound of screeching must've got the attention of Khadafi's soldiers because they all came running out of the house.

"What the fuck is this?" Cease asked when he saw me sitting on the curb, covered in vomit and blood. He pulled his gun from his waistline and walked over to me. "Go get Khadafi!" he screamed.

The guards rushed into the house to get Khadafi while Cease tried to free me from the chair. "Who did this to you?"

I was too hysterical to answer him, too full of terror and grief to say anything. I mumbled, "Drakey . . . they killed Drakey."

Khadafi came running out of the house. He ran over to me and dropped to his knees. He looked into my eyes. Khadafi eyes began to water, but no tear dropped.

Cease got the last pieces of tape off my wrists and held them up for Khadafi to see. My wrists and ankles were bleeding and raw from being tied so tightly to the chair.

Khadafi picked me up and carried me into the house.

"They killed Drakey. Khadafi, they cut him up—they just cut pieces of him right in front of me," I wrapped my arms around his neck.

A teardrop fell down the side of Khadafi's face. "Did they touch you?"

I quickly shook my head no.

He exhaled deeply. He didn't even ask me who did it.

"It needs to stop," I said softly as I cried in Khadafi's arms.

He kissed my forehead. "I know, I know. It will." He lay me down gently on the bed and watched as I curled up in a fetal position. Khadafi didn't say anything to me. I guess he knew that he'd put me directly in harm's way.

There was a small knock at the door. "Come in," Khadafi said softly.

Cease opened the door slowly and entered his mentor's room. I could see the rage behind his eyes.

If he was there, this shit wouldn't have happened, I thought angrily as I pictured Drakey's lifeless eyes staring at me.

"I'm on it, Khadafi; I can take care of it." Cease wanted to go after the men who'd done this.

Khadafi paced the room and rubbed the back of his neck, "No, I'll take care of it—this is personal . . . too personal. I have to put an end to it. Tell everybody to get out. Go home, young blood; I'll call if I need you."

Cease nodded his head up and down and said, "Okay," before walking out of the room.

Khadafi walked into the bathroom that was attached to our bedroom and ran a bath for me. By the time he came back out, the crying had stopped, and I was lying on the bed, staring out into empty space.

"Remy . . ." he said in a deep and soothing tone. He picked me up off the bed and carried me into the bathroom. He placed me in the bathtub and washed me gently. I felt his hand tense up when he noticed the bruises on my back.

"They killed Drakey . . . and told me to tell you it was a message from Poe."

I began to blame myself for Drakey's death. *If I hadn't begged him to take me shopping, he would still be alive.*

"They stopped us and said that the roads were blocked and then they—" My words broke off, and I lowered my head to my chest. "Drakey didn't do nothing to anybody. You told me to stay in the house. You've been telling me. I'm so sorry, Khadafi. I didn't know. I thought you were being overprotective. I should have listened to you."

Khadafi rubbed my hair. "Relax, it's all over—I am going to handle this." He finished giving me a bath and then helped me get dressed.

I lay back down on the bed and cried until the tears ran out. I couldn't sleep that night, and Khadafi stayed by my side, watching me, trying to help me get some rest.

"Try and get some sleep. I'm right here."

"No, I don't want to go to sleep." I was scared and, although I knew nothing was going to happen while he was with me, I didn't want to close my eyes.

Khadafi didn't sleep that night. He guarded the house with his life, determined to keep me safe from any more harm. I stood in the living room entrance and watched Khadafi as he sat in the living room. He had two 9mm handguns sitting in his lap, an assault rifle on the coffee table, and a pint of Hennessy at his feet, and talked to himself. "I wish you muthafuckas would come in my house. You had the audacity to take my woman, my Remy! She is mine! She belongs to me! You don't put your fucking hands on her!" Khadafi saw his reflection in the wall that was made out of glass mirror and he cocked back his gun and shot out the glass. The loud sound of glass shattering went through the house. I had never seen Khadafi like that. He stayed up all night, talking to himself and making threats to the empty room, and I stayed up listening, hoping that he would keep me safe.

For the next couple weeks Khadafi cracked

down on his security. He didn't trust anybody. Only Philly and Cease were allowed in the house. His other guards stood visible outside. Khadafi did everything in his power to make me feel comfortable, but it was hard for me to shake the image of Drakey lying lifeless on the wooden table.

Things were spiraling out of control, and nobody seemed to be able to stop the madness. I heard countless conversations between Philly and Khadafi. Poe was knocking off half of his crew; the other half was being shaken up by the Feds. I was scared out of my mind and didn't want to leave the house under any circumstances.

No matter what Khadafi did, it still didn't calm my soul. If he added more people to his security, I would say, "How do you know you can trust all those people?" If he had Cease or Philly guard me while he was away, I would say, "Philly and Cease can't protect me by themselves." I never felt safe and wanted the war to end. I couldn't feel secure until it was over.

Khadafi was stuck. He couldn't make a move without the Feds watching, but if he didn't do something soon, Poe was going to make his move. I was sitting on the living room couch reading *Dirty Money* by Ashley Jaquavis, trying not to think about the past couple weeks that had sent our world into a frenzy.

The phone rang, and Khadafi answered, "Hello?"

When I saw his face turn to dismay, I knew it was bad news.

"What's wrong?" I asked him when he hung up the phone.

He didn't respond.

"Tell me, Khadafi." I was tired of him keeping secrets about his business. Since his actions were beginning to affect me, I thought that I deserved to know what was going on.

"Netty's house is being raided. The Feds are starting to shut us down. I need to go down to the police station and post her bail."

I closed my book and shook my head from side to side. "It seems like this war that you're in is hurting everybody except you."

He walked over to me and grabbed my face gently with both hands. "I'm going to handle this. It will all be over soon. Right now, I have to go handle some business. I'm going to pick up Philly."

Tears began to form in my eyes when Khadafi said he was leaving me.

"Stop it. You're safe here. I'm going to call Cease over to sit with you and I have security outside." He kissed me passionately on the lips and said, "I love you more than anything. Nothing can keep me away from you. We will always be together, no matter what. This bullshit is going to end. I love you."

I smiled softly and wiped my eyes. "I know. I love you too."

* *

Cease sat in the living room staring at me. My whole attitude had changed since my encounter with the Colombians. He could sense my fear. "I'm not gon' let anything happen," Cease said, trying to reassure me.

"That's what Drakey said."

"I'm not Drakey. If somebody run up in here, they dying."

It was the first time Cease ever said more than a sentence to me, and for some reason, I believed him.

Chapter Ten

January 2002

I saw the flashing lights pull up to the house, and my heart began to pound. I knew the Feds were harassing Khadafi, but he'd told me that he was going to take care of it. He said they didn't have proof, but they had to know something if they were coming to the house. I was glad he wasn't at home. I knew that the Feds were coming to arrest him.

Cease finally noticed the flashing lights and mumbled, "Shit!" There was nothing that he could do to stop the police from coming into Khadafi's home, so he looked at me and said, "Don't talk. They are going to ask a lot of questions—don't answer them. No matter what they tell you—"

Ding Dong

Cease looked at me to make sure I understood.

I nodded my head yes.

Cease then walked over to the door and opened it.

A brown-skinned man in a leather jacket pulled

out a badge and said, "Good evening, sir. I'm Detective Reggie Coleman. I'm here concerning Khadafi Langston. We are looking for his next of kin, perhaps his wife."

Even though me and Khadafi were not married, I said, "That's me—I'm his wife. What are you here for?"

The detective looked at Cease and then at me. "Mrs. Langston, on behalf of the city of Flint, Michigan, I regret to inform you that Khadafi Langston was killed tonight. He was involved in a shootout."

I looked at the detective and the old me came out. "What did you say? What! You regret to inform me? You've been hounding him for months now and you come to my house all nonchalant and say that you regret to inform me!" I ran up on the cop and smacked him hard in the face. "He is not dead! Do you know who Khadafi is? He cannot die!" I yelled hysterically.

Cease grabbed me from behind and tried to keep me standing as my knees gave out in his arms.

"He's not dead . . . he said he wouldn't leave me." I moaned and cried painful tears of sorrow. The heartache I felt was indescribable. It hurt so badly, it felt like the pain was going to kill me.

"Get the fuck out!" I yelled at the detective. "Get out of my fucking house." I screamed forcefully as he turned around and left.

"Remy . . ." Cease began. He sat down on the couch and put his face in his hands. I think we both were in a state of disbelief. I had lost my soul mate, my father figure, my friend, and my lover. Khadafi was all of these things to me.

He watched as I curled up on the couch and hugged my knees to my chest, rocking back and forth as the tears started to fall. I looked at him and shook my head. "He promised me . . . he said we'd always be together," I said softly to myself. "Just leave."

Cease hesitated. "I don't think you need to be by yourself right now." He sat down next to me and pulled me close.

"It feels like I'm dying."

"I know. I'm hurting too, but you gon' get through this shit."

"I just wanna be alone. Just please leave."

Cease said, "Okay," and got up and left.

The only person I wanted to be around was Khadafi, but he was not there and would never be there for me again. He was the cause of my grief and it was squeezing at my heart; squeezing way too tight. I was choking on the feeling of a lost love. Tossing and turning, threatening to empty its contents, my stomach felt like it had been removed, and I could feel the pressure building up behind my eyes.

I lay on that couch all night wide awake, just thinking about Khadafi. I thought about when I first met him and how quickly and easily I had fallen in love with him. I thought about every day we'd spent together for the past three and a half years. I tried not to focus on the obvious, but to focus on the love that would never be replaced in my heart. Khadafi was the only person who had ever loved me. The first in my life to show me I was worth something.

I didn't even realize I had stayed up all night until Philly came knocking at the door. Weak from anguish and not wanting to move off the couch, I got up and slowly walked over to the door.

I opened it to a red-eyed Philly. He and Khadafi

grew up together and were extremely close. "Remy, I'm so sorry," he said as he embraced me. His hug made me cry all over again and gave me an excuse to break down.

"Why, Philly? Why did this have to happen?" I sobbed and leaned against him for support. He held my head tightly as I cried on his shoulder.

"Look, Remy, you have to remember how much Khadafi loved you. I never thought he would have settled down—he had always been a ladies' man. But from the first day he laid eyes on you, he fell in love. You are beautiful and definitely different than so many other skeezers who were only with him because of his money. I know we've had our differences, but I would not lie to you about something like that—he loved you very much.

"Listen, if you need anything, you call me, all right."

I nodded my head up and down, and the tears continued to fall down my face. My love for Khadafi was genuine, and I went from a hood rat to a queen when I started fucking with him.

"Anything . . . you call, I don't care what it is."

I opened the door and let Philly out. I was a mess. I yelled out to him, "Philly, will you um . . . will you come with me to view his body? I don't think I can do it alone."

Philly stopped dead in his tracks. "I don't think that's a good idea, Remy. When I spoke to the police, they told me that Khadafi was shot over sixty times. There's nothing left—you're gonna have to plan a closed casket."

I blinked vigorously, trying to stop myself from crying. I closed the door and walked back over to the couch. *Sixty times . . . oh my God.* I couldn't believe the amount of pain that Khadafi had gone through before he died. I walked over to the bar and poured a glass of Rémy Martin. I grabbed the glass and the bottle and sat down in Khadafi's office, behind his desk.

I took sips of the alcohol, hoping to lift my spirits or at least help me forget what was going on. I opened his desk drawer and pulled out a manila folder that was labeled "Payments." I opened it and found a bunch of receipts. It was nothing of interest to me, so I kept digging. I found a picture of me and Khadafi inside another drawer—the picture we had taken three years ago at the mayor's ball.

I traced the outline of his face with my finger. "I love you," I said, wishing that he could hear me. I reached over the top of his desk and swept everything off of it in one frustrated movement. I screamed at the top of my lungs then lay my head on top of the desk, weeping. I poured another drink and wallowed in my own grief.

I did this same routine day and night for two days before Cease decided to check up on me. I heard the doorbell ring but was too hung over to move. My head hurt so badly, I couldn't even open my eyes. I heard Cease's voice yell my name, but I knew if I opened my mouth to speak I would throw up before the words even came out.

He walked in and saw me passed out over Khadafi's desk. I could smell the alcohol coming out of me; it was fuming from my pores. He rushed to my side. "Remy." He picked up one of my arms and let it drop loosely to my side. He picked me up and took me up to the bedroom.

"Umm, stop, Cease. Put me down; I can walk."

He ignored me and lay me down on the bed.

I opened my eyes and tried to sit up and immediately felt the results of a hangover. "Cease . . . whatcho' doin' here?" I asked, my speech slurred.

"I'm just checking on you. Nobody's heard from you, so I came over here to see how you're doing. You have to start making arrangements for the funeral." Cease helped me to sit up.

"The . . . funeral . . ." I pointed at him, my finger shaking. "Khadafi's dead . . . he's gone . . ."

Cease rubbed the cold towel on my forehead. "I know you going through a lot right now, but you gotta get yo' shit together. You gon' have to start planning the funeral."

I nodded.

"I'ma give you some time to sober up. I'll be downstairs when you wake up."

I slept off the liquor and woke up later to a dark room and a banging headache. "Aww, shit," I said as I made my way to the bathroom and hurled in the toilet. I must have been heaving and choking real hard because Cease rushed up the stairs and helped me back to bed. "I'm sorry," I said.

Cease laughed and replied, "You got fucked up." Then he got more serious. "This is hard for everybody—Khadafi was like my father; I know how you feel, but you have to pull yourself together."

Once I realized time was still moving without me, I began to grieve in a more healthy way. I began making the funeral arrangements and although it was hard, I wanted to be the one to do it—Khadafi was my man and I at least owed him that. I didn't want to accept the fact that he was gone, but the more arrangements I made, the closer I got to saying my final goodbyes.

The day of the funeral was one big blur. I wore a black Valentino dress and dark oversized glasses so no one would see how bad I was doing. I got into Khadafi's black Lexus and drove down to Mt. Pisgah, the church that he'd supported. There were flower arrangements everywhere. I walked inside the beautiful church, with fear and pain in every step. Walking down the center aisle I heard the whispered comments.

"That's Khadafi's wife," one woman said.

Another answered, "Uh uhh, they weren't married. She used to strip down at Magic City."

"You can't turn a ho into a housewife," added another woman.

I couldn't believe those women had the audacity to come to my man's funeral and talk shit. I wanted to throw them out on their asses, but I knew that they had a right to pay their final respects.

I walked up to the closed casket that sat at the front of the church and gently placed the single red rose I held in my hand on top of it. The night before I had written Khadafi a note saying exactly how I felt about him. I kissed it, leaving my lipstick on the envelope, and then placed it next to the rose. "I love you, Khadafi. I love you so much."

I turned around and saw Cease walking down the aisle. "How have you been?"

"I'm just trying to take it day by day."

"Look . . . after the funeral, I'm leaving town for a while; I have to let things die down. Khadafi has a lot of enemies right now, and they are gonna be trying to get his camp—it's not safe here. And the Feds are waiting for somebody to make a move."

"I thought you were supposed to take over after . . ." My words broke up; I couldn't even speak his name without breaking down.

"Ain't nobody gon' be taking that over no time soon—his empire is over. I'm gon' have to build my own up from the bottom."

"I understand." I grabbed onto his suit jacket. "Thank you for everything."

He kissed me on the cheek. "Take care of yourself." Then he went to the casket to pay his last respects.

I took a seat in the front row next to Philly as the service began. I looked around the church and recognized all the faces that I had come to know over the years. Everyone, from the mayor to the police chief, was present. Sophie and her husband were seated in the back. She gave me a warm smile when our eyes met.

Reverend Hill's sermon had everyone in the church in tears. I cried softly, hiding behind the darkness of my sunglasses. My lip quivered, but I tried my best to be strong.

The service ended after a torturous two hours, and I, Netty, Philly, Cease, and a couple other members of Khadafi's entourage went to the cemetery to watch them lower his casket. I fell to my knees when Khadafi hit the dirt, all the pain over the last week mounting in me at that one moment. It was a piercing feeling. One that hurt me to the depths of my soul.

While the pastor was speaking and the body was being lowered, Cease was marking a black limo that pulled up about a hundred yards away. Cease's trigger finger began to itch. He touched Philly to get his attention. "Yo, Philly, look at that shit, man." Cease discreetly pointed his head towards the limo.

Philly looked over, and the limo pulled off. Philly leaned close to Cease and whispered, "They are going to die. They just came to make sure Khadafi was dead."

Philly put his arm around my shoulders.

I looked at Cease. His hand was shaking uncontrollably. I could tell he was furious. I knew he wanted to chase down the limo and light it up. The muscle in his jaw tensed and he gritted his teeth. I saw a teardrop on Cease's face.

When I made it back to what was now my house, it was crowded with mourners.

"I am so sorry for your loss," Sophie said as soon as I walked in the door.

"How did everybody get in here?" I asked.

"Maria let us in; we just want to be here for you."

"Thank you, but I really just want to be alone right now," I said as politely as possible. I hadn't planned on having a dinner and wasn't ready for everyone to be in my face.

Sophie cleared the house for me, but despite my request, Philly insisted that a couple of Khadafi's soldiers stay back and guard the house.

"Can I get you anything, Ms. Morgan?" Maria asked.

"No, thank you, Maria. You can take the rest of the day off."

I went outside and sat on the back patio and looked out onto the beautiful lake. I had been with Khadafi for so long, I didn't know what to do by myself.

I cried for a week straight and fell into a state of depression. That was not a place that I wanted to be, so each day that passed I tried to pull myself together a little more.

* * * * * * * * * * * * * * * * * *

I walked into the kitchen and opened the refrigerator. It had been three weeks since Khadafi had died, and the pain was still weighing down my heart. The inside of the refrigerator was pathetic. I had been accepting food from the neighbors for so long, I forgot to go grocery shopping.

Besides the few neighbors that stopped by, I hadn't heard from anyone since the funeral. Philly had called once the day after, but everybody else moved on with their lives. Cease left town, and Khadafi's workers all found other jobs.

I grabbed my purse off the counter and grabbed the keys to Khadafi's Benz and drove to the ATM. When I tried to take out some money, the machine said insufficient funds. "As much money as he got in this account, they better quit bullshitting!" I yelled out in aggravation as I parked the car in front of the bank and walked inside. I sat in the waiting area so that I could see the bank manager.

Five minutes later, a young white man, wearing a black suit with a blue tie, greeted me. "How can I help you?"

I walked into his office, sat down, then said, "I just tried to take money out of my husband's account and it wouldn't let me. The machine said insufficient funds, but I know that is impossible—he has millions of dollars in that account."

The bank manager said politely, "Okay, I'm sure we can clear up this mess. What is your husband's name?"

"Khadafi Langston."

The man didn't even enter his name into the computer. He looked at me and said, "Miss, your husband's account was frozen by the government yesterday morning."

My eyes opened wide in bewilderment. "What?"

"We cannot allow you to take out any money. This account now belongs to the government."

"What the fuck do you mean?—I need to talk to the person in charge."

"I am the district manager ma'am—there is nothing we can do."

I wanted to snatch his little white ass by his collar, but that was no longer me. I had to handle the situation with class. I gathered my purse and walked out of the bank embarrassed and not knowing what to do. *What the hell am I supposed to do without any money?*

I didn't have one red cent to my name. It had all been Khadafi's money.

I was frantic as I sped down the highway back to my home. I stormed into the house and went directly to Khadafi's office. I rummaged through all of his papers and went through his desk.

I went from room to room, trying to find some money. After I tore up the entire house I only managed to find $440. There was no way I could live on that. Hell, I spent that on my nails and hair each month! I had to figure something out.

I paced back and forth in Khadafi's office and tried to think of a way to make some money. I remembered that Khadafi always kept an extra stash of cocaine in the house, one of the only secrets he had shared with me about his business.

I remembered his words like they were law. "You always keep a stash for yourself . . . in case you fall on hard times."

I rushed down to the wine cellar under the basement. I opened the steel safe behind a picture that Khadafi had installed in the wall and saw fourteen kilos of pure cocaine. I didn't know what to do with it, though.

My first thought was to call Cease, but I remembered he said that he was leaving town until things calmed down. He didn't even leave a number for me to reach him. *I would have to call Philly.* Although we had our differences I knew he would help me.

Philly answered his phone on the third ring.

"Philly, the Feds have frozen all of Khadafi's accounts. I don't have any money; I need a favor."

"Anything."

"Khadafi kept a secret stash of cocaine in the wine cellar. I need you to sell it for me—I'll give you half of what you make."

Philly immediately came over to the house and took the cocaine out of the wine cellar. There was a look of greed in his eyes.

I knew I called the right person.

Just as he was getting ready to walk out the door, I asked, "How long do you think it will take?"

"I don't know . . . a month or so. I'll call you when I sell half of it and drop the money off to you."

I nodded my head. "Okay." When I closed and locked the front door behind him, a feeling of relief fell over me. I began to feel better now that I knew

I wasn't broke. I walked upstairs to my bedroom and sat in my bay window, thinking about Khadafi. I had no idea he was in so much trouble and still couldn't grasp the fact that he was no longer in my life.

I didn't hear from Philly for two weeks and tried my best to manage off the little money I had in my pocket. I picked up the phone and called him just to see how it was coming. He didn't answer, and after the fifth ring I hung up. I figured he was out hustling and decided to try back in a couple days.

I walked around the lonely house. I never really realized how big it was until Khadafi died. It was way too big for just me.

A couple of months before Khadafi passed, he'd added my name to the house deed. I thought about selling it, but the thought quickly faded when I remembered how many memories lay within the walls.

A knock at the door startled me. I expected it to be Philly, but when I opened the door I saw two white men and a bunch of people standing in the yard.

"I don't want whatever you're selling."

The men bumped past me and made their way into my house.

"What the hell are you doing?" I yelled as I followed them into my living room.

"We are from the United States government," a man announced. He shoved a piece of paper in my face. "We're here to seize this property."

Men started to fill my home.

"What?" I yelled, outraged and confused by their intrusion. I felt my pocket to make sure that the money was on me. "What the hell are you doing? This is my stuff. This is all that I have left. You can't just come in here and do this!"

The agents loaded up my belongings.

I rushed up to my room, grabbed the set of diamonds that Khadafi had bought me when I first met him, and stuffed them into my purse. I didn't care what else they took, but those were special to me.

Just as I was getting ready to pull out a suitcase and pack some of my clothes, one of the agents came upstairs and said, "Ma'am, you can't take those—everything in this house is being seized."

I watched helplessly as they emptied my house of its possessions and stripped me of the little dignity I had left.

"You have to be off the property when we're done," one of the agents said to me.

I just shook my head and sat on the curb and watched them do their job.

The neighbors quickly gathered outside their homes and made the situation even more unbearable for me. I instantly became the target of their disapproving stares and heard the rumors as I stared at the scene. I stood up and looked at the neighbors and yelled, "What the fuck y'all looking at?"

The white neighbors went back into their homes, terrified that I would start acting a fool.

I caught myself and noticed that I was acting exactly how Khadafi had taught me not to. I gathered my composure and sat back on the curb, watching the government move everything out of the place that I once called home.

I didn't know what I was going to do—I had no family, no friends, no money, and was alone, with nowhere to go. I wandered away from the house in utter despair. I was broke in every sense of the word—my pockets were short, my heart was shattered in pieces, and my house had been taken away.

I would have gone to Betty Netty for help, but she was arrested before Khadafi died and showed up at the funeral with a police escort.

I walked down South Saginaw, trying to make my way into the city. I had nothing but the clothes on my back and four hundred dollars. Grand Blanc was twenty minutes away from Flint, which made it around a three-hour walk. *I need to get to a hotel.*

Once I got into the city limits, I caught the bus to Dort Highway. I went to the Sleep Away and got a room at $39 a night. I frowned when the woman behind the desk handed me a dingy-looking keychain. I expected a plastic electronic card. *What kind of hotel still uses keys?*

I hesitantly walked outside and found Room 810. I opened the door and walked into the room. *Hell no! I am not staying in this run-down-ass hotel.* The room had one queen-size bed with red covers and sheets, one TV, and a small bathroom attached to it. I started to walk back out the door, but I didn't have the luxury of being picky; it was the only place I could afford since I didn't know how long it was going to take for Philly to sell the dope.

After paying for five nights in the hotel, I only had $205 left. I went straight to the phone and called Philly.

Ring ... Ring ... Ring ... Ring ...

I got no answer and hung up. *It's only been a couple weeks; he must still be hustling. I'm just gonna have to hang tight until he can get me the money.*

I lay down on top of the covers, afraid at what I might find if I lifted them up and tried my best to go to sleep. It had been a long day and I was stressed out. I didn't have any clothes or food and I barely had enough cash to make it.

I woke up the next day and tried not to think about what had been happening to me lately. *When Philly gets me the money, everything would be okay.* I tried to reassure myself that my situation was only temporary.

I walked out of the room and over to the gas station across the street from the hotel. I walked in and bought a toothbrush and stacked up on chips, water, and frozen sandwiches. I spent twenty-five dollars and walked out with two full bags, one with junk food, another with personal supplies. Hopefully, it would last through the next four days I planned on staying in the hotel.

I spent the next four days waiting patiently, giving Philly enough time to do what he had to do, and living off of junk food, and wearing the same clothes for days. The fifth night in the hotel I called Philly. When I received no answer, I decided to buy three more nights in the hotel. I went up to the front desk and paid them $117. I counted the money that I had left in my pocket—*$63 left.*

Philly needed to hurry up.

I was tired of living off of chips, cookies, and noodles, so that night I walked up the street to the local Coney Island. I didn't realize how hungry I was until I smelled the food in the restaurant. I ate like it was the best food I ever tasted in my life.

When I was done I walked back to my room and called Philly. I only had $52.

"*The number you have dialed is not in service. Please hang up and try your call again.*"

I hung up and redialed his number—slowly this time, to make sure I called the right number. "Two, three, four . . . nine, three, five, five."

"*The number you have dialed is not in service. Please hang up and try your call again.*"

I slammed down the phone and began to cry. It had been a while since I had given the dope to Philly. I knew that he'd made some kind of profit. *Why was his muthafuckin' phone disconnected?* I was frantic, but deep down I already knew what was up—I was getting jerked. I had given Philly too much credit; now his fat ass had fucked me over.

I couldn't figure out what to do next. I knew I was in trouble.

That night I tried to wash my clothes out with the soap from the hotel. I had been wearing the same panties for almost two weeks. I scrubbed my underclothes and my shirt and jeans and then hung them over the shower curtain to dry. I decided to keep calling Philly, even though I knew I wouldn't be able to find him.

The next day I went out to look for a job. I had to find a way to make some money—I couldn't survive without it. I went to stores, restaurants, and even dry cleaners looking for work, but nobody would hire me. I looked like hell.

I ended up spending my last few bucks on more nights in the room. I didn't even have money for food. I stole food from the gas station every day, hoping

I wouldn't get caught. After days of scrounging and struggling, I couldn't take it any more. I was hungry and on my last night in the hotel.

I knew what I had to do, but I cried every time I thought about going back to my old life. I was so hungry I began to feel weak and could hear my stomach growling. I basically had to say, "Fuck it—I refuse to die on the streets." I had to use what I had to get what I wanted or, in my case, needed.

All that prissy shit that Khadafi instilled in me wasn't worth shit without him—I needed to get on the grind—it was my only chance of survival. And so I went back to stripping. Which meant that I had to go back to Dock.

Chapter Eleven

March 2002

I thought as I sat on the hotel bed. *I don't have enough money to buy another night. Where in the fuck is Philly? He would never have pulled this if Khadafi was alive. I can't believe this! I need to come up on some bread quick.*

My situation had changed so drastically in a short period of time. I just had the world in the palm of my hands and saw it all slip away right before my eyes. It was all too overwhelming.

It was hard for me to plan my next move because all I could think about was my Khadafi. Those three years had been the highlight of my life. Khadafi showed me how life was supposed to be and treated me like a queen.

I stood up and began to pace the room, walking back and forth, thinking about what I would do next. All of a sudden, I burst out into laughter remembering how Khadafi used to pace the room when he was in deep thought. Being around him so much, I had picked up some of his habits. The laughter soon turned into sadness as I realized how much I loved and needed my man.

I knew that if I was going to go back to stripping, Magic City was the only club worth stripping in. It was the only strip joint that made any money. It was where the ballers went, and if I wanted to eat, I would have to go and ask Dock for my job back.

I caught the city bus down to Magic City, where I knew Dock would be, and stepped off the bus at the corner of Stewart and North Saginaw and proceeded to walk to the end of the corner. When I finally reached the club, I noticed that it looked a little different since the last time I had seen it. There was a new sign in front and the building was a different color.

Definitely an upgrade, I thought. I stood in front of the club and a tear formed in the corner of my eye as I grasped my own reality. I entered the club and saw dozens of half-naked dancers scattered all over the room. I felt the butterflies form in my stomach.

I didn't think I could do this again. I had come too far to wind up right back where I started. None of the women in the club were on my level, but there I was ready to do whatever for a dollar. I turned around and headed back towards the exit. I stopped dead in my tracks and realized that I had no other options. *If Dock didn't want to deal with me, I was fucked.*

The last time I was in Magic City, I was a totally different person. I remembered the last time that I saw Dock. The look on his face when I gave him that blast to his sweaty-ass balls was unforgettable.

All eyes were on me when I walked to the back of the club. My elegant appearance shocked the men and also the women in the club. It was something about my swagger, I think, that made me stand out from the rest of the women. I caught the attention of the men in the club—even with all of my clothes on.

I reached Dock's office and knocked on the door.

The door opened, and a familiar face came out of the office. She was crying.

"Don't come back asking me for money either," Dock yelled.

I looked at the light-complexioned girl. I had seen her somewhere before. The girl's eyes had bags under them, and she looked very frail. We made eye contact and then just kind of stared at each other for a few seconds.

"Layla?"

Layla fidgeted nervously. She quickly tried to fix her hair and wipe her tears away. "Hey, girl, long time no see."

She looked bad. She'd lost a lot of weight and didn't have that same sparkle in her eye. You could tell she was messing with drugs. I gently grabbed her by both shoulders and looked into her eyes.

Layla's nervous twitch prevented her from keeping steady eye contact with me.

"Are you okay?"

She put on a forced smile. "Yeah, I'm fine. Look at you, looking all glamorous and shit. I heard you got a good man and a big house in Grand Blanc—what you doing down here?"

The sight of Layla like that made me uncomfortable. She looked like a straight-up crackhead. "I came down here to see if I can get my old job back."

Layla was just about to say something when a bouncer grabbed her by her arm. "Dock said that you bet' not come in here no more begging. I don't know how you snuck past me, but you got to go. Let's go!" The bouncer pulled Layla away and put her out the club.

I felt so felt sorry for Layla, but I had my own problems to worry about. I quickly focused my attention on the present task. I dropped my chin into my chest as I stood outside of Dock's door. The club's musty scent filled my nostrils reminding me how much I hated my previous profession. I raised my fist to the door and knocked three times.

"Come in," a voice yelled from the office.

I opened the door and slowly walked into the dimly-lit room Dock called his office. There he was—Dean Murdock, a.k.a. Dock.

Dock looked at me and squinted his eyes in disbelief. "Well, well, well . . . What do I owe for this surprise?" Dock sat back in his chair.

The sight of Dock still made me tremble. My adrenaline began to pump and I couldn't stop the tear that was forming in my eye. A single tear slid down my face causing my mascara to run.

"I haven't seen you in . . . about four years. I heard you were big-time now with Khadafi." Dock had a slight grin on his face, and he began to rub his goatee. "Sorry to hear about your loss."

Insincerity was written all over his face.

I replied in almost a murmur, "Thanks." I looked in Dock's eyes. "Look, I need a job, Dock."

I stood directly in front of his paper-scattered desk. My whole demeanor had changed—I was a seasoned woman now. I no longer avoided eye contact when speaking and I was more confident.

It instantly turned Dock on, and his manhood began to harden. I could see the imprint in his pants begin to rise. "So after all these years you want to come back to me? What? Khadafi didn't leave you any dough?"

I could tell he enjoyed every minute of it. I turned around and hastily stormed towards the door. I stopped at the door and broke down crying.

Dock didn't say a word. He just stood there and watched me suffer.

I gathered myself and with a raspy voice said, "Please, Dock, I need the money."

The sight of me needing him amused him even more. He stood up, leisurely unzipped his pants, and smirked at me. "One favor deserves another. If my memory serves me correctly, you had some unfinished business the last time you were in this office."

I knew what favor he wanted done and contemplated leaving.

Dock walked over to me and stood face to face with me and the scent of his cheap cologne floated into my nose. "If you want a job, I want a job."

I wanted to walk out but thought to myself, *I have no choice*, and hesitantly dropped to my knees and . . .

* * * * * * * * * * * * * * * *

Cease violently ripped the page of Remy's diary and balled it up in the palm of his hand. His heart began to beat. He gritted his teeth in pure rage. He put the book down and began to walk around the room. He picked his gun up from off the dresser and cocked it. He wanted so bad to go down to Magic City and pay Dock a visit, but he realized that it wouldn't do anything but bring more heat on him. He calmed himself and sat at the end of the bed with his gun in his right palm. He gripped his gun so tightly that it began to hurt. "Remy, Remy . . ." he mumbled in a shaky voice. Trying to keep himself from dropping a tear, Cease looked at the diary and put his gun down. He slowly picked the book back up and continued to read.

* * * * * * * * * * * * * * * * *

I sat in front of the vanity mirror where I sat four years earlier and applied my makeup. Dock bought me a two-piece see-through teddy to dance in. It had been so long since I had danced. I wondered if I still had it. My shape was even more enticing, so my body wasn't the issue—I knew I didn't belong there and I despised every second of it. I stood up and prepared to go onto the dance floor when I heard someone yell my name.

"Remy!"

I turned around to see who was calling me. I couldn't believe my eyes. I hadn't seen her since the last time I was in the club. "Peaches?" I looked harder to see if it was really her.

Peaches ran over to me with her arms opened, and we embraced each other. "Hey girl, I ain't seen you in so long," Peaches looked me up and down.

Peaches was a little heavier than I remembered, but all the weight was in the right places. I grabbed her by her shoulders and asked, "Girl, what you been up to?"

She waved her hand over her body and replied, "As you can see . . ."

I smiled and shook my head.

"I heard you were rich and living good."

My smile slightly dropped, and so did my head. "Yeah, well, things change and people do too."

Peaches tried to lighten up the mood. "We are going have to catch up. But for now, I need to go and make this money."

"Fo' *show*," I replied, and we exited the locker room and headed to the front.

As soon as I reached the main floor I became nervous and uncomfortable. I noticed things had changed since the last time I stripped. There were all new dancers and staff. The crowd had changed too, and having Peaches there with me made my situation a little better. *I can't do this shit. Look at all of these girls in here. It's going to be hard for me to get back into it.* The girls danced differently and had new tricks. Tricks I had no idea how to do.

After a couple of shots of Hennessy, I was back in my comfort zone. I hit the stage and didn't miss a beat. I made $500 dollars in tips that night—I stole the show. And the fellas in the club were waiting in line to get a lap dance from the new girl. All night I heard comments like, "I'll take care of you," and "You don't need to be in here, you should let me take care of you."

Once upon a time, comments like that would have flattered me and maybe I would have taken them up on their offer, but now I was much smarter and wiser.

When the night finally ended, I sat in front of the vanity mirror in the locker room. The back was full with naked dancers walking around and preparing to leave for the night. I let my hair down and took off my black high heels. My feet ached from standing on my feet all night dancing for dollars. I pulled the money from my bra and thong and counted the scrunched up bills.

I had a good night. I just need a month of nights like this and it's a wrap—I hate doing this bullshit. I had it set in my mind that I would hustle hard for a month and stack enough dough to survive off of; I was just waiting for Philly to come through with the money. I prayed to God that he hadn't taken Khadafi's dope and left me on "stuck."

Philly was Khadafi's right-hand man, and I just refused to believe the obvious—I had got "got." I blocked out all of the conversations that were happening around me and just stared into my own eyes in the mirror.

Dock walked around the locker room, collecting his cut from his workers. He made his way over to me and put his hand on my shoulder, snapping me out of my daydream. He put his hand on me, causing me to jump. "Relax," he said, running his fingers through my hair.

I wanted to tell him to stop, but he had my job in the palm of his hand. "Dock, here is your cut." I handed him his share, and while he was counting the money, I got up and went into the bathroom stall. When I came back out he was gone. *Thank God. I'm just ready to go to the room and go to sleep.*

After I got on my clothes and gathered all of my things, I headed out of the club. I stood at the curb, trying to flag down a cab. A silver Denali truck pulled up.

Who is this? I squinted my eyes to get a better look.

The window rolled down, and Peaches stuck her head out. "Need a ride?"

Her chrome wheels glistened, and the street lights bounced off the shiny paint job on her truck. After I finished admiring Peaches' car, I yelled, "Hell, yeah," got my duffle bag, and walked over to the passenger side of the car.

Twista pumped out of the speakers, and the smell of new leather filled my nostrils, reminding me of the nights me and Khadafi used to roll around the streets of Flint in one of his luxury sedans.

"It looks like you living good," I said, examining her ride.

"I'm maintaining." She pulled off the block and onto North Saginaw Street.

Damn, it looks like she doing her muthafuckin' thang. Either that or she fucking with a get-money nigga—I know she can't afford this on a stripper salary. I mean she was getting dances, but not like that. Whatever or whoever Peaches was doing, it paid very well.

"Girl, a bitch hungry as hell. You trying to get something to eat?" Peaches asked as we rode down the city streets at 2:30 in the morning.

I didn't have money to blow, but I didn't want to throw a wrench in the program. "Yeah, I guess I am a lil' hungry."

Peaches turned up her system and headed to the Coney Island in downtown Flint.

The restaurant was empty except for two truck drivers sitting down at two different tables. We sat in the smoking area, and a waitress walked over to us.

"Uhmm, uhmm, give me some bacon and eggs . . . and—nah, give me a five-piece wing ding dinner," Peaches said after searching the whole menu.

The waitress looked at me and waited for me to order.

"Just give me a bagel."

Peaches shot a look over at me and yelled, "A bagel? I know you didn't get all of that back there by eating bagels."

Both of us burst out laughing.

"It's just I'm kind of short on cash. I gots to get on my hustle for real."

Peaches looked at the waitress and said, "She'll have what I'm having."

The waitress took the menus and walked away.

"It's on me, girl." Peaches winked her eye at me.

"You didn't have to do that."

Peaches pulled out a Newport and lit it up. "You get it the next time."

"Excuse me, ladies, we are about to close," the waitress said to us as we conversed at the table.

Peaches looked at her phone and noticed it was 4:00 A.M. "Damn, look at us . . . running our mouths. We been here for over an hour."

During the conversation I told Peaches that I was staying at the motel, and she offered her home, just until I got on my feet. We came to an agreement that I would pay what I could each week and it was settled—we were roommates.

When Peaches and I arrived at her home, I noticed that her house was small but nice. She had black leather furniture and the living room was well decorated. *Peaches definitely had taste.*

"Get comfortable," Peaches told me as she dropped her bags and headed to her blinking answering machine. She pressed the buttons and started taking off her shoes.

Yo, Peaches, get at me when you get in. I'm tryin to get it in with you this weekend. One." BEEP!

Baby girl, I need you at this party on the fifteenth. Call me, let me know what's up! This Eric. BEEP!

This Qua—if you tryin to get down call me.

"You can sleep in the room to the right. The towels are in the closet, and you have to jiggle the toilet to make it stop running." Peaches began to undress right in front of me.

I looked around and thought, *This sho' beats staying at that crusty-ass motel. She cool as hell; I think we are going to get along fine.* I sighed and almost in a whisper said to Peaches, "I'm tired as hell. I think I'm going to call it a night. Thanks for everything, Peaches. You really looked out by letting me crash at yo' spot."

Peaches smiled and opened her arms. "It's nothing. You my girl, right?—we gotta look out for one another."

I hugged Peaches and retired to the room. I took off my clothes and stripped down to my bra and panties. I lay in the bed and started to think about my life, how many obstacles I had encountered, and how fucked-up my hand was. I was dealt a bad hand and had no control over my destiny. The one time I was comfortable and had something special, it was taken away from me in an instant.

Not one night passed that I didn't think about Khadafi. Most nights I cried myself to sleep. He was the last thing on my mind when I went to sleep and the first thing on it when I woke up.

Chapter Twelve

July 2002

I remember the night that Peaches and I had a party to do on the Southside. It was a summer night and we had the windows down while Peaches system blasted Lil' Kim. We had our hand out the window, waving it as we chilled on the strip. (The strip was where everybody who was anybody went on Saturday night.)

Earlier, Peaches mentioned that she had some friends that wanted to have a little fun. The way Peaches was talking, these niggas was some ballers. I couldn't let the opportunity pass, so I agreed to go with her.

I remember that night clearly. After we left the strip, we cruised down I-75, talking about how much money we would make that night. At that point nothing was off limits for us—we were willing to do anything if the price was right. We finally arrived on at the Ramada Hotel on the north side of Flint. Obviously, whoever was throwing this party had chips, because the Ramada wasn't cheap at all. Usually ballers stayed at the Ramada or wealthy people passing through Flint stayed there.

We valet parked and entered the lobby of the hotel. Peaches looked at me and I looked at her. We both smiled at each other, knowing we were stepping into a gold mine.

I hadn't been in a place so luxurious since Khadafi was alive.

Peaches looked at me and said, "I'm about to go to the ladies' room."

I waited for her in the lobby, my duffle bag in hand.

The butterflies no longer existed in my stomach before we did private parties. The first two or three times I was nervous as hell, but I eventually got used to it. I was there for one reason: to get money.

Peaches always had something lined up for us on the weekend. With the money I was making at Magic City and our side hustle, I had saved up a little piece of change.

Peaches walked out the bathroom and came out with a trench coat on.

I already knew the deal—she had only a thong and bra on under it. That wasn't the first time I had seen her with that coat on. "Girl, you got dressed already?"

She grinned and said, "Yeah, I already know how these niggas get down. They don't want to see no striptease or stripping. This is going to be straight-up wham, bam, thank you, nigga . . . feel me?"

I nodded my head and followed her to the second floor.

Peaches looked at the door number and said, "Okay, this is it. 810. Yep, this is it. You ready?"

"Let's just get this shit over with."

Peaches knocked on the door.

A brown-skinned, medium-built cat with neatly twisted, short dreads answered the door. The chain resting on his chest was the first thing I noticed. It was iced-out and blinging in the light. The weed aroma flowed out of the room. He looked at Peaches and smiled. "What up, baby girl? Come in."

"Hey, Jodi." Peaches walked in first; I was right behind her.

I noticed the room had about five niggas inside. I immediately grew nervous. They were looking at us like we were pieces of meat.

Peaches and I walked into the back room. Before I could put on my outfit Peaches pulled out a small vial and emptied some coke between her thumb and her index finger. She sniffed the contents into her nostrils and held her head back to prevent her nose from running. Peaches did this every time we had a party to do. She claimed it made her have a better time.

She offered me some, but just like every other time, I turned it down. I had learned my lesson from that shit.

"Cool—more for me," she would always say when I refused.

Before I could even get my high heels on tight, Peaches was walking out of the door. The trench coat came off and the only thing she had on was a smile.

I heard the music playing in the other room as I was getting prepared. When I finally walked in,

Peaches had her head buried in a nigga's lap and her ass was in the air. The other men were ranting and raving over the show Peaches was giving. Everyone except a guy in the corner smoking a blunt.

As soon as I walked in, two guys left Peaches and walked over to me with wads of money in their hand. I slowly started to dance and shake my ass. Out the corner of my eye, I saw the man that was sitting in the corner walk my way. I felt a strong arm grab me by the elbow while I was dancing. It startled me because he wasn't just getting a free feel in; it was hostile.

"What the fuck?"

He pulled me into the back room. He did it so quick, I didn't even see his face.

The men outside yelled, "What the fuck you doing, man?"

He pushed me into the dark bedroom, and I fell onto the bed. When he switched on the lights, I finally saw his face. It was Cease, with a disgusted look on his face. "Remy, what the hell are you doing here?" He threw both of his hands up.

I was at a loss for words and couldn't believe that he was standing in front of me, trying to stop my hustle.

"You know this wouldn't be going down if Khadafi were still alive!"

This nigga was seriously mad. The look in his eyes was genuine. I couldn't think of anything to say, I was so embarrassed. I didn't want him to see me like that. I was humiliated.

He turned his head and said, "Put on some clothes."

He waited for me get dressed, and we began to talk.

"Remy, how did you end up fucking around with Peaches. She's got a reputation, ya know?"

"Well, after Khadafi died, the Feds came in and took everything. I didn't have a dime to my name. They took the house, the cars, and they seized the bank account. I literally got put out on the streets."

"I didn't know it all went down like that. I had to get out of town for a minute—things were getting too hot. If I stayed I would have went down with Khadafi's operation." Cease paced the room, fingers over his goatee. "Okay, we need to get back in that house. Khadafi had some—"

"I gave it to Philly."

Cease's face frowned up. "What?"

Almost in a whisper I repeated, "I gave the dope to Philly. He took all the dope and I haven't seen him since."

Cease dropped his head knowing I'd made a big mistake. "I would have never let you live like this. I owe that much to Khadafi. You're coming with me."

I thought about what he said and knew that Cease probably didn't have more money than me . . . and I was barely getting by. "No thanks, I'm doing fine —"

Cease grabbed me by my shoulders firmly and looked in my eyes. "You're going with me. I promised Khadafi that if anything ever happened to him I would make sure you're okay. I can't break my word for nobody. Understand?"

I wanted to tell him to step out of my way, but the look in his eyes was so honest and he wasn't taking no for an answer.

"Just until I find Philly. He has to pay what he owes. He would have never pulled that shit if

Kha—" Cease's eyes turned red. He gathered himself and continued. "Khadafi was like a father to me and you have to help me help you."

With that, we left the room and the hotel. Although they probably wanted to, nobody said anything to Cease when we walked out. Half of the guys in the room were too busy taking turns on Peaches.

We reached the parking lot and hopped into Cease's car. He had Tupac blasting out of his subwoofers. His '85 Cutlass had a big rust stain on the side of it. Only thing that was nice about it was the 20-inch rims that it sat on. Honestly, the rims looked liked they cost more than the car. I was skeptical about getting into his hooptie, but was in no position to complain.

Cease picked up his cell phone and made a call. I eavesdropped trying to hear what he was saying. "Yo', I need a favor. A close friend of mine is going to stay at yo' place for a minute."

"Who the fuck is you talking to?"

"I pay them bills. I was being nice by asking yo' ass, but now I'm telling you. I'll be there in a minute. Bye."

Cease looked over at me and said, "You're going to stay with my lil' ma until I get this shit straight with Philly, a'ight?"

As much as I wanted to refuse the offer, I realized that anything would be better than doing what I was doing now. I kind of felt bad for leaving Peaches at the room by herself, but she would have done the same thing to me in a heartbeat.

We pulled up to a small apartment complex.

"This is only temporary," Cease explained. "You should stay here for a while. Ol' girl is a lil' hot-headed, but she good peoples. I just want to make sure you stay out of harm's way until I find out what happened with Philly. Word on the street is he making moves in Detroit. I never knew how he got on so fast. But when you said you hit him with them bricks, it all started to make sense. He eating off Khadafi and he did it by robbing you. You should have called me, Remy."

"I know, Cease, but you were nowhere to be found and I never thought Philly would pull this snake shit. Not on me. I was in a tight situation and trusted him. Khadafi kept that nigga around for years and he ate well off of my man. He and Khadafi were friends since childhood. He ain't real like I thought. Some niggas just ain't built like that."

We got out the car and went into the apartment complex. Cease knocked on the door.

"Remy!" she yelled, wrapping both of her arms around me.

I couldn't believe who answered. "Shay!" I shouted in excitement at the sight of my old friend.

I immediately recognized the aroma in the apartment. It was a smell I knew well. I saw the four boiling pots on the stove and already knew what was up. *This is where Cease probably cooked his dope.*

Shay and I sat down in the front room. We immediately clicked and began to catch up on old times. I hadn't seen her since I left the girl's home. She had cut her hair and had a tattooed rose on her neck.

Cease stood there amazed that we knew each other. "How y'all know each other?"

"We were locked up together," Shay told him.

Cease went to the back while Shay and I talked.

It seemed as if we were never apart. We talked and talked for hours. Shay was one of the friends that I had really missed over the years. We were cut from the same cloth. For real. That was my girl, and it was a relief to see her again. She embraced me with open arms and was excited to have me stay there for a while.

"It will be just like old times. Except this time we ain't cramped up in a lock-up facility," she said to me.

It seemed like a massive weight was lifted off of my shoulders, and I immediately felt at home.

A couple of hours later, Cease had emerged from the back room with two brown paper bags in his hand. I guess he had been back there cutting up the dope that Shay had prepared for him. When he entered the room, our conversation stopped, and we both looked at him.

"It seems like y'all are getting along. Remy, you can stay here for a while. I am going to get at Philly's ass—that's my word."

I nodded.

Cease then told Shay to talk to him in the kitchen. The kitchen was only a couple of feet from where we were sitting, so I heard the whole conversation.

"I don't want no shit out of you, Shay."

"Don't worry about it—Remy's my girl."

"Yeah, you say that now, but I know yo' ass."

"Cease, it's cool."

"I owe this to Khadafi. You know what he meant to me."

"I know. I know."

"All right. I want you to put the rest of the dope in the attic."

"Okay."

They both motioned towards the living room.

I immediately picked up a magazine and pretended I was reading.

Cease was young but, I had to admit, was wise beyond his years. He sort of reminded me of Khadafi. Of course, he didn't have money like Khadafi, but you could tell that Khadafi had mentored him. Cease was a little more street, though; he was a rough neck, and it wasn't a secret. He had a tattoo of his name across his neck and always wore a hoody. Well, at least every time I saw him he had one on. He wore his fitted cap low, almost covering his eyes and had a low, raspy tone. He was walking out of the door and, just as he was about to exit, looked at me and said, "I'll see you tomorrow."

"Okay," I replied.

When he left, Shay and I picked up where we had left off. I felt like a little girl again. We stayed up until five in the morning talking. She told me what she had being doing the past few years and explained to me how she met Cease.

They had been dating for about eight months, and eventually he began paying her rent. But it wasn't because he was pussy-whipped or a sucker for love—they had an agreement—she let him stash his product at her home and cooked it up for him, and he paid all the bills.

By the end of the night, I had told Shay all that happened since the last time we had seen each other. Telling my story brought tears to both of our eyes. For some strange reason that long conversation was therapeutic for me. I needed it.

The next day Cease took me over to Peaches' home to get the rest of my clothes and the little belongings that I had.

Peaches had a little attitude when I told her that I was moving out. "What the fuck am I supposed to do about rent? I budgeted this month for half of the bills." Peaches waved her hands in my face.

I was about two heartbeats from snatching that blonde weave right out of her head, when Cease stepped right in the middle of us. "How much is half?"

Peaches put her hand on her hip. "About seven hundred."

Without hesitation Cease pulled out a wad of money and flicked off seven crispy hundred-dollar bills onto the floor and picked up my bag. We both headed out of the door and that was the last time I saw Peaches. I kind of felt bad leaving her there, but I knew deep inside that I was making the right decision. All of the late nights at the club and tricking at private parties had me ashamed to look in the mirror. It felt like I was being saved for the second time, the same way I felt when Khadafi showed me the better side of life.

A couple of weeks had passed, and Shay and I were getting along well. I saw the type of relationship Cease and Shay really had. Shay was madly in love with Cease, but it didn't seem like Cease's feelings were mutual. He would come over about every other day to pick up and drop off drugs. It seemed like he was more worried about my well-being than Shay's.

The first thing he would do was ask how I was and he would make sure I was taken care of. I guess Shay began to notice it too and that created tension in the home.

I also sensed that there was a problem when

Cease asked me to start cooking up the dope, since I used to at Netty's house. Shay messed up so many batches of dope, Cease started to take losses. Me on the other hand, I was a professional at cooking dope. Every time I cooked it up, it came back right. It was an art to that shit. I had learned from the best—Betty Netty.

One day while I was in the house watching the Cosby Show, Cease came in. I had to admit Cease was beginning to become attractive to me. He wasn't the boy who followed Khadafi anymore, and his demeanor was so thugged out—that's what turned me on. He asked, "Where is Shay?"

I explained that she was at her sister's house getting her hair braided.

He shook his head and walked to the hallway under the attic entry. He pulled down the small string that was hanging from the ceiling and the attic stairs came down. He went halfway up the stairs and pulled down a shoebox.

I saw him in the corner of my eye glance over at me to see if I was looking.

He pulled a wad of money out of his pocket and put it in the box. He also grabbed a plastic bag down. I assumed that it was his dope that he stuffed into his coat pocket. He closed up the attic door and headed out.

When he reached the door, I called his name. He looked back, and that's when I slowly walked to him and grabbed both of his hands. "Cease, thank you for everything."

Our eyes got stuck on each other's, and I went for it. I kissed him on his soft lips, and he kissed me back.

Then the unthinkable happened—he turned his head and slapped me silly. "What the fuck is you doing?" He avoided eye contact with me.

I knew I deserved that, but I couldn't help myself. I looked at him and his eyes gave him away.

He softly said, "Look, I'm sorry for hitting you, but you can't do that, Remy. You can't!" He turned and walked towards the door and before leaving, he turned around and said, "When I find Philly, you are going to be straight. Just give me a minute." With that he walked out of the door.

I hate to admit it—but the kiss was worth the slap. His lips were so soft, despite his thuggish look. When he left I ran over to the couch and screamed as loud as I could into the pillow. I was so embarrassed.

* * * * * * * * * * * * * * *

Cease smiled remembering how much he had liked that kiss. He wanted to take off all her clothes right there and break her off, but he couldn't bring himself to do it. He remembered the time that he brought Remy over to his cook-up spot. That was at a time when he was trying to make a name for himself in the streets. He remembered how he and Jodi used to post up on the block, alternating crack sales for hours. He had come a long way from that point. He once was a corner hustler with short pockets; now he had become one of Flint's best-kept secrets. He rose to the top of the dope game over the years, and no one actually knew except for his close circle, how much dough was coming in.

Cease had learned from Khadafi's mistakes and realized that to be a successful drug dealer he needed a low profile. Actually, he lacked Khadafi's charm, but made up for it with his "get down or lay down" mentality. Of course, Cease didn't have the political connections like his former mentor, but his money spoke for itself. His pockets just weren't as long as Khadafi's.

Cease stayed out of the limelight and refused to flash his money. He still drove that same '85 Cutlass that he been had. He got a nice black paint job and the interior done, but nothing too flashy. He refused to go out like Khadafi. He didn't let his death go in vain, he learned from it.

Chapter Thirteen

Cease had a slight headache from reading for an extended amount of time. He slowly rubbed his temples to try to ease the pain. He thought about Philly's face when he and Jodi finally caught up to him. Cease chuckled, remembering Philly's facial expression when the chrome was at his forehead. Cease thought back to that night.

"Yo, Cease," Jodi's voice blared out of the phone speaker.

Chirp

"Yeah."

Chirp

"Guess who in the fuck I'm looking at right now?"

Chirp

"Fuck the guessing game, Jodi boy—what's up?"

Chirp

"Philly fat ass up in here buying out the bar—he flashing big cash."

Chirp

"Straight up?"

Chirp

"Straight up!"

Chirp

"Where you at?"

Chirp

"I'm at the Purple Moon."

Chirp

"Don't let that nigga outta yo' sight, son. I'm on my way."

Cease felt his adrenaline begin to pump, not in fear but in anticipation. This is the type of shit he got a kick out of. He pushed his Cutlass through the back streets of Flint, heading to the club Purple Moon to pay an old friend a visit. With his chrome .357 sitting in his lap, he bumped Tupac's notorious song, "Hail Mary."

When he made it to the club, he saw Jodi's car in the back of the parking lot. He pulled right next to it and called Jodi on to let him know he was outside. Within minutes Jodi walked out and joined Cease in his car. They patiently waited for Philly to leave out of the club.

Finally, he walked out with two Latino females following him. Philly was iced-out—he had a gigantic rock hanging off his ear and a platinum chain that hung down to his belt buckle. He had major dough and wanted the whole world to know. Philly and his girls jumped into his new Mercedes Benz and took off.

Cease and Jodi jumped into Jodi's car and followed him. They switched cars because they didn't want Philly to recognize Cease's car and took the extra precaution of staying two cars back at all times.

"Yo', I'm 'bout to get at this nigga." Cease cocked his gun. Cease knew Philly was in Detroit making some noise in the dope game. But Cease knew his boundaries and refused to look for him in his new territory. He knew that word would spread quickly that someone was looking for him, so he let Philly come to him. He knew it wasn't going to be too long before he returned home to show off.

"Cease, let's just pull up next to him and light his car up and get this shit over with!"

"Nah, we still need to get the rest of the dope. I need to find out where his spot at," Cease said, piecing his plan together in his head. He didn't think Philly moved all fourteen kilos in a matter of months. So he assumed Philly still had the dope—or a nice piece of change at his spot. Either way, Cease didn't care. He also wanted to give Remy what was rightfully hers. He felt he had to do it for Khadafi.

Philly pulled up into the Ramada Hotel and had his car valet parked. Philly and his two friends got out the car and entered the building.

Cease and Jodi pulled into the Coney Island restaurant across the street and parked Jodi's car. Cease didn't think Philly had the money or the dope on him, so they decided to wait and follow him home. The Ramada had a glass entrance, so you could see the whole lobby from the front. Cease observed Philly check-in with the desk clerk and noticed something helpful.

"Jodi, ain't that the crazy chick you used to mess around with?"

Jodi squinted his eyes to try to get a better view. "Where?"

Cease pointed to the hotel and said, "The desk clerk."

"Yeah, that's her. But I know what you thinking. Fuck that! I had to move because of that bitch—she slashed my tires every other day because I quit her ass." Jodi grabbed his dreadlocks with both of his hands and took a deep breath. He looked at Cease and knew that he was gon' have to take one for the team. "Fuck you, Cease." He jumped out of the car and headed towards the hotel.

Cease smiled at all of the stories about her stalking and terrorizing his best friend. He sat back and watched Jodi work his magic.

When he walked in her facial expression wasn't a pleasant one, but eventually her cold stares became smiles. Within five minutes, Jodi was walking back to the car with a card key in his hand. He shook his head in disgust. He got in the car and said, "Yo, you owe me, son. I told that bitch I would pick her up after work. She gets off in an hour, so whatever we going to do, we need to do it now."

Philly was participating in a ménage à trois. His butt in the air jumping from one crotch to the next, pleasing both of the females, he was so busy having his face buried in between their legs, he didn't even see Cease and Jodi walk in.

Cease flicked on the light switch, and the moans quickly turned into screams. Cease pointed his pistol in their direction. "Shut the fuck up if you want to live."

Philly quickly reached for his gun on the dresser, but Jodi had already taken it while he was having his little orgy.

"Cease?" The sweat dripped off Philly's forehead. "What the fuck you think you doing?"

Cease reached for Philly's pants and pulled out the money that he had. It had to have been about a thousand dollars. He gave it to the girls and told them to catch a cab home.

The two girls grabbed their clothes and hurried out. As the girls passed, Jodi's eyes followed their asses. Under different circumstances he would have tried to get at them, but he had to handle his business.

Cease pointed the gun at Philly's dome. "Put some clothes on, you fat muthafucka."

Philly put on his pants, all the while keeping his eyes on Cease.

"Now where's the dope, Philly?"

"Man, what you talking 'bout, nigga?"

Cease put the pistol to Philly's dome and pressed the cold steel to his temple. "Don't fuckin' play with me!"

Philly put both of his hands up, realizing he couldn't weasel his way out of it. "It's all at the spot, Cease . . . in Detroit. Take it!"

Cease smiled and said, "Put on yo' shoes—we about to take a ride to Detroit."

Jodi threw Philly's shoes at him, and Philly quickly put them on. They made their way down to the lobby and, at gunpoint, Cease directed Philly to the exit.

Before they could reach the revolving doors, a woman's voice yelled, "Jodi!"

Jodi turned around, and the desk clerk had her arms crossed, tapping her feet.

Jodi put a pretend phone to his ear, signaling he would call her, but she knew better. She began to talk loudly as they all walked out of the door.

Jodi told Cease, "Man, let's hurry up and get out of here."

Jodi and Cease laughed, but the situation wasn't funny to Philly. He knew Cease was a killer who'd been putting his murder game down since back in the day. He didn't want to make a wrong move—it could be his last.

They got to the parking lot and walked to the back of the car. Jodi opened the trunk.

Cease pressed the gun against Philly's back and looked around to see if anyone was watching. When he saw the coast was clear, he yelled, "Get in!"

Philly got in the trunk, and before he could even position himself comfortably, Cease slammed it down.

When they got to the Detroit exit, they pulled to an abandoned parking lot and let Philly out so that he could direct them to his spot. Cease let Philly get in front so he could keep the pistol on him at all times.

Philly regretted ever going back to Flint and was sweating bullets.

All of a sudden, blue and red lights flashed behind them.

"What the fuck?" Jodi slowly tried to put on his seat belt before the cop came. He pulled over to the side of the road and kept his eye on his rearview mirror. "What the fuck we gon' do, Cease?"

Cease pressed the gun to Philly's side to let him know it was still there. "Just stay calm. You got yo' L's, so we straight; just stay calm."

Just then a white police officer knocked on Jodi's door with his flashlight. Jodi rolled down his window. "What seems to be the problem, officer?"

"You got a busted taillight back there—license and registration, please."

Cease became enraged. Philly had broken the light to get attention from the hook.

Jodi reached over Philly's lap and grabbed his information. He gave it to the cop and smiled.

The cop said, "Wait right here," and walked back to his car.

Cease struck Philly in the head with the butt of the gun. "Bitch-ass nigga."

Philly's head hit the glass hard and caused a thud sound. He was instantly knocked unconscious, his head resting on the passenger side window.

All of the commotion drew the officer's attention. He turned around and quickly returned to their car. "What's going on?" His hand hovered over his gun.

"Nothing, officer. Our friend over here just had a little bit too much to drink." Jodi looked over at Philly.

The cop flashed his lights on Philly's face. To him, it looked as if Philly had passed out from drinking. The cop gave Jodi back his papers and told him to hurry up and head home.

"I can't believe this nigga tried to pull that shit. He lucky I didn't dead his ass right there." Jodi looked at Philly and spat in his face.

The massive wad of spit made Philly come to. He looked around, not knowing where he was at. But Cease quickly brought his ass back to reality by putting the pistol to the back of his neck so Philly could finish directing them to his spot.

They pulled into Philly's two-story mini-mansion right off Seven Mile road. Philly told them that the dope and the money were stashed in his safe in the back.

Philly was living well from Khadafi's money. His crib was plush as hell—from the plasma TV that hung on the wall, to the bearskin rug that lay in the center of the floor, it was nice.

They followed him to the back room. Philly walked over to the closet and got on his knees. He moved a rug that lay over a secret compartment in the floor and started turning the combination dial. It finally cracked. He stuck his hand in the hole and said, "This is all I got. Just let me go and this—" Philly pulled out an all-black handgun and swiftly swung it around at Cease. He fired a shot that grazed Cease and entered Jodi's left shoulder.

Cease jumped on the bed and aimed his gun at Philly's head in the middle of all the chaos. A .357 slug entered Philly's head, instantly splattering blood onto the closet door. Philly dropped with his eyes wide open.

Cease focused his attention on his wounded partner.

Jodi was on the ground, holding his shoulder. "I'm cool—it went in and out," he said, returning to his feet.

Cease examined the wound. "We need to get you to a hospital—but let's get what we came here for first." He grabbed a duffle bag from the closet and began filling it with the kilos of cocaine and money.

By the time they were done, they had thirty-two thousand in cash and twelve kilos of dope. Cease thought to himself, *This nigga is lazy. It is no way I could be sitting on this amount of dope for this long. If I had this, I would have had the whole city of Detroit high by now.*

Cease and Jodi headed towards the hospital with a trunkful of opportunity.

The doctor explained to Jodi that he was lucky

that the bullet went in and out. "Your arm's going to be sore for a while," he said, "but it would eventually heal."

When they returned to Flint, Cease needed someone to drive Jodi's car home for him, so he called Shay's home.

Remy picked up the phone. "Hello?"

"Yo, Remy, where Shay at?"

"I don't know. She just got up and left about ten minutes ago."

"Where did she go?"

"She didn't say. Something was wrong with her, though—she was acting all jittery and shit."

"You know how she is anyway. But . . . um . . . I need you to ride with me and drive Jodi's car home."

"Okay. But why he can't drive?"

"I'll explain that later. I'm on my way."

"I'll be ready."

Cease and Jodi headed over to Shay's house. Jodi sat in the passenger seat, knocked out from the painkillers the doctor had given him.

Cease pulled up to the apartment and saw something suspicious. There were two black vans parked in front of the apartment and two men were talking on walkie-talkies near the bushes. He knew what was going on—they were about to perform a raid. He immediately picked up the phone and called Remy. "Remy, listen close—flush the dope down the toilet now! Go, Remy—the hook is outside." He heard the phone drop and couldn't do anything but wait. With twelve kilos of dope in the trunk and thirty-two thousand in cash, he was federal as hell. He woke up Jodi and slowly drove out of the apartment complex.

An hour later he sent one of Jodi's girls to bail Remy out. The bail was $30,000—just about what they got from Philly.

Cease, Jodi, and Remy sat in Jodi's living room talking.

Remy explained to him what went down. "I tried to flush all the dope down the toilet, but it all happened too fast. They busted in and kept asking me if there was something in the apartment I wanted to tell them about before they found it. I kept saying no, and they went in the attic and took the shoebox full of money."

Cease closed his eyes and took a deep breath, relieved. He knew that they didn't have anything to go on—except some unaccounted cash and a little bit of coke. *That would be tax evasion and possession at the most.* "You did good, Remy. I owe you my life. You didn't snitch or nothing—that's real.

"I have some good news, though."

Jodi walked over to the closet and pulled out a duffle bag. He handed it to Cease, who then exposed its contents to Remy. "Philly is sleeping with the fishes, but we have enough dope here to get a lot of money."

* * * * * * * * * * * * * * * * * *

Cease remembered that night so vividly. It was the night his game got took to a whole different level. With the go-ahead from Remy, he flooded the streets of Flint with pure cocaine. The streets demanded what Cease had. They hadn't had a taste of this flavor since Khadafi's demise. So when Cease hit the streets, he hit 'em hard. It got to the point where fiends wouldn't buy any other dope in the whole city. They couldn't deny the pure, "un-stepped on," Colombian flake that once was Khadafi's.

Cease managed to move six kilos of dope in an eight-month span. On the low, the city was his. The street called him "the man that made it snow," and that's exactly what he did.

Unlike Khadafi, he wasn't selective about his clientele—whoever had the bread, had the dope. And if there were any problems, he would shoot first, ask questions later.

Cease looked at the clock on his living room wall and saw that he had been reading all day. It was 2 A.M., and he had to be in court at 8 in the morning. He closed the book for the night and went to sleep.

Chapter Fourteen

Jodi sat on the stand with a smug look on his face. He hated the police and everything that was associated with them, including the courts.

The defense attorney stood up and approached the witness chair with a friendly look on his face. He knew that the character witness on the stand was about to paint a pleasant picture of his client. "Jodi Smith, can you explain to the jury how you are associated with the defendant?"

Jodi shifted in his chair and said, "We grew up in the same hood; he's like my brother."

"In all your years of knowing him, have you ever known Mr. Ceaser to be violent or jealous?"

Jodi shook his head and replied, "Nah, Cease ain't the violent type, and he definitely ain't jealous of nobody. Only dumb-ass niggas are envious."

The audience gasped in unison at Jodi's bad language.

The attorney walked over to where Shay was sitting in the crowd and said, "But earlier this week you heard this young woman state that Mr. Ceaser has an uncontrollable temper. She stated that she experienced traumatic and violent encounters with him. She also stated that she saw him commit such acts against Mrs. Remy Ceaser."

"That bitch was lying—Cease would never put his hands on Remy . . . maybe on any nigga who looked at her wrong, but not Remy. He loved her. She was his reason for doing everything. He wanted to make life better for Remy; they were getting ready to start a family. He was proud of that, he was proud of her, and it showed. Ask anybody in the streets. Everybody who knows Cease knows that he was in love with his woman—you could see it all over his face—she made him happy."

The lawyer paused to let that last statement stick in the jury's mind and then said, "So, in your opinion, do you think he murdered his wife?"

"No, that's impossible," Jodi quickly replied. "You don't see a love like theirs every day. Remy was a real woman. He would kill himself before he let anything happen to her. He didn't do it; she made that man whole."

The defense attorney looked at the judge and said, "No more questions, Your Honor."

The judge then handed the floor over to the prosecution. "Would you like to cross-examine?"

The prosecutor stood up.

The tall, white man in the black suit made Jodi sick to his stomach and he immediately tensed up.

"Mr. Smith, how would you explain us finding Mr. Ceaser's prints all over the gun that was used to kill Mrs. Remy Ceaser?"

Jodi shook his head in utter disbelief and said sternly, "Of course, his prints were on the gun—it was his gun! It was a registered, perfectly legal weapon, and it was his right to own one; it's only natural that his fingerprints be on his own gun. That don't mean that he's the one who shot it the day that Remy was killed."

Jodi's words had tugged at Ccase's heart as memories of Remy flashed through his mind. It was so hard for him to sit up in the courtroom and listen to other people talk about his wife.

The defense attorney smiled when Jodi said those key words.

Jodi stepped off the stand and walked towards the exit of the courtroom. He saw Shay sitting on the end of the last row. He smirked at her and whispered, "Pow, pow," in her ear when he walked by.

Tears came to Shay's eyes as soon as she heard the threat.

Cease's eyes began to burn from staying up all night reading Remy's book. He looked over at the prosecution, and then looked at the jury, who seemed to believe Jodi's testimony.

After more hours of hearing cross-examinations and viewing evidence, the court adjourned for the day.

The prosecution walked over to Cease's lawyer and whispered into his ear.

Cease looked at his attorney and asked, "Did we have a good day?"

His attorney laughed. "We had a great day—the prosecution wants to deal. They are offering manslaughter instead of first-degree murder. This is the type of offer we've been waiting for."

Cease buttoned the jacket to his Sean John suit. "Fuck that—tell them, 'no deal.' I'm not admitting to the murder of my wife. I didn't kill her." Cease began to walk out of the courtroom.

"Take the deal," his lawyer said, grabbing his arm. "If we lose, you will get life."

Cease snatched his arm away. "I'm paying you very well to get me off. Do your job." He walked out of the court room.

"Man, you all right?" Jodi asked.

Cease shook his head. "Man, I don't know. I been reading Remy's diary. Man, it's fucking with me. I need her, man. I need my shorty."

Jodi had no clue how it even felt to love a woman, so he definitely didn't know how it felt to lose one. He'd never seen Cease so weak—that's what made him know Cease did not kill Remy.

"I'm about to head to the crib. Thanks for everything, Jodi; I appreciate it, boy."

Jodi and Cease shook hands gangster-style and went their separate ways.

Cease rushed home to pick up where he left off with Remy's story.

****

December 2002

"Take the deal, Ms. Morgan. All the police need is the name of the person you were making the drugs up for. Tell them that and you can walk out of here today—no jail time and no probation."

I felt the tears welling up and getting ready to fall. I was scared. I didn't want to go to jail, especially not for fifteen months.

"Take the deal," my lawyer urged once more.

As desperately as I wanted to be free, something inside me would not let me turn Cease in. I shook my head and said, "I told you I don't know! I don't know whose drugs they were."

The lawyer sighed and replied, "Well, then I can't help you. I hope he was worth it."

The tears fell when a police officer put my hands in cuffs and escorted me to a small holding cell.

A couple weeks later my trial began, and Cease and Jodi showed up every day. The trial was short and sweet. Within a matter of a month, I had received a fifteen-month sentence for possession with intent to sell, and tax evasion. The police had managed to scuffle up three grams of cocaine throughout the apartment.

When the judge gave me the sentence, I looked back hopelessly at Cease. There was a look of guilt behind his eyes, and I lowered my head as I was escorted in cuffs out of the courthouse.

"In a couple days, you will be shipped to the women's detention center in Saginaw," the officer told me.

I just put my face in my hands and cried silently as the reality sunk in. I would be spending the next year and three months in a maximum-security prison. I thought about Shay and wondered why she wasn't charged with anything. I didn't really know why I covered for Cease, I knew I just couldn't tell on him, so I took the fifteen months, hoping the time would go by as quickly as possible.

Three days later, I stepped into captivity. I saw the snipers standing high in the towers and the fifteen-foot barbed wire fence surrounding the facility. I followed the line of women into a building, where I was ordered to strip. (I was not self-conscious—it wasn't the first time I got the command to take off my clothes.) I was then told to bend over and open my legs.

The male guard bent down and took his time as he inspected me, licking his lips as he peered inside mine.

When I stood up, I was face to face with the guard. He was so close to me, I could feel an erection in his pants. The feeling made my skin crawl.

He stepped back, smirked, and handed me a green jail suit. The color was dark, depressing, and ugly, but after the violation from the guard, I hurriedly put it on and followed the rest of the women as we were processed through the prison system.

I didn't expect to have any visitors, but I put Cease on the list just because he was the only person I had on the outside.

I was actually relieved when I finally reached my cell. It was small, way smaller than I thought it would be. There was literally no room to move around, and the room stunk. I saw that the bottom bunk was already taken, so I began to put my sheets on the top. I sat down on my bed, trying to settle into what was now home . . . at least for the next fifteen months.

I heard a buzzer, and my cell door opened. A dark-skinned woman who looked to be in her forties walked in slowly, mugging me, and shaking her head.

What the fuck is you looking at? I thought to myself. I wanted to say it aloud, but I was new and wasn't trying to create beef. At least not just yet, and definitely not with my cellmate.

"You must be the new girl that everybody talking about. You Khadafi's bitch, right?"

I didn't respond. The situation reminded me of the first time I met Shay.

"Yeah, you Khadafi's bitch," the woman said, sure of herself; "we done heard all about your 'sew ditty' ass—Betty Netty talk about you all the time. She said she read in the papers how you got caught up in some bullshit."

The sound of Netty's name caught my attention. The last time that I visited her, she was locked up in Jackson.

"Betty Netty is here?"

"Yeah, she got moved a couple months ago. Anything that goes down, she knows about it."

I smiled. *Maybe the year wouldn't be that long after all.* I looked at the woman and said, "I'm Remy."

"De'Andrea—Dee for short."

I sat on the edge of my bed and looked her in the eye. "Dee, can I ask you something?" I paused, thinking about the long year that lied ahead of me. "What's it like in here?"

"I'm not goin' to lie to you—it's hell . . . especially for a little pretty piece of something like you. I used to look like that, but hell, I've been in here for five years and every day it's a new battle. A different struggle. The days just keep getting longer and longer. I have twenty more to go before I can even apply for parole. That's why you've got to be careful in here. These women in here don't care whose woman you are; they are already hopeless— more time being added to their sentence don't mean nothing.

"You don't need to make no enemies in here, cuz as soon as they find out you not in here for the long haul, you become their target. Stay low-key and keep to yourself. Once people find out you roll with Netty, then they won't fuck with you too much anyway; she has a lot of pull in here."

I didn't respond, but the words stuck in my head like glue. Even though Dee seemed cool, I still had my reservations, and until Netty told me she was okay, I planned on keeping her at a distance.

My first night was hell. I couldn't sleep at all. I had too much on my mind. I didn't know anything about surviving in prison, so I knew I had to learn quick. I tried to convince myself that I'd made the right decision by protecting Cease.

The next morning I scanned the cafeteria for Betty Netty, but she was nowhere to be found. "This is some bullshit," I mumbled to myself. I sat down at the corner of the closest table. I was hungry as hell, but I definitely wasn't about to eat the slop that was put on my plate. I picked at the food, thinking that the next year was going to be long.

I felt someone pull on my hair. I turned around to see a Hispanic girl walk by me and sit at the table directly behind me. I didn't say anything about it, assuming that it was an accident, but when I felt it again, I turned around with an attitude. "Bitch, what the fuck is up?"

The Hispanic girl turned and laughed at me to her friends and said, "Oh look—Khadafi's little girlfriend wants to know what's up." The clique of girls started laughing too.

I wanted to smack the shit out of her for even mentioning Khadafi's name, but I wasn't trying to create beef and let it ride.

"Oh, are you too good to talk to us? Did we hurt your feelings? Is Khadafi's bitch sensitive?"

I felt another pull at my hair that set me over the top. I picked up my tray of food and smacked the girl across the face with it. "Bitch, don't ever mention Khadafi's name." I gave her a right hook to the face.

Before the fight could escalate, it was broken up by the guards.

I could see by the look in her eyes that she had it out for me. "You are dead, bitch! Dead!"

My heart was pumping. A sense of fear went through me when she made the threat, but quickly passed. Just because I was in jail didn't mean I was going to start letting people punk me. *That bitch could kiss my ass.*

The guard said, "Come with me."

I didn't know where I was going. I figured I was going to see the warden since it was only my second day there. I thought they were going to send me to "the hole," to teach me a lesson.

The guard led me down some steps into a wet, dark, basement-looking room. She pointed to a door and said, "Go in there."

I reluctantly walked towards the door. When I opened it, I saw Netty and De'Andrea sitting, waiting for me.

"Netty?" I approached her and gave her a hug.

A Virginia Slim hung from Netty's mouth. "Hey, baby!" she said, hugging me.

"I'm glad you here; I thought I was gon' go crazy up in here."

Netty smiled. "We ain't gonna let that happen. What the hell you doing in here? What's this I hear about you covering for some nigga?"

I shook my head, almost regretting that I had

turned down the deal. "It was Cease; I was covering for him—you know snitching was not an option."

"Why the hell did that boy have you cooking up dope? He know your position—you are Khadafi's woman."

"Netty, shit has changed since Khadafi died. Nobody speaks of him anymore. After he died the Feds came and took away the house and the money. I had nowhere to go. I was stripping back at Magic City, just to eat. It's been hard.

"I ran into Cease about six months ago. He gave me a place to stay and paid me more than enough to cook up his goods. I wasn't on the street, and I had money in my pocket—that's all I could ask for."

Netty shook her head in a disapproving way. "Khadafi didn't mean for it to be like this."

"I know, but this is how it is."

"He loved you—you know that, right?"

"Netty, it's time for y'all to head back to the cell block," a guard yelled.

Netty looked at me and said, "We'll talk in the yard."

I hugged her again, relieved that I had seen her, and then walked back to my cell with Dee. When I got back to the cell, there was an envelope sitting on my bunk. I looked at the return address, but there was only numbers; the name had been left off. I opened the letter, wondering who the hell wrote me.

> *Remy,*
> *Shit, I don't even know how to start this. What do you say to somebody that you owe your life to? You a real one, Remy. Not many*

women would have done what you did. I appreciate it. You took a year for something that I would have gotten twenty for. I've been losing a lot of sleep wondering if you okay. I've already filled your commissary, so if there's anything else you need, let me know. Don't hesitate to ask. I owe you.

    Cease

I put the letter back in the envelope and placed it underneath my pillow. It felt good to hear from Cease. I was glad to know that he was going to look out for me while I was locked up. Cease could have easily said, "Fuck you," but he wasn't a ho-ass nigga; he handled his business.

"Hey, Dee, you got some paper?"

Dee handed me a piece of notebook paper and a pen.

I didn't know exactly what I would say to him, it just felt good to have somebody to write to.

    Cease,
    There isn't much to say about what happened. I know the rules of the streets just as well as you. Prison was my only choice because snitching was not an option. It ain't no bad feelings, though; I'll be okay. Betty Netty got transferred here, so the time shouldn't be that bad. It feels weird being locked up in here. No matter how bad things got, this was one thing that I never would have thought could happen to me. Please don't lose too much sleep, just do you and continue to get money. Thanks for filling my commissary, you didn't have to but it's nice to know that somebody's think-

ing about me. Oh, and thanks for writing me. It made this day a little bit better, just to hear from you.
　Sincerely,
　Remy

I folded the letter and borrowed a stamp and envelope from Dee before giving it to the guard to be put in the mail.

"You coming out to the yard?" Dee asked.

I nodded yes and then followed her out, where we met Betty Netty. "I got a letter from Cease," I told her.

Netty looked at me and said, "Did he say something about cashing you out when you get out of here?—he owes you some kind of compensation."

"No, he didn't say anything about that. He just said he felt bad about it and that if I needed anything to let him know. He filled my commissary too."

Netty shook her head and left the subject alone. "Khadafi never wanted you to be exposed to the bullshit part of this game. He says that you done experienced enough bad stuff in your life."

I smiled at the thought of Khadafi, but it quickly faded. "His side of the game was no better; maybe worse—it got him killed. I don't have him, and that's all I really wanted."

Netty looked sincerely at me and said, "Khadafi loves you. Always has and always will—you remember that. Seven years or so from now when you thinking that you might move on, you remember that."

Even though it was hard for me to talk about Khadafi, I didn't have any intention of forgetting him. He was my love and I knew that the memories of us would always dwell in my heart.

The first couple of months in prison were like hell. It was hard for me to grasp the fact that I couldn't do what I wanted to do. Prison ain't no ho—if anybody has ever told you that it's not as bad as it looks, let me be the first to tell you, "They lying to your ass." All the training and etiquette that Khadafi instilled in me went out the window. It was like survival of the fittest and the old Remy Morgan emerged.

I had a lot of leeway because people knew I was with Netty's clique, but in order to gain my own respect, I had to prove that I should not be fucked with. A lot of women tried to test me—I even had to go as far as cutting a bitch up in the shower for running up. But eventually people just started getting it and left me alone.

Netty and I grew even closer from the time that we spent together. I had a lot of hard days in those first couple of months and I don't think I could have made it without her. She would pull out her chessboard and it was like therapy for me. I would pour my heart out to her about everything from Khadafi, to beef in jail, to not knowing my plans when I got out. Betty Netty was my rod in prison, and she gave me strength when I thought I had none.

I was four months into my sentence when I received another letter from Cease. "Morgan, you have mail," a guard yelled as she handed it to me.

"Who you got writing you?" Dee teased.

I smiled. "The nigga I'm in here for, but it ain't what you thinking." I hopped onto my bunk and eagerly opened the letter.

Remy,
Sorry that I haven't kept in touch with you more often. These streets have been keeping me busy. Me and Jodi boy have been clockin'. I've been thinking about you. I got you when you get out. I'ma make the year that you spending in there worth it. I feel like I'm responsible for what happened to you. I hope that Netty is taking care of you in there. You are Khadafi's woman, you deserve better. Some men can't handle prison, so I can't even imagine what you're going through. Don't let it break you, Remy. Don't let it make you a different person. Stay the same, stay beautiful. I hope that you have everything that you need.
Cease

His letter made me smile. He was right about one thing—prison was capable of hardening you. His letter motivated me to not become that hardened convict. I put the letter underneath my mattress and wrote him back . . .

Cease,
Thank you for writing me. I smiled when I got your letter; it feels good to know that you're still thinking about me. For a minute, I thought you had forgotten about me. It's nice to know that you and Jodi are doing y'all thang in the hood. Tell him I said hi. But I'm good, you don't owe me shit. I'm just happy to hear that you are doing okay. It's funny how everybody expects me to be so different just because I was Khadafi's woman. That don't mean too much in here. At first it made

things worse. I guess it's funny how things change, how people change, how I've changed. Anyway, Betty Netty has been well, and of course she's been good to me. She's what keeps me going sometimes. But I'm glad you decided to write me.

Sincerely,
Remy

I met Netty at our table at dinner time. Dee and a couple other chicks that we chilled with joined our table and we all sat down, trying to entertain each other as if we were not locked up like animals.

"So, Remy," Dee said, "what are you in here for? I know you said you got caught up in some bullshit, but you never actually told us what it was."

Hesitant about answering her question, I took a bite of the nasty prison food. I didn't know if I wanted everybody at the table in my business like that, but I said fuck it. "I used to cook dope for a hustler in Flint and I got caught in the house during the raid. They wanted me to tell them who I was working for. I wouldn't talk, so they threw me in here with y'all bitches."

Dee replied, "Shit! Girl, you a good one because I would have told them the name that they wanted to hear—was it your man or something?"

Netty's eyes cut low when Dee said that.

"Nah, just somebody I know from around the way."

Dee added, "Shit, that's some ol' 'I-love-you' type shit right there. I wouldn't be doing time for a nigga unless I was in love. He would have to be laying the pipe real good for me to do some shit like that."

We were interrupted when a group of Hispanic women walked past me mugging. Thalia, the girl I fought with on my second day in jail walked past last. It seemed like they were afraid to say anything because Netty was sitting there. Netty didn't say anything; she just let it play out.

I looked at Thalia and waved her away. "Bitch, keep it moving." I was waiting for her to say something smart because I was ready and willing to go in her mouth. I knew our beef wouldn't end until the day I got out.

Netty laughed loudly and said, "Her mouth ain't so big anymore."

After lunch I lied in my concrete-like bed, thinking about what I was going to do when I was released from prison. Cease said that he would have something waiting for me, but I figured it was probably just talk. I had learned my lesson—I never wanted to have to depend on a man for shit. (Philly made sure I learned the hard way when he fucked me out of my money.)

I started thinking hard about a way to make some cash. I had to save up some kind of money so that when I finally got out, I wouldn't be left on stuck.

"Hellooo?" I heard Dee say loudly.

"What?" I replied.

"Damn, girl, what you thinking about? You look like you in a trance or something."

"I'm just thinking about what I'm gonna do when I get out of here, how I'm goin' to survive, you know. I need some money."

Dee frowned her face. "Ain't your boy supposed to break you off when you get out?"

"That's what he says, but that ain't guaranteed—that's his money; I need to make my own chips."

Dee smacked her lips and said, "You tripping—that nigga keep your commissary full. I'm sure that his word is bond. He ain't gone just ho you when you get out. And if you so unsure about it, just call him and see what he says."

I dismissed that idea. I wasn't trying to call Cease begging—that shit just wasn't me.

Dee seemed to read my expression. "I'm not telling you to beg him, but at least call him. You can tell if a man got your back or not just by the way he sounds."

* * * * * * * * * * * * * * * * *

Cease put down the diary. He was thinking about the times that he had just finished reading about. The year Remy was in jail was the same year he himself started coming up strong in the game. After getting the best dope from Philly, he and Jodi had the streets locked. Cease and Jodi knew that the twelve kilos they took from Philly wouldn't last forever, so they started mixing other dope with Khadafi's product. The streets seemed to love that combination even more.

He and Jodi were slowly but surely building an empire, and they did it without bringing unnecessary attention to themselves.

"Jodi boy, pull out that machine so we can count this money."

Jodi got the money machine out of the closet and watched as Cease dumped the money out of the bag. Hundred-dollar bills were all over the table, and Cease couldn't wait to count it up.

Cease was precise when dealing with his money. He always counted it two different ways, once on the machine and once by hand. The activity was strenuous and took hours to accomplish, but Cease didn't mind. There were only two people in this world that he trusted, and that was himself and his right-hand man, Jodi.

Cease watched the bills flip through the machine. He was intrigued with his cash and loved the smell of money. He took the stack out of the machine and began to count it by hand as Jodi put another stack in.

After a couple hours of this same routine, Cease put his money in a safe he kept in the basement, behind the furnace.

"Fuck with me tomorrow," Jodi said as he left, and he took his money and went to the crib for the night.

Cease sat back in his house and watched *Sports-Center*. It felt good to kick back in his spot. Business had been hectic lately as the streets craved what he had to offer. He had the rawest product out, and the crackheads couldn't get enough of it.

When Cease first got back on the grind after Khadafi died, a couple people tried to test him. Cease didn't talk too much and he wasn't loud or flashy. After making a couple examples out of little niggas trying to be hard, niggas knew not to step on his toes. He knew that the niggas who walked around talking about what they did were usually the ones who weren't doing shit. There was no need for him to talk about it, he lived it. It wasn't something he was proud of, but that's just how shit was.

Cease walked out to the mailbox to retrieve his mail. He noticed a letter from Remy.

Cease snapped out of his memory and looked at the diary he held in his hands. He felt so conflicted. Halfway through her story, he decided he was going to read till he reached the end.

* * * * * * * * * * * * * * * * * *

After a couple days of worrying about my financial situation, I decided to call Cease. I wasn't going to ask him directly about any money, I just planned on calling to see if he would mention it. I waited patiently for the pay phone during my "rec" time. When it was my turn to use the phone, I dialed Cease's number collect.

"Remy," I said when the operator asked me to say my name. I waited for a minute hoping that he would accept the charges. He did, and when the call was connected, all of a sudden, cat got my tongue.

"How you doing?" he asked.

"I'm doing okay. I mean as good as I can be. How are you?"

"I'm good."

There was an uncomfortable silence between us. I didn't really know what to say to him.

"Thank you for writing me. The letters help. It reminds me that somebody is thinking about me, even if it's just you."

"Oh, it's like that?" He laughed. "I see you haven't lost that smart-ass mouth."

"I'm just playing. But seriously, your letters do help. It's not that much to smile about in here.

When I get a letter from you, it gives me an excuse to smile."

"Why haven't you called before now? You been in for four and a half months. I been expecting your call."

"I don't know. I wasn't trying to interrupt what you doing. Cease, you don't owe me anything; I don't even know why I called you today."

"I owe you everything. Anything you need. All you have to do is ask—you know that. You don't need a reason to call either. You doing some real shit for me, Remy. Don't let them walls fuck with you. When you walk out of there, I want you to be the same woman you were before you walked in."

"I don't want to be that girl either."

I don't think he knew how to respond to that statement because he didn't say anything.

"Look, I'm coming up there next month to visit you," he said. "I want to see you."

His words made me smile. *It would feel good to finally have a visitor*. "Okay, I'd like that, but I got to go."

I hung up the phone and walked back to my cell. It felt good to talk to Cease. It sounded like he was doing well. I was glad to know that he hadn't forgotten I was doing time for him.

Netty came to my cell. It was still rec time, so all the cells on the block were open.

"Hey, Netty."

"Hey, baby, where you been? I was looking for you in the yard."

"I was on the phone. I called Cease today."

Netty cut her eyes low, the way she always did when I mentioned Cease's name.

"He's coming to see me next month," I told her.

Netty shook her head. "Khadafi would have a fit if he knew that Cease had you serving time in jail for his bullshit mistake."

My eyes began to water. "Khadafi isn't here . . . he's been gone for a while now."

"Just because he's not with you here don't mean that his love has to go away. He loves you more than I've ever seen him love anybody. Your heart still belongs to Khadafi, and his to you," Netty said, stirring up emotions I hadn't felt lately.

"I know, Netty. I know."

When Netty left the room, I was left alone with my thoughts. *Would I ever be able to let Khadafi rest in peace? He's on my mind constantly.*

The next day I was in the shower. It felt so good to finally be able to wash my body and hair. In prison, we were only allowed to shower twice a week, and I felt dirty all the time. The water felt good as it hit my body. I scrubbed my skin until it hurt.

There was a difference between stripping in the club and handling your business in a room full of women. It didn't matter to me; I had gotten used to that the first couple of weeks. I was enjoying the shower so much. Just then I suddenly felt something sharp cut deep into my side. A stabbing pain shot through my side. Next thing I knew, blood was running down the drain. "Aghh . . ." I screamed in pain and dropped to my knees. I felt the kicks to my stomach and back. I tried curling up, to protect my body from the blows. The pain was too great, and my vision became blurry.

I woke up a week later in the infirmary. The lights were blinding when I first opened my eyes, and the pain was almost unbearable.

"So you finally woke up?" I heard a voice say.

I looked towards the door and saw the prison doctor standing in the entry. "You've been out for about a week. You're in pretty bad shape."

I tried to sit up in the bed and it hurt like hell. "What's all wrong?" I asked.

The doctor sat on a stool next to me and began to examine my vital signs. "Well, you have two fractured ribs. Twenty stitches in the abdomen from the stabbing, five stitches underneath the right eye, and lots of bruising on the back. Can you remember who did this to you?"

My mind flashed back to the shower scene. I didn't see anybody's face, but I knew exactly who'd done it. *That bitch is dead.* I looked at the doctor. "I don't know who it was. I didn't get a chance to see their faces. They jumped me from behind." My heart was set on "murking" that bitch. "When can I get out of here?"

"Maybe in another week. We don't want to put you back into general population yet, because the slightest thing can cause those wounds to bust open. In a week you will be well enough to move around safely. There'll still be pain, but you won't be at a great risk."

I nodded my head and laid back. I was ready to go to war with Thalia and was pissed that I had to wait a week to do it.

The next seven days crept by slowly. I was counting each second as it passed by. My body still hurt, and I was grateful I had at least a week to try and recuperate. The doctor gave me Vicodin to ease the pain, but that wasn't strong enough—it didn't really soothe the throbbing in my body; it only put me to sleep. I slept more than fifteen hours a day and when I was awake it was torture.

Being in the infirmary was worse than being in a cell. There was no human interaction whatsoever. The only person I encountered was the doctor—and that was only when it was time for him to give me more medicine. I was going crazy in there not having anybody to talk to, and that was killing me. There was no TV, no books, no magazines, no nothing. Just me, four walls, and an odor that I came to notice on the fifth day. That stench—a mixture of blood, germs, cleaning supplies, and sweat—fucked with me for two days, and I was suffocating in it. When I was finally allowed to go back to my room, I was relieved to smell the pissy scent of the cell. It was funky, but it was still better than that shit.

Dee looked at me with concern as I climbed slowly onto the top bunk. "You okay?" she asked.

"Yeah, I'm cool. I'm just ready for tomorrow."

"I know what you thinking, but Netty told me to tell you not to do nothing until she talks to you."

I turned around on the side that didn't hurt and went to sleep.

The next day, one of the guards escorted me and Dee to the basement of the prison. Netty was waiting there, sitting at a round table. I took a seat, and the guard sat down too.

"We have a situation here," Netty said. "Thalia needs to be taken care of."

I spoke up quickly. "That's on me—I can handle it."

"I know, but we need the opportunity." Netty

looked at the guard. "We don't want to make it sloppy."

The guard replied, "It can be done in the kitchen. She has kitchen duty tonight. I can make sure that the other two girls that she's working with are occupied at that time."

Netty nodded her head. "Good. Tomorrow the situation should be settled."

I nodded my head and slowly got up from the table. Before I walked out the room Netty said, "Be careful."

I didn't reply and just kept walking.

That night at dinner, Thalia and I did not take our eyes off each other. I knew she was plotting something, and she must have been assuming the same thing about me because we were both on our p's and q's.

It seemed like everybody's eyes were on my table. Everybody in the prison knew about what went down and they were all waiting to see how I would react. I wanted to get up and snatch Thalia's Mexican, burrito-eating ass out of her chair, but I kept my cool. I knew that in about an hour, she would no longer be so tough.

After dinner the guard gave me the signal that Thalia was alone in the kitchen. As all the inmates filed out of the cafeteria and headed back to their cells, I crept into the entrance to the kitchen. The kitchen was cluttered with a stack of pots and pans as high as the ceiling. I hid behind them and watched as Thaila loaded the dishwasher. I grabbed a knife from the chopping block and crept up behind her.

I planned on making it quick—*slice the bitch's throat and get back to my cell before anybody realized I was missing.* I knew I was doing some hot shit—I only had ten months left in prison. My heart was pumping, and the knife started to feel slippery in my hands. I knew I had to kill Thalia. If I didn't, there was a good chance she would kill me, *and I was not dying in jail.*

I got directly behind her, put my hand over her mouth, and the knife to her neck. "You should have killed me," I said. I stabbed the knife into her neck and sliced across.

I felt her flesh rip. The feeling made me sick to my stomach. I dropped the knife and let Thalia's body drop to the floor. "Oh my God . . . what did I just do?" I said softly to myself as I watched her blood seep onto the concrete floor. I was shaking and my breath was shallow. *I have to get the fuck out of here.*

Thalia's eyes were wide open. It seemed as if she was staring at me.

I quickly picked up the knife and rinsed it off in the sink. I scrubbed it good and then wiped it down thoroughly, making sure I didn't leave any prints. Then I put the knife in the dishwasher with the other dishes that Thalia had already started loading, and started it up. I didn't even look back at her.

I met the guard outside the kitchen and was escorted back to my cell.

"Is she dead?" the guard whispered to me.

I nodded yes and quietly replied, "You'll find her body in the morning."

My nerves were bad that night. I kept thinking I would get caught. I had done some dumb shit. I was so hooked on getting Thalia back for jumping me, I didn't think about the fact that I was putting myself at risk. If I got caught, that was a guaranteed life sentence. That was the only thing that kept going through my head, and I was scared.

I kept picturing Thalia's eyes staring back at me. I had taken a life, and now the guilt was weighing down heavy on my soul. My ribs hurt. I was still bruised, and the stitches felt like they would break at any second. But I couldn't complain—I was breathing, and Thalia was not—I had gotten the good end of the stick.

The news of Thalia's murder spread quickly through the prison. Everybody knew that I had done it, and that made them fear me. Even Thalia's old crew was showing me respect. Once I found out that the warden was not pressed to find Thalia's killer, my nerves eased up a bit.

Cease showed up that next month during one of the visiting days. When my name was called, I was eager. It felt good to have somebody waiting to see me. I was escorted into a room, where I saw Cease waiting at a table. When he saw me, he stood up.

I smiled at his presence. He was still the same Cease. Dressed in baggy light jeans and a white T, he was fresh to death. The diamonds that hung low around his neck and in his ears made him look even better. His dark-brown skin seemed flawless.

He greeted me with open arms, "What up, shorty?" He held me close.

It felt good to be in his arms, and I didn't want him to let me go. I sat down across from him.

He looked at the small scar below my eye. "What happened to you? Who put they hands on you?" The anger was apparent; I could hear it in his voice.

"It's been handled already—I took care of it."

Cease reached across the table and grabbed my hands. His touch sent butterflies up and down my spine. "You shouldn't have to take care of it, Remy. I want you to be all right. It's hard watching you struggle in here."

"It's so good to see you. I didn't know how much I missed you until today." Cease looked at me. He stared deeply as if he was seeing me for the first time. "I miss you too," he said. "It seems like since you got in here, time has been moving slow— it's been fucking with me— you shouldn't be here."

I held his hands tighter and said, "Neither should you. We both know that you would have gotten locked up way longer than me. It's worth it, Cease. I wasn't trying to do that to you."

It was something about Cease that drew me to him, something real about him that made me realize that he was the only person on the outside that I could depend on.

"How's Netty?"

I shrugged my shoulders. "She's the same. This place doesn't really bother her that much. Most of the time, she's the one keeping me sane."

"Do you need anything?"

I shook my head and asked playfully, "Do you?"

"Right now, all I want is for you to be easy until you get out. Then I can take care of you."

I smiled, but I didn't know if he was saying it because he felt he had to or if he wanted to. "How's business?" I asked.

"Business is good. Life is good right now."

I thought about when I first met Cease back in the day, when he was working for Khadafi. "We've come a long way—I remember when you wouldn't say more than two words to me."

Cease sat back in his chair and said, "It wasn't my place back then—you were off limits."

I raised an eyebrow. "Oh okay, and now . . . ?"

Cease laughed softly and said, "You still off limits to everybody else; I haven't figured out what you are to me yet."

"Well, you let me know when you figure it out."

We sort of looked at each other for a minute; it seemed like we were both intrigued with each other.

"Morgan! Time's up," the guard yelled.

The sound of the guard's voice snapped me back to reality. I rolled my eyes and looked at Cease, "I have to go."

He stood up and gave me a long hug.

"Thank you for coming to see me."

He put his hands on my face and looked down at. "Take care of yourself."

I nodded my head and walked away, wishing we had more time to talk. When I got back to my cell, the only thing that I could think of was Cease. His visit made being locked up even harder, and I began counting each day.

"I'm just tired of this, you know. I'm ready to live my life again. It feels like I'm just waiting to die in here," I told Netty one day when we were sitting in the yard.

She was smoking a cigarette, listening to me gripe about being locked up. "I know, baby. You got to hold on to that one thing that makes you strong, though—and that should be your love for Khadafi."

I rolled my eyes at Netty. It seemed like every time I talked to her about something, she had to remind me of Khadafi. I had closed that chapter in

my life and was trying to move forward. I hugged
Netty and went back to my cell. She didn't understand how I was feeling. Netty had ten long years
to serve; I only had six more months. She didn't
know how it felt to be so close to freedom, but at
the same time, be so far away.

When I walked into my cell I saw a letter on my
bunk. I knew it was from Cease—he was the only
person I talked to. I opened the letter and read.

> *Remy,*
> *I'm not gon lie to you. Ever since I saw you*
> *a couple months back I've been going crazy*
> *thinking about you locked up in there. I don't*
> *know if it's right for me to be thinking like*
> *this. My head is all fucked-up. I know that*
> *you are Khadafi's woman and I respect that,*
> *but Khadafi ain't here to take care of you and*
> *for some reason, I'm feeling like I need to be*
> *that man in your life. You deserve the best of*
> *everything, and I'm in the position to give*
> *that to you. I'm not half as big as Khadafi*
> *was but I'm getting money. I don't know*
> *what your plans are after you get out, but I*
> *do want you to know that you got a nigga*
> *waiting on you.*
> *Cease*

I couldn't believe what I'd just read. My heart
was racing and I was confused; but it felt good. I
don't think I ever felt like that in my life. I was beginning to think that I was feeling Cease . . . on a
deeper level than I was willing to admit. I sat down
and wrote him back.

Cease,

I know what you feeling. You don't have to explain it to me because I've been feeling the same way. You say that you don't know if it's right for you to look at me like that and I know where you coming from. As Khadafi's woman, I don't know if it's right either, but will it ever be right? How long am I supposed to wait before I can move on with my life? I don't want to wait anymore. I've dealt with the death of Khadafi and it was hard. I cried myself to sleep many nights over that man and yeah, he will always have a place in my heart, but that don't mean that I don't have room for you either. Khadafi is gone; I can't just put my life on hold. I can't put my feelings for you on hold. I don't know if I'm feeling you because I'm locked up or because it's real, but I do know that I want to find out. I want to be with you and I hope that you give us a chance so that you can find out if you want to be with me.

Remy

The next day I sent the letter to Cease. I waited to see what he would say, but he never wrote back. My thoughts were consumed with him. I couldn't stop myself from falling in love with him.

The months passed slowly, and the walls of the prison seemed to be closing in on me day by day. Being locked up for twenty-one hours out of the day will make a person crazy, and I was beginning to think I was getting there. All I wanted to do was see Cease, to know how he reacted to my letter.

Netty and I grew extremely close while I was in

jail. Her advice and kind, wise, listening ear was what helped me through. I'm sure that without her I would have died.

The night before my release, Netty arranged for the guard to let me, her, and Dee have a little farewell party in the basement. We all sat around and sipped on some Rémy Martin, Betty Netty's favorite, which one of the guards snuck through in a coffee mug.

For the first time, I thought about how much I was going to miss those two. "Thank you both for everything," I said as I hugged them both.

"Don't go getting all soft on us. As long as you write me every once in a while, I'll be fine," Dee said.

Netty downed a cup of Remy. "Just remember an old girl. I'm fine. I want you to remember Khadafi. His love is alive, Remy."

I laughed at Netty's drunk ass and hugged her tightly. It was the last time I would see her for a while, because after that night I was a free woman.

Chapter Fifteen

March 2003

I couldn't believe how good it felt to be outside the walls of the prison. I looked rough—my hair was in braids straight to the back, and I had on the same jeans and T-shirt that I'd worn in there fifteen months earlier. I walked down the long driveway to the prison, not knowing where I was headed. It didn't really matter to me, as long as I was free to do what I wanted.

When I reached the end of the driveway, I saw an apple-red, convertible Mercedes Benz. Cease leaned against the car, his arms crossed. I smiled when I saw him. I can't even begin to describe my feelings when he smiled back. Cease looked fresh, as always. He wore baggy Sean John jeans, a crispy white T, a fitted hat, and some tan Timberland boots. The long, diamond-studded cross that hung from his neck made him look even better.

I ran up to him and hugged him tightly.

He practically picked me up off the ground.

"What are you doing here?" I was surprised to see him waiting at the gates for me.

"I told you what it was gon' be like when you got out." He held up a set of keys.

I looked at the car that sat behind him and said, "You lying! Cease, quit playing with me."

He opened the door to the passenger side for me then walked around to the driver side.

I looked around the car and practically screamed in delight at the custom-style inside. My name was engraved in the leather headrests and on the dashboard. There was a CD player, and a flip-screen DVD player in the car. "Oh my goodness—you didn't have to do all this."

"Look, Remy, I'm sorry you had to go through this shit, but life is gon' be good from here on out—"

"Cease, let's just go—I'm not trying to remember anything that went down while I was in that place. We don't even have to talk about it. Just get me as far away from here as you possibly can."

Cease nodded his head and sped off. We did ninety down I-75, heading towards Flint. The car ride was silent. Neither of us said a word, but we both nodded our head to Jay Z's "Reasonable Doubt."

Two hours later we pulled up to a hair salon called "The Bold and the Beautiful."

He looked over at me, and insecurity swept over me as I looked down in embarrassment. I knew I looked hit—hell, I had been locked up for over a year and looking good hadn't really been on my agenda.

He put his hand underneath my chin and lifted my head. "I'll be back to get you in two hours. Ask for Margo."

I smiled, knowing that my hair needed some serious work. I walked into the hair salon and over to the receptionist's desk. "Hi, I have an appointment with Margo."

The girl sat with her legs crossed, flipping through a hair book and popping her gum. She looked up at me and frowned in disgust.

I wanted to tell her about her damn self, but she was young—she couldn't have been a day older than seventeen, so I let it slide. *Hell, five years ago I was her age and I would have reacted the same way.*

She checked the appointment book. "Remy?"

I nodded my head yes, and she directed me to a room in the back.

When I walked to the back of the salon, Margo was finishing up a client's hair. "You must be Remy," she said. She took some money out of her smock to give her other client change. Margo had a warm voice, and just by her look, I could tell she was down-to-earth. A heavy-set woman with dark, chocolate skin and long, thick, pretty hair, she appeared to be in her late forties.

"Yes, I'm Remy," I said as I sat in the shampoo bowl.

She stood over me and unbraided my nappy hair. I knew she was gon' have a time taming my hair—I hadn't had a perm in over a year, and my 'kitchen' was wrecked.

She let a relaxer sit in my head for like five or ten minutes, and I quickly began to burn. I didn't care, though, I was gone let that perm marinate in my damn hair until it got all the kinks out. When the pain became unbearable, I leaned back over the sink and the stylist began to rinse and wash my hair.

"So you are the famous Remy," Margo said. "I remember hearing all about you. The streets couldn't stop speaking your name a few years ago. Everybody was talking about Khadafi's new girl. My whole shop was filled with gossip about you."

I laughed. Everybody had something to say when I first hooked up with Khadafi. It had been years, though, and people in Flint were still talking out the side of they neck. I replied, "Yes . . . that was a long time ago."

Margo rinsed my hair and applied conditioner to it, and I closed my eyes, relaxing while she massaged my neglected scalp.

"I remember when Khadafi first met you. Girl . . . he was so infatuated with you."

"You knew Khadafi?"

Margo smiled. "Child, please—I knew Khadafi for twenty years before he died. We went to school together in Lansing; we were close."

Then why the hell don't I know anything about you? "That must have been a long time ago. We used to talk about everything and he never mentioned you." I tried not to sound too rude.

She laughed and replied, "I imagine he wouldn't have, but like you said, that was a long time ago." She turned off the water and I got up and walked to her styling chair. Margo turned me toward the mirror and I saw her standing behind me in the reflection. Her face was solemn and her striking features were turned down in sadness. "Khadafi was a good man—he always took care of home."

The tears in her eyes told me they really had been close.

"Yeah, he did," I said, remembering the days I didn't have to worry about anything.

"He would turn over in his grave if he knew about you and Cease."

Her statement caught me off guard. I hadn't even talked to Cease about how I felt and people were already running off at the mouth. "What is that supposed to mean? What makes you think that Cease and I have something going on?"

She sensed my disposition and quickly stated, "I know my son—Cease has grown fond of you. For the past three months all he's been doing is running around here doing stuff for you, preparing for when you came home."

I smiled.

"Plus," she added, "that grin you got on yo' face is giving you away. Anyway, I know about what you did for him, and I commend you for that. But I still don't think it's right. Khadafi wasn't close to many people, but he loved you and he loved Cease—you and Cease need to think about that before y'all make some big mistakes."

I looked at her in the mirror and remained silent. Her words had left me with enough to think about. Margo and I talked for about an hour and a half about different stuff. I was saying anything just to prevent her from bringing up Khadafi's name again. She put me up on game about what had been happening in Flint while I was locked up. A lot had gone down, and she had informed me on all the new gossip.

Just as she finished up my hair, Cease walked in the door. The sight of him made me nervous.

"Hey, ma, you done with her?" Cease kissed his mom on the cheek.

"Yeah, I'm done with her."

I got up out the chair and said, "Thank you, Margo," and then followed Cease out the shop.

"Why didn't you tell me that I was getting my hair done by your mother?"

"My fault. I didn't think it mattered. Why? What did she say to you?"

"Nothing, we were just talking. She's nice."

Cease reached in his glove box and pulled out two rolls of money and placed them in my lap. "Can you handle that?" He leaned back in his seat and continued to drive.

I took the rubber bands off. It was all hundred-dollar bills. There had to be twenty G's in my hand. I smiled at him and said, "I think I can do something with it."

An awkward silence fell over the car. It was like we didn't know what to say to each other.

We drove out to Jennings Road, where Cease pulled up to a red brick, two-story house with a two-car garage. After Cease parked, I stepped out of the car. "Is this your house?"

"Yeah, I made you up a room. I figured you would be staying with me for a while."

I threw my arms around his neck. I was glad that Cease was taking care of me. I didn't know what I was going to do when I got out of jail, but it didn't seem like I was going to have to worry about anything. The place was fully furnished in brown and tan. It needed a woman's touch, of course, but other than that the house was plush and I was impressed. I rushed from room to room, trying to take it all in. It felt good to be in a real home again, to be looking at something other than four compact walls.

"Thank you for letting me stay with you."

He sat down on the couch and said, "Look, this is for everything. You keep thanking me, but I owe you this. You deserve this. You have been very loyal to me. You could have snitched like most people but you didn't. I appreciate that."

I looked around the three-bedroom, two-bathroom house and said, "I can't believe this. I'm gon' be real with you—I didn't know what was gonna happen to me when I was released. Thank you for helping me."

I sat down on the couch and looked around the house, still in disbelief. Before I went to jail he had been staying in a small apartment, trying to stay low-key. I knew that he had purchased the house because of me. He didn't have to do it, but I was glad that he did. "If you don't mind I'm gonna go and take a long, hot bubble bath."

Cease turned on the 72" flat-screen TV and replied, "I'm chilling; take your time."

I walked into my bedroom. It was a big room with a cherry oak bedroom set, a big screen TV, and a computer in the corner. I walked into the attached bathroom and ran a long, hot bath. I wrapped up my hair so that it wouldn't get wet. I got in and literally lost track of time. It felt so good to be bathing alone, in the comfort and safety of a private bathroom. I didn't have to look over my shoulder every five minutes, all I had to do was relax.

After a long, hard year of survival, I was finally home. I wanted to feel safe but the thoughts of how harsh prison had been stopped me from feeling secure. I lay my head back on the porcelain tub and closed my eyes, hoping to ease some of the tension that had formed in my mind and body while I was locked up. The steaming hot water was like heaven to me; it was slowly putting me to sleep. I felt my mind drifting off, taking me to a place I didn't want to be—I was dreaming of prison.

Thalia's face flashed through my head and I recalled the day I ended her life. I tried to put that day behind me, to forget what I had done, but this dream was reminding me of the horrid act. I pictured myself, Netty, Dee, and the security guard sitting at the round table. I saw the blood draining from Thalia when I slit her throat. Thalia's face morphed into mine and I felt myself choking as she stood over me with a knife in her hand. I knew I was dreaming but I couldn't make myself wake up. I couldn't return to the comfort of the bathroom.

I opened my eyes gasping for air as I forcefully woke up from the dream. I was frantic and took deep breaths to calm down. The guilt was a heavy burden on my heart. I slowly got out of the tub and grabbed a towel out of the closet. I looked in the mirror at a face that I hardly recognized. It was my face, but in a way my eyes had changed. Prison had changed me and I was no longer the sheltered woman that Khadafi had transformed me into. I really didn't know who I was, but I knew that I was not the same. I unwrapped my hair and let it fall down my back and then I walked back into my room. I didn't have any clothes, so I wrapped the towel tightly around my body then walked out of the room and into the living room where Cease was watching *SportsCenter*.

"Damn, I thought you died in there."

I laughed and sat next to him.

"I haven't taken a bath in over a year."

He looked at the towel I was wearing and said,

"We gon' get you fresh tomorrow. I'm gon' take you shopping."

I put my hand on the side of his face and rubbed gently, mesmerized at the way he was making me feel. I knew he was feeling the same way, but I could see the conflict in his eyes—he didn't know if he should be feeling me, if it was right to feel something for me because of Khadafi.

He grabbed my hand, but before he could remove it from his face, I kissed him. He turned his head away from me.

I turned his face back, "It's okay . . . I want you to." I kissed him softly on the lips.

He resisted for a minute, but eventually grabbed the back of my head and kissed me intensely.

I crawled onto his lap and straddled him as he gently pulled at my hair, his tongue caressing mine. His touch sent butterflies fluttering through my stomach. I felt myself getting wet as he reached underneath the towel and put both of his hands on my ass. I felt his hard abs tighten as I pulled the white T-shirt over his head.

He pulled his gun out of his pants and placed it on the living room table. Then he picked me up and lay me down on the floor. I was ready for him to be inside of me. My insides were on fire, and I needed something hard inside me. I wanted him to make me feel good.

I put my fingers on my clitoris, knowing that sight would entice him and make him want me more. I cringed when he finally put his big, hard dick inside me. My legs tightened as he moved rhythmically, in and out, making my toes curl. I moaned as he sped up and slowed down, trying to find out how I liked it.

He kissed me slowly as he grinded into me. I could feel every inch of him and it felt good. It was meaningful. And the closer I came to an orgasm, the more I fell deeper and deeper in love with Cease. I rolled on top of Cease and moved my ass up and down, riding him slowly while he gripped my backside, smacking it gently, letting me know I was doing my job. He bit his lower lip as I rode him in circles. I felt him stretch his legs and I knew his toes were curling as he felt himself getting ready to climax.

"Shit!" he said as I rode him harder, lifting my pelvis and lowering it with intensity.

I myself was getting ready to cum. I felt his dick get harder and harder, like he was getting ready to burst. I moaned loudly when my juices flowed over him, and we both tensed up as our bodies released an orgasm.

"Damn, girl," he said as I lay on his chest and laughed. He put his arms around me.

There was no guilt in my heart—Khadafi was gone and I had moved on.

Cease kissed the top of my head as we both lay there in silence. A comfortable silence, one that said, "we're completely satisfied with one another."

I was in love with Cease. I first felt it when I was in jail, but that night made it all real to me. I was itching to tell him how I felt because I was almost one hundred percent sure he felt the same way. "Let's go into the bedroom." I stood up and wrapped the towel back around my body.

He walked up behind me and kissed me on my neck. I couldn't believe the way he was making me feel. I never felt like this in my life—every spot he touched tingled, and I wanted him again.

Before we could reach the bed, Cease had me up against the wall. My monkey was thumping and I was ready to go another round. He picked me up, and I wrapped my legs around his waist as he put his manhood deep inside me.

"Cease," I said as he fucked me against the wall, "I love you." I was scared to say it to him, thinking he wouldn't say it back, but I had to get it off my chest. When he didn't respond immediately, I started to explain, "I don't know how you feel about me, but I wanted you to know—"

Cease put his hands on his face in frustration. "Fuck! Man, this shit ain't right—you belong to Khadafi. You are his woman. I know this ain't right." He got up from the bed and abruptly said, "I got to go."

I wrapped myself up in the bed sheets, got up, and followed him into the living room. "Wait. Cease, don't leave. You don't have to go!" Cease fumbled putting back on his clothes and tried to avoid looking at me.

My heart was breaking, I had just told this man that I loved him and this wasn't the response I had been expecting.

"Look, Remy, I can't do this; he don't deserve this."

I rushed over to Cease and stood in front of him. "Cease, stop! Just wait. I don't want you to go. I love you. Cease, I love you, and you don't have to say it back. I just wanted you to know how I felt." I wrapped my arms around his neck.

Cease looked down at me and shook his head from side to side, pain in his eyes.

"Cease, stay with me—I want to be with you."

Cease cupped my face in his hands. "It's something about you."

I put my hand on his face, trying to reassure him it was all right. "I belong to you now; Khadafi is a part of my past. I did love him and a part of me always will, but that doesn't change or stop the way I feel about you or the way I know you feel about me. I don't have to hear you say it to know how you feel. He's gone, Cease. He has been for a long time now. I love you. I'm trying to be with you."

He didn't respond, so I left it alone, leaving him to think about what I said.

We went back to the room. That night I slept close to him, never wanting to leave his side. I knew I wanted to be with Cease. Everything about him intrigued me—the way he walked, the way he talked—his whole style. I was attracted to his thuggish nature, and the feeling was too strong to stop.

Chapter Sixteen

November 2003

Cease never told me how he felt about me, but I could tell he was feeling me. He was taking care of me and doing way more than he had to do to make me comfortable. I guess his lacing me with jewelry and cash was his way of letting me know where he stood. I wasn't stupid, though. I knew if he was spending money on me the feeling had to be mutual.

I quickly grew accustomed to the lifestyle that Cease provided for me. I was back on my high horse, but in a much different way than with Khadafi. I had become the queen of the streets, just by association. I never heard him call me his woman, but the streets quickly labeled me "Cease's girl." I got respect in the deepest parts of the hood. From Selby Hood, Merrill Hood, the fifth ward, and even to the South, niggas knew who I was. I tried to stay low-key though. I didn't fuck with too many females—over the years I had come to learn that they couldn't be trusted.

Cease was my everything, and just by living with him, we grew close as hell. He was my man and my best friend, and instead of letting him change me like I had allowed Khadafi to do, we compromised and changed each other.

His "get money" mentality became my mentality. I began to keep his books for him. That way he would know how much profit he was making off of his product each month.

The dope game kept him busy. He always had business to take care of. He stayed gone a lot, but when he came home, he always brought home stacks for me to count. I couldn't say shit. I knew when he wasn't at home he was out hustling with Jodi. Cease wasn't selfish at all. Anything I asked for he gave it to me, no questions asked. I loved Cease, he knew that. He had a swagger about himself that attracted me.

After a couple of months, I could hardly believe how well I had put my life back together. When I was in jail I thought it would be impossible to feel normal again, but everything was fine. *I'm loving life right now. I'm with Cease and everything is good.*

Cease interrupted my thoughts. "What you got up for today?"

"Nothing really. I think I'm gon' write Betty Netty today. I haven't talked to her since I got out. I don't want her to think I'm acting funny." I walked into my room and grabbed a pen and pencil off my desk.

Cease walked up behind me and put his arms around my waist. "You gon' cook yo' boy something to eat?"

"Yeah, I got you," I said sweetly. His lazy speech made me smile.

Cease sat in the living room and played his XBox while I cooked him breakfast fit for a king. He wandered into the kitchen just as I was fixing his plate. He kissed my cheek, smacked my ass softly, and took his plate back into the living room.

That's when I took the opportunity to get pen and paper to write Netty.

> *Dear Netty,*
> *Hey, how have you been doing? I hope everything is going okay for you. I know it's been a couple months since you heard from me, but I've been trying to get my life back together. I'm cool now and everything with me is going well. Cease met me at the gates the day I was released and ever since then he's been taking care of me. I love him so much. I didn't think I could love somebody else after Khadafi, but I do and it's real. I know you are not going to like what you are reading, but you are like a mother to me and I don't want to lie to you. Cease makes me happy, which is something I thought I would never feel after Khadafi. Everything about Cease is real and he is good to me. Other than that I haven't been doing too much.*
> *I am glad to be out of prison, but I do miss you. You have helped me out so much and I want you to know that I will never forget that. I'm not fake, I was close to you in there and I plan on continuing our friendship now that I'm out. You are one of the only people*

*who was there for me at my lowest moment,
you are one of my only friends. Tell Dee I said
hi and that I haven't forgotten about her ass
either. Anyway, I just wanted to let you know
that I am doing okay and tell you that I am
here when you need me.*
   Remy

I got up from the table feeling better. I felt guilty
for not writing Netty, but now it was done, it felt
like a burden was lifted off my heart. After mailing
the letter I went into my room, which I had turned
into a writing space, my personal spot in the house
where I went to clear my head and express my feelings. The same room I chose to write this story in.

I went into the bathroom to get dressed, put on
a pair of Diesel jeans, a black camisole top, and
some black Manolo Blahnik heels. I combed my
hair down so that it fell in layers down my back
then placed a pair of sunglasses on the top of my
head. I grabbed my purse and was ready to go.

"Cease, I want to go shopping today—I need
some new jewelry." I walked over to him and sat
on his lap.

Cease knew my game, though. He smiled slyly
and replied, "I guess this means you want me to
come."

"It would be nice."

Cease sighed, rose from the couch, and walked
over to his safe. He pulled out three large stacks of
money and we left the house.

We drove down to Auburn Hills to go to the
Great Lakes mall. We went from store to store on a
mini shopping spree. Anything I liked, Cease pur-

chased for me. I led the way into Jared's—the bling of the showcases caught my eye.

"Hi, can I help you find something today?" a friendly white woman asked me.

I shook my head no. "No, I think I know my way around. I'll let you know when I find something."

I walked around the different showcases, looking for something I liked. I found a 5ct diamond necklace. "Cease, what you think about this?"

I waited for a response but got none. I turned around in the crowded store. Cease had a look of suspicion on his face. "Cease, what's wrong?" He looked at me and put his arm around my shoulder. "Nothing . . . let's go."

We walked out of the store and made our way back to the car. Cease didn't say anything as we walked through the mall. I could tell something was wrong. As we walked out into the dark parking lot, a creepy feeling ran down my back. I looked up at Cease and asked, "What's wrong?"

He didn't reply, but just continued to lead me towards the car.

Cease got onto the expressway and headed home. There was an unusual quiet in the car. His mood had changed in the blink of an eye, and I didn't know what was going on. He kept looking in the rearview. I looked in the side mirrors but didn't see anything out of the ordinary. There was a line of cars behind us, but nothing seemed to be wrong. Cease got off on the exit before the one that led to our house and drove around the city streets.

I noticed he'd made four left turns. "Why are we driving in circles?"

All of a sudden Cease stopped the car. Headlights shined through our car as another car pulled up behind us. Cease reached in his waistline and pulled out his gun. He reached out of his window and shot at the car behind us.

I screamed as I put my hands over my ears.

The car behind us backed up, turned around, and raced away. Cease turned around and followed the car speeding down the long, deserted street.

I gripped the side of the door and cringed in my seat as he raced to catch up to the other car. Cease had an angry expression plastered on his face. By the time he turned the corner, the other car disappeared.

"What the hell was that? What is going on?"

Cease grabbed my hand and said, "Don't worry about it. I'll handle it."

My heart was beating fast from fear. "Let's just go home."

Cease took the long way to our house.

"What the hell was that? Why is somebody following you?"

Cease walked into the room and sat on the bed. "I don't know, but I'm gon' find out."

I put my hands on my hips. "What you mean you don't know? Cease, you just shot at another car in the middle of the damn street. You been acting funny since we were at the mall. Was somebody following us there too?"

Cease didn't respond. He pulled out a different gun and loaded it with shells.

His behavior was scaring me. I had never seen him like that. "Cease! Why won't you answer my questions?"

He walked over to me and kissed me on the lips.

"Calm down—it ain't nothing wrong. Everything's good, all right."

I kissed him back and rested my head on his chest.

"Stay in tonight, okay," I said, hoping he would stay home. I had a bad feeling and didn't want him to leave the house.

"All right, go take a bath and get comfortable; we'll chill tonight."

That night in bed Cease had his arm around me and was stroking the top of my head.

I sat up suddenly and asked. "Why did you drive in circles earlier?"

Cease looked at me and said, "If you ever wanna see if someone is following you, make four left turns. You will drive in a circle, and if the car behind you does the same thing that means that they are tailing you."

I nodded my head as I listened to his logic. I guess it did make sense. "How did you know that someone was following us through the mall?"

"I just got this feeling that someone was watching me. You got to be aware of your surroundings, and you got to trust your own senses. If you ever feel that something ain't right, you get the fuck on down. I don't care who you with."

"Cease, I don't want anything to happen to you."

He kissed me on the bridge of my nose and said, "I know you thinking about the shit that happened to you when you were with Khadafi—ain't nothing gon' happen to you, not while you with me. You are safe with me. I'm not gon' let nobody touch you."

I was deep in thought.

"Stop thinking about that . . . I'm here with you. I got you."

I closed my eyes and went to sleep feeling safe in his arms.

A week later I received a letter from Netty.

> *Dear Remy,*
> *I'm glad that you doing okay and I was glad to receive a letter from you. I knew you wouldn't forget about an old woman when you got out. It's nice to know that you are doing good, but it seems that Cease is doing a bit too much to make you happy. It's funny how fast people will stab you in the back once they think you're gone. Anyway, who am I to judge, I'm just an old-timer sitting in a jail cell. It sounds like you're happy, and that's what Khadafi always wanted.*
> *Sincerely,*
> *Betty Netty*

I smiled and folded up the letter. I knew that she would not like the fact that I was with Cease. She had always been Khadafi's advocate. She was always telling me how much he loved me. Netty was something else. She and I kept writing each other at least once a week. When I was in jail, Cease's letters helped me make it through and I was hoping my letters did the same for Netty.

We talked about everything, and I kept her updated on what was going on in Flint. She was the type of person who had to know everything about everybody, so I tried my best to keep her updated. I enjoyed talking back and forth with Netty. She was one of the only people besides Cease that I trusted.

Cease walked in and saw me writing back to Netty. The phone rang and I got up to answer it.

"Hello?"

No one replied and I grew irritated. That wasn't the first time someone had called, playing on the phone. It had been happening all week. Cease was getting the same calls on his cell phone and it was starting to get on my nerves. I hung up the phone and looked at Cease. "That shit is starting to bug me."

"I got to handle some business tonight, so make sure you stay in the house."

I nodded my head and replied, "Okay."

Cease grabbed the keys to his black Escalade and before he walked out the door said, "I might be out late, but I'll call to make sure you are okay."

"Okay." I closed and locked the door behind him.

Cease had been extra cautious since the incident at the mall. All week he was paranoid—I knew something was up. He was constantly checking up on me, making sure nothing happened. I knew that there was something he was not telling me, but I didn't press him for information. I just did what he said. I did not want to be caught up in no type of beef, so the less I knew, the safer I felt.

This behavior went on for weeks, but I tried to keep my mind off of it by continuing to talk to Netty. I knew that I was supposed to get another letter from her some time soon and they always helped me remain calm. Netty was a wise woman who been around the block a couple times, so whenever I needed advice, I always asked her. I told her about what was going on in one of my letters. She assured me I was safe.

I waited for days for her next letter, but oddly, it never came. I decided to write her again to see what was going on, but that letter went unanswered as well. I didn't know what to think, I knew that she would not be ignoring me on purpose, so I thought that something happened to her. I wanted to go see her, but I was not trying to go back to that jail. It was a place that I had sworn to never step foot in again and I was not making an exception for Netty. Besides, Cease was so very protective of me lately, I knew he would never let me visit Netty in jail. So I just waited for her to respond.

Cease continued to be alert. He told me, "It feels like somebody is out to get me."

That's when I became scared. I didn't want anything to happen to him and I knew that for him to be talking like that, something was definitely not right.

Things were becoming almost intolerable. The prank calls increased and Cease's temper was getting worse by the day. He was frustrated because he didn't know who had beef with him. It would have been so much easier if he knew who he was going up against, but he had no clue.

Jodi too seemed just as clueless. He started seeing a girl named Neicy, and late at night when Cease and Jodi had to be out in the streets, Jodi would bring Neicy to our house. Cease and Jodi thought we both would be safer if we were together.

And so on one of the many nights we spent together, she said, "I don't know what's up. All I know is that Jodi been acting paranoid for like a month now."

"I don't know what to tell you." I shrugged my

shoulders. "I don't know much more than you do. I know that Cease will eventually handle it, though, but until then I'm staying in the house. I've been in this situation before and I'm not gon' make it easy for whoever is after Cease to get to him by getting to me."

Neicy was cool. Tall and light-skinned, her hair was cut medium length, and she wore it down around her face. She was cute, and surprisingly we got along very well. She'd been talking to Jodi for about six months, and it actually seemed like Jodi was into her. You never knew when it came to Jodi, though— he had too many women to keep count.

We both sat back thinking about our present circumstance.

"Them niggas could have left us with the car keys or something," she said.

I had my own car parked in the garage, but it wasn't gon' be moved that night—I wasn't going anywhere until Cease told me it was okay. Neicy had no clue just how big Cease and Jodi were. She probably just thought she was fucking with a nigga with money—every bitch in Flint was trying to get their hands on a "get-money nigga."

Cease and Jodi, two of the biggest faces in the drug game, had clout in Flint, and now that someone had it out for them, we had to be extra careful. Any little mistake could easily become a big mistake, and I was hoping that everyone involved realized that. Especially Neicy.

Chapter Seventeen

Cease remembered the exact night he'd just read about. Still trying to figure out who was fucking with them, he and Jodi were riding down Clio Road. They were on their way back to Cease's house.

"Man, this shit is crazy how niggas is fucking with us. I've been getting them calls too. I'm ready to dead me a muthafucka," Jodi said.

"Niggas is bitches—that's why they doing this childish shit—playing on phones and all that."

Cease drove past Beaver's, one of the craziest clubs in Flint. That particular night it was jumping. The strip was filled with cars parked on both sides of the street.

"Damn, we need to fall up in there tonight," Jodi said as he looked at the line to the club.

"Jodi!" a group of girls yelled out as Cease crept past the club. Traffic moved slowly.

Jodi through two fingers out the window saying, "What up," and they continued to creep down the street. Jodi saw a car full of girls parked on the side of the street, chilling on top of their car. "Let's hit the club tonight."

"You know I ain't fucking with the club. If my gun can't get in, you know I ain't going in—I ain't trying to fuck with them skeezin'-ass bitches anyway."

Jodi laughed and said, "Shit, I know you ain't trying to fuck with them with Remy thick ass living with you. Shit, nigga, I would be in that shit every night!"

Cease shot Jodi a look. "Watch yo' mouth, nigga. It ain't like that. Remy ain't like that; she's different."

"My fault, man. I ain't mean no disrespect. So that's you—that's yo' girl now?"

"Nah, we just kicking it. It ain't on no serious shit or nothing like that."

Jodi looked at Cease like he was crazy. "Get the fuck out of here! She living with you, ain't she?"

"Yeah man . . . but—"

"You fucking her, ain't you?"

"Yeah—"

Jodi interrupted again, "She goes shopping with your money, don't she?"

Cease laughed at his friend and replied, "Yeah man, but—"

Jodi threw his hand at the air. "Nigga, but nothing—that's your muthafuckin' woman. You might didn't see it coming, but it happened. That's you, cuz!"

Cease shook his head and laughed, but Jodi's words made him think. He hadn't really looked at their relationship like that. He knew he cared for Remy. Shit, he was in love with the girl, but he was so busy he hadn't had the time to put his thoughts together.

They finally passed the couple blocks near the club where it was crowded and stopped at a red light. They were both nodding their heads to a 50 Cent CD. Cease heard an engine rev up and saw two dudes on a motorcycle ride up next to them and stop at the red light.

"Look at these daredevil-looking-ass niggas." Jodi pointed to the dudes on the bike.

One of them was driving it, the other was riding on the back—facing the other way. They both wore dark helmets and big, puffy, black coats. The light turned green and the motorcycle pulled off.

Cease drove off too.

The guys on the motorcycle sped up and cut Cease off from the front, causing him to slam hard on his brakes. His Escalade screeched to a stop, and the dudes on the motorcycle rode around the entire car, spraying bullets through the body. They shot the car up with M-16's, firing off round after round.

Cease reached for his gun but couldn't get a shot off. Bullets sprayed through the car and glass broke as the dudes rode around the truck shooting from every angle. After thirty seconds of nonstop shooting, the motorcycle sped off, leaving the truck looking like Swiss cheese.

Cease's door opened first, and he stumbled out the car. "Fuck!" he yelled out loud, feeling the many cuts on his arms from the shattered glass. He felt the spots that the bullets hit and was lucky they hadn't penetrated.

"Jodi!" he yelled as he pulled his friend out of the car.

"Fuck! Nigga, you bloody as hell." Jodi looked at Cease's arm and neck.

"Are you hit?" Cease asked, patting his best friend's body.

"Nah, man. I'm straight."

They both walked to the side of the road and examined each other. Cease and Jodi took off the bulletproof vests they wore for protection and tossed them down the sewer opening—it was a federal offense to own one if you wasn't a cop, and Cease knew that the hook would be on their way. He picked up his cell phone and called Remy.

* * * * * * * * * * * * * * * * *

Cease shook his head at the memory. He opened the book and continued to read.

June 2004

The house phone rang loudly, waking me and Neicy up from our sleep. I looked at the clock. It was 2:30 in the morning. I got up from the couch and answered the phone. *This better not be no damn prank call.* "Hello?"

"Remy . . . I need you to come and get me and Jodi," Cease said.

I knew something went down. "What happened?" I asked, worried that he was hurt.

"I'll tell you when you get here. We on Clio Road by Stewart Street. Hurry . . . and Remy, be careful."

When I hung up the phone, Neicy looked at me and said, "What? Who was it?"

I grabbed the keys to my red Benz from the counter. "It was Cease—we got to go."

Neicy didn't ask any questions. She just kicked on her shoes and followed me to the garage. We hopped in the car and I sped down Jennings Road. My heart was racing. Cease had never called me in the middle of the night to come get him, so I knew it was something serious.

They weren't far away, so it took me about five minutes to get there. I pulled up to the intersection of Stewart and Clio and saw Cease's car filled with bullet holes. "No!" I yelled as I parked the car and jumped out. "Cease!" I screamed. My heart sank. I could not believe that it was happening again. I couldn't be losing Cease too. I ran to the car and felt relieved when he emerged from the back of the car with the license plate in his hand.

"Cease . . ." I yelled as I ran up to him and hugged him tightly. "Baby, what happened? What happened to you?" I saw that his arms and neck were covered in blood.

Cease kissed my lips and said, "I'm okay—get back in the car."

I watched as he and Jodi stuffed a piece of paper in the gas tank and lit the end of it with a lighter.

They both ran to the car and hopped in. "Drive, Remy. Go, go, go!" Cease hollered.

I took off towards home and watched in my rearview as the car blew up.

"Oh my God!" Neicy yelled when she heard the explosion. "Jodi, what happened?"

He put his arms around her. "Nothing . . . don't worry about it."

I looked at Cease but didn't ask him any questions. I figured he would tell me when we were alone.

When we arrived back at the house, Jodi and Neicy went into the bathroom in the hall, and Cease and I went into the one inside our room.

"What happened?" I asked Cease as I took my tweezers and pulled out pieces and bits of glass stuck in his skin.

"We got shot at," he said calmly.

"By who? Cease who is doing this?" I began to tear up.

He pulled me close and said, "Don't worry, we gon' leave town for a while. For a week or two . . . just to let shit cool down."

"Can we leave tomorrow?"

"Yeah, we'll leave first thing tomorrow."

I finished cleaning Cease up, and he stood up and hugged me tightly.

We walked out into the living room where Jodi and Neicy were sitting. "Jodi, we need to leave town, boy." Cease sat down on the couch.

Jodi nodded his head. "Where to?"

Cease looked back at me.

I said, "Vegas."

That night Jodi took my car to his house to get some cash, and Cease and I packed enough clothes to last two weeks.

The next morning we were on the first flight out of town.

We arrived in Vegas the next night. We pulled up to the Caesar's Palace Casino and Resort and I was blown away at how plush it really was.

"Damn!" Neicy said as we grabbed our bags from the rental car.

I looked up excitedly at Cease and he grabbed my hand and led me into the hotel.

"Aghh!" I screamed out of excitement.

The first thing we heard when we stepped inside was the sound of the slot machines ringing. We walked into the lobby and over to the front desk. The rooms were five hundred dollars a night, and Cease and Jodi each cashed out $7,000 for two weeks worth of stay.

I was amazed when I walked into the suite—it had the best of everything. I knew that I would be in heaven for the next two weeks. Cease sat down on the bed and leaned over in deep contemplation as I began to unpack our clothes.

I walked over to him and said, "Baby, relax— we're in Vegas. Leave all the bullshit in Flint and deal with it when we get back. We came here to get away from all that."

Cease grabbed me and sat me on his lap. I kissed his forehead and he sighed deeply.

I walked out onto the balcony and looked out over the city. "Cease, come look at this. Ain't this crazy?—it's late as hell here, but the whole city is awake."

He smiled and pulled me close to him.

I knew what he wanted; I could feel it through his jeans.

He picked me up and leaned me against the sliding door that led to our room.

I opened my legs and wrapped them around his body.

He ripped off my panties and entered me easily. He was hard and I felt his aggression as he moved in and out of me. I felt the stress leave his body as I moved rhythmically with him. Cease's body was unbelievably sexy, and I wanted to kiss every inch of him. He opened the sliding door and carried me inside, never taking himself out of me and still grinding me slowly. He lay me down on the bed and went into me harder and harder.

"Daddy," I screamed. Then I turned him around and rode him gently.

He put his hands on my hips and moved them for me, letting me know how he wanted me to ride it.

I kissed his neck and made my way down until I reached his dick. I swallowed all of it and made it appear and disappear over and over again.

"Damn, ma . . . Remy, shit!" he squealed as I sucked on him. He turned me around and entered me from behind.

As soon I began to bring it back, he nutted inside me.

He pulled me close and said, "I love you, girl."

I looked up at him in surprise. It was the first time he'd said that to me. I didn't know if he meant it or not.

"You don't have to say that just because we fucking, Cease—I want you to mean it."

He looked at me and said, "I love you. I loved you since the day you stepped foot in my house—maybe before then—I just needed time to figure some things out. You belong to me now."

I smiled and said, "I love you too, Cease."

We both got up and took a shower together and our sexual act resumed in the bathroom. Once we were both exhausted we crawled in the bed and went to sleep.

Early the next morning when the phone rang loudly, Cease got up and answered it. "Remy," he mumbled, "it's Neicy."

I reached over him and grabbed the phone. "Hello."

"Hey, Remy, I wanted to know if you wanted to go shopping with me?"

"Hell yeah, I'll be ready in an hour." I got up and got in the shower.

When I got out, Cease was up eating room service. "What you hop up for this morning?" he asked.

I walked over to him and grabbed a piece of bacon off his plate. "I'm going shopping with Neicy in a few. Can I have some money?"

Cease shrugged his shoulders. "It's in the safe."

I opened the hotel safe and looked at him. "How much can I take?"

"Take as much as you want. I brought fifty G's, so you got twenty-five thousand to spend. That's for the whole two weeks; you can do what you want with it."

I took a stack of five thousand out of the safe and put it in my Dooney and Bourke.

Just then there was a knock on the door. It was Jodi and Neicy. "You ready?" Neicy asked.

"Hell, yeah." I was anxious to spend some money.

Just as I was walking out the door, Cease yelled, "We gon' meet in the lobby for dinner at nine."

Neicy and I yelled, "Okay!"

We took the rental car to Fashion Show mall and immediately began hopping from store to store. The mall was huge, and we planned on conquering it all before it was time to go. We went into Neiman Marcus, Macy's, Saks Fifth, and Dillard's. I was in a zone—I could have easily spent the whole five thousand in one store, but I decided to shop lightly.

I left the mall with a Christian Dior dress and a pair of Manolo glasses. Neicy left the mall with a new pair of diamond earrings and a pair of Baby Phat jeans. We still had a couple hours before it was time to meet back up with Cease and Jodi, so we decided to get makeovers at the hotel spa. I couldn't wait to get a full body massage, after all the drama that had happened in Flint—I needed one. We both paid for the full package and spent the rest of the day pampering ourselves.

The masseuse who did me had strong hands. The experience was almost orgasmic. He kneaded all the kinks out of my body, and I planned on showing Cease how limber I was later that night.

We got mud baths, Brazilian waxes, and facials. We also got our hair, nails, and feet done. When I slipped into my new dress, I knew that I was going to be looking good.

After our day of nonstop primping it was almost time to go to dinner.

"I'll come to your room in an hour," Neicy said, "and we'll walk down together."

I didn't have to do all that much, since the spa had done everything. I slipped into my black cocktail dress and put on a pair of silver and black heels that I'd brought from home. I put on my diamond necklace, tennis bracelet, and anklet and was ready to go. I didn't take any more money from the safe because I still had $1,000 left. I figured I would gamble with that. I didn't want to lose all my money in one night.

Neicy came over to my room an hour later as

promised. She looked fly too—she had on a pink baby doll dress with silver, strappy shoes, and diamond and platinum accessories.

We walked down to the lobby together and spotted Jodi and Cease. I could tell by the look on Cease's face that he approved of my makeover. I kissed him on the lips and he put his arm around my waist as we walked towards the restaurant.

We all sat down together and ate dinner. We conversed about everything and drank Cristal champagne.

"Shit, I'm ready to go win me some money at the casino," Neicy said after getting a little tipsy.

"This one's on me," Jodi said. He placed three hundred-dollar bills on the table.

We all got up and walked over to the packed casino. We split up—Neicy and I went to the slot machines; Jodi and Cease went to the tables.

I was having fun. Just the possibility of being able to win some money made it worthwhile to me, and I was actually doing pretty good. I hit for thirty-three hundred on one of the high-stakes machines. After that I was done for the night. I was not going to bet my money back and lose.

I found Neicy and she was broke. "Girl, I lost three thousand tonight."

"I lost five hundred and hit for thirty-three, so I did pretty good."

After hours of playing different machines, I was tired, and so was Neicy. I was sitting down at the machines nodding off. I was so ready to go back to my room, I didn't know what to do.

We searched the casino for our men and found them at the same damn crap table that they'd been on all night. A smiling Cease stood beside Jodi, who was shaking the dice and throwing them. Cease was laughing at the sight of Jodi losing all of his money.

"Hey, baby," I said as we approached them.

"What up." Cease sipped his drink in his hand. "This fool done lost about twenty G's."

Jodi shook his dice and put his hand by Cease's mouth. "Blow, Cease."

Cease looked at him like he was crazy. "Man, I ain't 'bout to blow them damn dice."

Jodi turned to me and asked me to blow them. I blew them and he threw them across the table.

"Seven. Crap out," the table dealer yelled.

Cease had seen enough. He grabbed Jodi by the arm. "Come on, my nigga."

Cease laughed at that nigga all the way to the room.

Jodi had a salty look on his face. He kept saying, "That ain't shit."

I had to admit that shit was funny. Even Neicy let out a few chuckles.

We all retired to our rooms to get some rest. It was four in the morning, and we were tired as hell. Cease and I took a shower together and did some other things. After that we lay down in the king-size bed and talked.

"Thank you," I said to him.

"What you thanking me for?" he asked me.

"For everything—you were there for me when I needed you. After I got out of jail, I didn't have anybody, but you were there. I love you so much and I need you."

"I love you too, Remy. I've never said that shit to anybody, but it's true. I'll do anything for you and will kill anybody who tries to harm you."

I lay directly on top of Cease. He ran his fingers through my hair and said, "We might as well make this shit official."

I sat up and looked at him. "What?" I thought I knew what he meant but wasn't sure.

"Shit, we already in Vegas."

I jumped up and yelled, "Oh my God, yes! Cease, yes, yes, yes!" I couldn't believe what I was hearing.

He laughed and said, "So we gon' do this? You ready to be my wife?"

I hugged him so tight, I didn't think he could breathe.

"Yes, baby . . . yes, I will be your wife."

We both got up and put on some clothes. I put on a white Valentino dress that I'd brought with me. It was short and hung around my neck, exposing my cleavage. I added silver Prada heels—and my diamonds, of course.

Cease put on a white T and some Diesel jeans with a fresh pair of crisp "Forces" and we were ready.

We knocked on Jodi's and Neicy's door. "Open up!" I yelled.

Jodi groggily answered the door.

"I need a best man, Jodi boy."

Jodi's eyes bucked. "Yeah, fucking right, nigga! Quit bullshitting—yo' ass ain't getting married."

Neicy heard the word and yelled, "Married?" She rushed to the door and saw me in my "wannabe wedding gown." "You getting married?"

I nodded my head in excitement. "I need a maid of honor."

Cease kissed the top of my head, and Jodi shook his head. "Congratulations, man." Then he looked at me and pointed to his friend. "You got yourself a good nigga right here."

"I know," I said, holding on to Cease.

We went to the wedding chapel and bought the most expensive wedding package. I was so happy that I was marrying Cease, I didn't know what to do. It was the happiest day of my life.

"I do," I said to Cease as I looked him in the eyes. Our kiss was long and warm.

Jodi and Neicy clapped loudly. Jodi hugged me. "You better take care of my nigga."

"I will."

The next morning we went and bought me a 7ct diamond ring with a platinum band. Cease got a simple platinum band. The rest of our stay in Vegas served as one big honeymoon. We gambled, shopped, and had sex almost every day. After two weeks of the fast life in Las Vegas, we made our way back home.

Things had settled down in Flint. I was hoping the phone calls and beef had stopped.

"I told you everything was gon' be all right," Cease said as he carried me over the threshold of our house.

Being married to Cease was like a dream. He was my best friend, and I couldn't have asked for a better husband. We fought sometimes, but by the end of the day we would make up. There was never one moment I thought he didn't love me.

After all the hardship in my life I had found my king. He made my world complete and I knew that I was going to be with him until the day I died.

<u>Chapter Eighteen</u>

Cease woke up and prepared to go to court. Today was the day that he would find out his own fate. Still mourning the loss of his wife and unborn child, a single tear slowly slid down his face as the image of Remy entered his thoughts. Cease got into the shower and let the steaming water hit his face. He wept as he sat in the corner of the tub and let the water hit his body.

The loss of Remy was too much for him to bear. He didn't even get to go with her to the hospital. The police had arrived on the scene first and arrested him on the spot. He didn't even get to pay his last respects to his wife—the police made it hard for him to post bail, and he missed the funeral service. Cease sat there thinking about Remy and feeling drained.

Cease pulled himself together as best he could and got out of the shower. He got dressed and thought about finishing Remy's book. He wanted to know how she ended it. He walked to her room, and picked up the book from the bed, and read the last page.

* * * * * * * * * * * * * * * * * *

It's been two years since Cease and I got married, and, I have to admit, I am happy with my life. All of the things I went through seemed to be worth it. Cease made me feel whole, and with him I've found complete happiness.

I found out this morning that I am three weeks pregnant. I am so excited. This is my chance to create a life for the child I never had. I can't wait to tell Cease tonight at dinner that he is going to be a father. He is going to be the happiest man in the world.

I can honestly say that my story has a fairy-tale ending. It's time for me to end my autobiography and start my new life with Cease.

THE END

* * * * * * * * * * * * * * *

"Do you swear to tell the truth, the whole truth, and nothing but the truth, so help you God?"

Cease stood on the stand, his right hand on the Bible and left hand in the air. "I do." He sat down.

The prosecuting attorney stood up and walked to the center of the courtroom and began cross-examination. "Will you please state your name, for the record?"

"Drayton Ceaser." Cease's low, raspy voice echoed throughout the courtroom.

The prosecutor, with both hands behind his

back, walked toward Cease and said, "Where were you on the night of November 28th, the night of your wife's untimely death?"

Cease dropped his head and answered, "I was with her."

The prosecutor continued, "Remy was murdered in cold blood by a .357 hollow point bullet through her chest, with a gun that was registered in your name."

Cease closed his eyes. The words that left the prosecutor's mouth felt like a thousand daggers to his heart. "I did not kill Remy! I didn't kill my muthafuckin' wife."

The Judge banged his gavel and warned Cease about his vulgar language.

The prosecutor walked up to Cease and began to yell, while pointing his finger at him, "You were the last person seen with her. The murder weapon is registered in your name, with only your finger prints on it. You also have a history of violence. You cold bloodedly killed your wife!"

Cease grew angrier with every word. He stood up and yelled at the lawyer, "Why are you saying this shit. Don't ever speak Remy's name again. Never talk to me like that. I did not kill Remy!" Tears flowed from his eyes.

The crowd chattered in awe as the prosecutor took two steps back to create more distance between himself and Cease.

Cease knew that his outburst would hurt his case, but pure emotions took over. He regained his composure and sat back in his chair. The prosecutor looked at the judge and nodded his head, signaling he was done examining Cease.

The courtroom was in an uproar. It seemed as if

everyone had something to say. The judge banged his gavel once again to bring down the noise level. He looked at Cease and asked, "Would the defense like to cross-examine?"

Cease's lawyer immediately got up and walked over to his client. He leaned on the stand right in front of Cease and asked him a question as if they were the only ones in the courtroom. "Mr. Ceaser, can you please take us back to that horrific night, the night in question, when your beloved wife was taken from you?"

Cease, without raising his head, nodded and whispered into the microphone, "Yeah." He closed his eyes and took the courtroom back to that painful night.

Remy sat in front of her mirror, fixing her hair. She looked in the mirror and watched as I loaded my gun and put it in my back waistline. "Baby, leave your gun at home tonight," she pleaded. "You always carry that thing."

"You know that ain't happening—wherever I go, it goes."

I walked over to her to help her put on her pearl necklace. She smiled and held the back of her hair up for me to snap the necklace together. I examined her beautiful eyes in the mirror as I stood behind her. I smiled at her and winked my eye. I'd finally found happiness with her.

Remy asked me earlier that night to go out to dinner. (She'd already made reservations at the most prestigious restaurant Flint had to offer.) She told me she wanted to talk to me about something important.

When I came out from the bathroom, Remy was sprawled out on the bed, lying on her stomach, writing in her book.

"What do you be writing about in that little book?"

She looked back at me and closed the book. "I'm writing my autobiography. I'm finally done. I just wrote the last page."

I looked her in the eyes and jokingly said, "Lately that book has been getting all of your attention."

Remy imitated a baby's voice. "Oh, is my boo-boo jealous? I sorry, baby. Come here." She got up with open arms and walked over to me.

Just then I tried to grab the book off the bed. She quickly snatched the book before I could get to it and burst out laughing. I snapped my fingers in defeat.

Remy held the book behind her back, guarding it from me. She stuck out her tongue. "I'm too fast for you."

I let out a small chuckle, and Remy left out and went to the next room, where she usually wrote. Moments later we walked out of the house on our way to dinner.

We sat at the restaurant table enjoying our dinner. I signaled for the waitress and asked for her to bring me a bottle of Remy's favorite champagne—Chardonnay.

Remy shook her head. "I don't want a drink tonight."

"What? You ain't getting tipsy tonight? That's something new."

She smiled at me. "I can't drink."

"Yeah, why is that?"

"You're not supposed to drink when you're pregnant."

I was about to put another piece of steak in my mouth when I paused. "What you talking about, Remy?"

She took a deep breath and smiled from ear to ear. "Cease, I'm pregnant—you're going to be a daddy."

"Stop playing, ma."

"I'm serious—I found out this morning."

I jumped up and embraced her in excitement. People stared at me like I was crazy, but I didn't care. I was ecstatic. I told her, "I'm too excited to eat," and dropped a hundred on the table and we left.

On the ride home, all I talked about was our child. "If I had a girl I would have a mink before she could wear it, and if I had a son, I would never leave him like my own father left me." I was the happiest man in the world at that moment. I just wanted to go home and lay my head on my wife's stomach.

When we got to the house, I hopped out and ran over to the passenger side to open the door for my queen. "Be careful, baby," I said as I grabbed Remy's hand and helped her out.

Remy snatched her hand back in protest. "I'm pregnant, not handicap."

I still helped her out of the car.

Remy complained about how bad she had to use the bathroom as we walked up to the house. When I opened the door, she brushed past me and shot upstairs to relieve herself. I walked into the living room and the smell of smoke filled my nostrils. But it wasn't smoke from a fire, it was smoke from a Cuban cigar.

I immediately grew suspicious and quickly scanned the living room. I saw the silhouette of a man smoking a cigar sitting on our couch. I immediately turned on the light switch and what I saw was unbelievable. I stared at the man in shock.

The man sat there with his legs crossed and took a long puff from his cigar. "Young blood," he said, "it's been a long time. I see you kept your promise—you're taking care of Remy as I can see." Khadafi's tone of voice wasn't one of gratitude, but one of anger.

"Khadafi? I thought you were dead," I whispered softly. I felt lightheaded and slowly walked towards him and stopped about three feet away.

He stood up face to face with me.

I didn't know what to feel. I reached out my arms to embrace him, but he pushed me away.

At that moment Remy came walking into the room, not paying attention to the situation. She walked in talking, without actually looking at me. "Baby, maybe we can turn my writing room into a nursery—" Her jaws dropped when she saw Khadafi's face. She grew lightheaded and fell to her knees.

I instantly rushed over to her. "Remy, are you okay?"

She just stared at Khadafi. "Khadafi?—you're supposed to be dead; I buried you four years ago."

"I had to deceive my enemies . . . for you," he explained. "They were after me, and if I hadn't done what I did, we all would be dead right now. I had to fake my own death."

Remy pieced together the painful memories and realized that she'd never actually viewed the body. "But the police came to my door and told me you were dead."

Khadafi walked over to Remy. "I have connections with the chief of police and he had it arranged for me. I never wanted to leave you, Remy, I was only protecting you." Khadafi sounded sincere in his every word.

Remy became furious, remembering all that she had to go through after his alleged death. She slapped him across his face with all her might. "Do you know what I had to go through after you left me? I was tossed on the streets with nothing. I was homeless and had to go back to Dock." Tears started to flow down her face. "I sold my body for money, you bastard! The Feds came and took everything. You left me without anything!"

Khadafi's eyes began to water.

"I never intended for that to ever happen. I didn't know the Feds got a hold of the money. I would have never left you to fend for yourself. I loved you, I still love you, and I came back for you."

I'd heard enough. "Things have changed since you've been gone."

Khadafi frowned his face. "What? When you thought I was gone you went after my woman—you're a fuckin' snake. All I did for you and this is what you do to me?"

"Khadafi, I thought you were dead. It wasn't supposed to be like this."

He had pure hatred in his eyes for me. He grabbed his gun out of his waistline and I went for mine. We stood toe to toe, with a gun pointed at each other's face.

"No! Do not do this!" Remy tried to plead with both of us, but there seemed to be no turning back. Neither of us took our eye off the other.

I told Remy, "Go upstairs and call the police. Tell them your husband just killed an intruder."

Remy began to cry and rubbed my face. "Baby, I love you. Please put down your gun. You are my husband; I am with you now and always—you don't have to do this."

Just as I glanced at her, Khadafi hit my hand, causing my gun to fly across the room. He hit me again, this time in the temple. I stumbled back and yelled for her to get out. I didn't want her or my unborn child to be hurt.

Khadafi kicked me in the mouth while I was on the ground. I was disoriented from the blow and tried to stand on my feet, but just before I could, the butt of his gun struck me across the mouth. My mouth immediately began to bleed.

He looked down at me and said, "Get the fuck up, young blood—you went behind my back and tried to take my place—stand up like a man." He tried to kick me again, but this time I dodged the kick and pulled his other leg from underneath him. He hit the floor, and the impact made him drop his gun, which slid underneath the couch.

The two of us began to fight, exchanging powerful punches to the face. We squared up in the living room like two boxers, trading hit after hit. I noticed that my gun was in the far corner of the room. Khadafi followed my eyes and spotted the gun too. Khadafi was closest to the gun and he ran for it. But before he could reach it, Remy kicked it away from him.

Khadafi looked at Remy for a split second, and

that's when I let him have it—a right hook to the face—and looked around for my gun. Remy ran over to it and picked it up.

"Baby, toss me the gun." I opened my hands.

Khadafi screamed, "Remy, please . . . please, give me the gun."

Remy wanted to give me the gun, but she didn't want me to kill Khadafi. Even though he'd disappeared from her life, a part of her still cared. She looked at me and knew who she had to ride for. She tossed the gun to me, but Khadafi jumped in front of it and grabbed it. We both struggled for possession, and in the midst of the chaos a shot was fired.

All movement stopped as we both looked at what just happened—a .357 bullet entered Remy's chest and she dropped to the ground, covered in blood.

Both of us screamed "No!" at the top of our lungs.

I rushed over to her side as she struggled for air and the blood gushed out of her mouth. "Cease," she said in a weak tone. Her body began to shake as I cradled her in my arms. Before I could even say anything, the shaking stopped and her eyes gazed into space, not focusing on anything. Remy died in my arms.

Khadafi just stood there in a daze and watched as I rocked Remy back and forth, crying loudly and praying to God that she would come back to me. A tear dropped down Khadafi's face, and he walked out of the door.

Cease opened his eyes and scanned the room. Some of the jurors had tears in their eyes; others didn't believe a word he said.

Cease's attorney paused and let his client's testimony sink into their thoughts. "Cease, why were your fingerprints the only ones on the gun?"

"Khadafi had on gloves."

The attorney turned towards the jury. "That would explain why there is only one set of fingerprints found on the weapon."

Cease nodded his head yes.

"So are you saying that Khadafi Langston is alive?"

"Yes."

The whole courtroom gasped at the far-fetched allegation. Khadafi's death was all over the news and published in the local paper years earlier.

Cease's attorney walked to the center of the courtroom and addressed the courtroom. "I have a surprise witness. Will the guards please let Khadafi Langston into the courtroom?" Cease's lawyer pointed towards the entrance, and all eyes immediately focused on the door.

After five seconds of complete silence, the lawyer spoke again: "The law states that if there is any reasonable doubt, my client should not be convicted. I noticed that every pair of eyes in this courtroom, including the jurors', went to the entrance. Therefore, it would be illegal for you, the jury, to render a guilty verdict." The lawyer looked at the judge. "That will be all, Your Honor."

Sitting next to Cease's mother, Jodi smiled and whispered to her, "He's good."

The courtroom was in awe of the lawyer's performance. He walked back to the table and sat down. He looked over at Cease and winked at him.

The prosecutor got out of his seat and asked permission to approach the bench. Next thing, both lawyers went to the bench to talk to the judge.

Cease's lawyer came back with a disgruntled look on his face.

"What happ—"

Before Cease could finish, the prosecutor shouted, "I would like to call Betty Lynette to the stand."

The guards opened the doors, and in came Betty Lynette.

Cease was confused. *What the hell was he calling her to the stand for?* He watched her stride to the stand.

She was sworn in, and the prosecutor began to question her. "Please state your name for the records."

"Betty Ann Lynette."

"Did you know Remy Ceaser?"

"Yeah, I knew her—she was like my daughter."

"Did she ever discuss her relationship with Drayton Ceaser with you?"

"Yeah. She would often tell me that she was scared for her life and Cease had become very violent with her."

Cease shot out of his chair and yelled, "What the fuck is yo' problem?"

The judge banged his gavel, and Cease's lawyer grabbed his client's arm and instructed him to calm down.

The prosecuting attorney smiled and continued, "Was she happy with Cease?"

"No, not from what she told me—she said she was about to leave him."

Cease could not believe what he was hearing.

The lawyer asked Betty Netty, "Did you know the late Khadafi Langston?"

"Yes, I did . . . God bless his soul."

"Do you believe he is still alive?"

"No. I'm sure he is not alive."

"How are you so sure?"

"I buried my son three years ago. I had to go down and identify the body. My son is in heaven." Betty dropped her head and began to whimper.

The lawyer handed Betty his handkerchief and told the judge he was done.

Cease's lawyer shook his head in defeat. He knew Betty Netty's testimony was damaging.

When Betty got off the stand, the judge ordered a recess for deliberation.

The jurors returned to the courtroom after an hour and a half. The head juror walked to the judge and handed him a piece of paper.

The judge banged his gavel. "Order in the courtroom. We have a hung jury—the jurors have not been able to deliver a verdict. The charges are dismissed, and a new case has to be filed. The defendant is free to go."

Cease hugged his lawyer, and Jodi soon came to congratulate his friend. Naturally Cease was happy he got off, and even though the probabilities of charges being filed again were slim, he still didn't find much to cheer about because of his lost love.

Alongside his mom and Jodi, Cease walked out of the courtroom to cameras and reporters. He hailed his mother a cab.

Jodi asked Cease, "Do you want to celebrate?"

"Nah, Jodi boy, I ain't really up to it. I need to go somewhere else right now. I'll see you a little later." They gave each other a pound and went their separate ways.

Jodi watched Cease walk away, knowing exactly where he was headed. He knew his friend was having a hard time letting Remy go.

Chapter Nineteen

Cease looked up at the courthouse and he was filled with grief. *I could have stopped it. I was supposed to protect her,* he thought to himself as he made his way to his car. He ignored the reporters and held his head down to avoid the cameras as he walked across the street and got into his car. He drove off and headed towards the cemetery. He had to be near Remy, and even though she couldn't speak back to him, he had to tell her he was sorry.

Cease pulled up to the cemetery and parked. He sat in his car for a minute not wanting to get out and face reality. He got out and walked over to his wife's grave. He knelt down and dropped his head as he felt the tears begin to well up in his eyes. He read the inscription on her head stone: "Remy Princess Ceaser, beloved wife and mother." The words stopped in his throat and choke him up. "I'm sorry, Remy." He gripped the top of her head-stone. "I love you," he said, hoping that she could hear him. He knew that he would never find another woman like her.

He heard the crunch of gravel and turned around to see his mother getting out of a cab. She walked over to him, and he kissed her on the forehead. "What are you doing here?"

"I thought you might need a little support."

Cease lowered his head and touched the headstone of his wife's grave. "I need her."

Margo put her hand on her son's shoulder and squeezed it reassuringly. She took a deep breath and sighed. "There's something you need to know," she began hesitantly.

Cease looked up at her with red eyes.

She wished she could take back her words. She saw the pain in his eyes and knew he wasn't ready to hear what she had to say. "You had his eyes." A tear slid down her face as she noted the similarity.

"What?"

"I have something I have to tell you."

"Now's not the time."

"The time will never be right for what I have to say."

Cease heard the serious tone in his mother's voice and gave her his full attention.

"You have to forgive Khadafi for what he's done, Cease."

He remained silent and waited for her to continue.

"There has been enough bloodshed already. You can't seek vengeance against him. Promise me that you won't."

Cease frowned. "Why is this so important to you?"

Margo lowered her eyes, unable to match her

son's stare and whispered. "Because Khadafi is your father."

* * * * * * * * * * * * *

Jodi rolled down the highway thinking. It hurt him to see his best friend go through his dilemma. He decided to go check up on him, even though Cease wanted to be alone. He noticed something different about Cease's eyes the last time he'd seen him. He picked up his phone and chirped Cease and got no response. *That's odd,* he thought as he exited the highway; *Cease always hits me back.*

He pulled into Cease's driveway and approached the door. He knocked and received no answer. Jodi noticed the door was slightly open and pushed it. "Cease!" He took a step into the home. He looked around and saw the house in a mess. Which was out of character for Cease. "Cease!"

Jodi quickly grew suspicious and decided to check for Cease upstairs. Many thoughts ran through Jodi's mind as he raced up the steps.

He reached Remy's old room and noticed a black book in the middle of the bed. He walked over to it and began to flip through the pages. He realized that it was Remy's diary and became frantic as he skimmed through the pages. Jodi flipped through the tiny book, looking for something that he prayed wasn't in there.

"What you looking for, Jodi boy?"

Startled by the voice behind him, he dropped the diary and turned around to see Cease standing there, watching him closely.

"Oh, my fault, man. I came over to check on you." Jodi sat the book back down on the bed.

Cease stared intently at Jodi, and the room was smothered with an awkward silence. "You sure?—it seem like you was looking for something."

Jodi shook his head. "Nah, I just came over here to make sure you was straight. You were acting kinda crazy; I wanted to see if you were all right—the shit you been through lately would fuck any man up." The tension between the two of them made Jodi shift his stance awkwardly.

Cease reached into his pocket and pulled out a crumbled piece of paper and threw it at Jodi forcefully.

Jodi frowned up and yelled, "Nigga, what the fuck up? What's wrong wit' you?"

"Read it!" Cease yelled in response.

Jodi bent down and picked up the paper. He opened it and began to read.

Dear Diary,
I don't know what to do. I just found out that I was pregnant and I don't know how Cease is gon' react to this news. I love him and I am finally where I want to be in my life. It seems like fucked-up shit always happens to me. I never should have slept with Jodi. This baby could be his, but I have no way of finding out. I can't imagine what Cease would do if he ever found out about this. It's been on my mind for the last couple days and I had to express it through words—if I didn't I would go crazy. I have no feelings for Jodi; it's just something that happened that—

"Remy was writing that the night she died. I walked in and knew something was wrong. I snatched the paper from her hands and look what I found out."

"Man, it wasn't supposed to be like that. It was a mistake. It was just something that happened—it ain't mean shit."

Cease laughed and shook his head. "'It ain't mean shit.' You fucked my wife and you telling me it ain't mean shit—what the fuck you do it for, Jodi boy!"

Jodi was speechless. It wasn't something he or Remy planned, and they both knew it was wrong right after it happened.

"All the questions about Remy . . . you wondering if I was with her or not—you been interested since the beginning." Cease was furious but tried to control his temper. "You made me do this to her, Jodi."

Jodi looked up and stared his friend in the eye. "What—"

Cease loved his wife more than anything, but the idea of her being with his best friend caused him to do something he regretted. "I just reacted, the thought of you and her—I just snapped." Tears began to accumulate behind his eyes.

Jodi's eyes opened wide in disbelief. "You killed her? You killed Remy?"

If Jodi had been any other nigga he would have been dead, but Cease couldn't even bring himself to reach for his gun. There were too many emotions going through his body and he didn't know which one to display.

He nodded his head and, for the first time, admitted to what he'd done.

"So Khadafi didn't do it?" Jodi asked, still trying to put the pieces together.

"Khadafi is dead. I killed Remy. I killed my wife. I caught her writing about you in her diary and I just snapped. We argued and I pulled my gun. I wasn't gon' shoot her, I just wanted to scare her. She kept saying she was sorry, but I had to teach her a lesson. I aimed the gun at her chest. The clip wasn't even in, but there was still one in the chamber. Remy grabbed the gun and it went off. I didn't mean to, the gun just went off . . ." Cease dropped to his knees, unable to finish his story.

Jodi walked over to Cease to try to console him. He knelt down next to him.

Cease drew his gun and pointed it at Jodi's head. Tears streamed down his face, and he shook uncontrollably. "Get out if you don't wanna die."

Jodi tried to explain. "I'm sorry. You're like my brother. I would never—"

Cease pulled back the hammer on the gun, letting Jodi know he didn't have that many words left.

Seeing the truth in Cease's eyes, Jodi knew there was no love left. He'd caused too much pain, and no matter how much time passed, he knew that Cease would never forgive him. He got up reluctantly and walked out of the room. Just as he got to the front door he heard a single shot. He jumped, startled by the sound of the gunshot. He dropped to his knees. "Nooooooo!" Jodi knew he'd just lost his brother.